PERSEPHONE LOST & FOUND

Goddessverse Fantasy Series
Book 2

CORALIE MOSS

Pink Moon Books

Published internationally by Pink Moon Books, British Columbia, Canada.

Cover art: Elizabeth Mackey

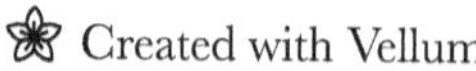 Created with Vellum

Contents

Content Notes

Persephone, the primary character, suffers with disordered eating, anxiety, and would be considered to be mildly "on the spectrum" by today's standards.

While there are no scenes of sexual intimacy in *Persephone Lost & Found*, in the Goddessverse Fantasy Series, women kiss women, men are coupled with other men, and tolerance is high for all manner of sexual and relationship preferences outside of the heteronormative.

This story also contains references to pregnancy and childbirth; to amicable separation and divorce; to past acts of violence perpetrated by goddesses and gods from the Greek pantheon.

Glossary of Mythological Figures

Bold= Figure/place has a role in *Persephone Lost & Found*

Italic= *Figure/place only mentioned in* Persephone Lost & Found

* Figure also appeared in book 1 of the Goddessverse Fantasy Series, *The Goddess & the Woodsman*

- **Achilles:** (Greek) Mortal son of Thetis and Peleus. Hero of the Trojan War.
- ***Airmid:** (Irish) Goddess of Herbal Healing. Member of the Tuatha Dé Danaan.
- *Aphrodite: (Greek) Goddess of Love and Beauty.*
- **Arkè:** (Greek) Messenger Goddess. Sister of iris. Sided with the Titans. Zeus punished her by cutting off her wings and remanding her to the Underworld's prison, Tartarus.
- ***Astrape:** (Greek) Goddess of Lightning. Shield Maiden to Zeus. Sister of Bronte.

- *Atalanta: (Greek) Warrior goddess. Said to be competitive + a runner.*
- ***Aušrinė (Rini):** (Lithuanian) Daughter of the Dawn. Daughter of the Goddess of the Sun, Saulė.
- ***Baubo (Babs):** (Greek) Goddess of Mirth. Crone.
- ***Bé Chuille (Bé):** (Irish) Sorceress and witch. Daughter of Flidais. Member of the Tuatha Dé Danaan.
- ***Bronte:** (Greek) Goddess of Thunder. Sister of Astrape. Shield Maiden to Zeus.
- **Charon: (Greek) Ferryman of the River Styx in the Underworld.*
- ***Creirwy (Ciri):** (Welsh) Daughter of Ceridwen (Goddess of Grain + Sows).
- ***Demeter:** (Greek) Goddess of Harvest and Agriculture. Mother to Persephone.
- **Dionysus:** (Greek) God of Winemaking, Theatre, and more.
- Dryad: (Greek) Tree nymph
- *Eleusis: Greek city Elefsina, and home to the Eleusinian Mysteries*
- *Elysium: A place separate from, but associated with, the Underworld where mortals and others related to the gods could reside.*
- *Gaia: Ancient Mother Goddess*
- ***Habonde (Habs):** (Celtic) Hearth Goddess, celebrated with fire and ale. In *The Goddess & the Woodsman*, she is the owner of Bone Fire Croft. Bruiser, her dog, was given to her by Hekate.
- ***Hades:** (Greek) God of the Dead. King of the Underworld.
- **Hekate: (Greek) Goddess of the Crossroads, and more.*
- *Hera: (Greek) Goddess of Marriage, Women, and Family.*

- **Hermes:** (Greek) Herald of the gods. Psychopomp. Soul guide
- **Iris:** (Greek) Goddess of the Rainbow, and servant to the other Olympians.
- **Kronos:** (Greek) Descendant of Gaia. Leader of the Titans. Patron of the harvest. Overthrown by Zeus and sent to Tartarus.
- **Lesser Mysteries:** (Greek) Secret, religious initiatory rites in the cults surrounding Demeter and Persephone.
- ***Minthe:** (Greek) Nymph (or naiad) associated with the Underworld river, Kokytus. Mistress of Hades.
- **Mount Olympus:** (Greek) Highest mountain in Greece, and home to the Greek gods and goddesses.
- ***Naiads:** (Greek) Spirits residing within bodies of fresh water (streams, wells, springs).
- **Patroclus:** (Greek) Friend and companion of Achilles.
- ***Persephone:** (Greek) Goddess of Spring. Queen of the Underworld. Married to Hades.
- **Tartarus:** (Greek) Prison of the Titans located far beneath the surface of the Earth.
- **Titans:** (Greek) Pre-Olympian gods/goddesses. The twelve children of Uranus and Gaia.
- **Underworld:** (Greek) The world of the dead.
- ***urisk:** (Scottish) Household spirits playing a tutelary role in the lives of humans and others.
- ***Zeus:** (Greek) King of the Gods, Rules from Mount Olympus. Also, god of the sky and thunder.

To Mr. Moss.
Simply, the best.

———

PERSEPHONE LOST & FOUND

Part One

Godsrest

A period of renewal entered into by beings graced with immortality. The location of their tomb, the length of their rest, and their method of reawakening is known only to the individual. During their Godsrest, the immortal cannot be contacted. Whether to partake of a Godsrest, or not, is a matter of personal preference.

Chapter 1
THE UNDERWORLD. LATE-FEBRUARY.

I STRIDE THROUGH HOUSE OF HADES' central foyer toward
my husband's half of the estate, my steps echoing against a
tableau of slate, metal, and sand-blasted glass. Goosebumps
pebble my forearms. The sleeves on my dress end above my
elbows and I almost spin on my heel, thinking I'll return to my
wing of the mansion and grab the sweater I should have added to
my outfit. But if I deviate from my mission, I might be tempted
to abandon it to the next day, and I'm already on a tight
schedule.

No amount of heat warms these rooms enough to make them
habitable for me, let alone hospitable. Briskly rubbing my arms, I
continue onward. Every time my stilettos connect with the floor,
the movement jars my bones and rattles my teeth, punctuating
the fact that I can't see myself ever referring to the architectural
monstrosity Hades designed as "my" house or even "our" house.
Though newly built and furnished, this place will be, always and
forever, The House of Hades - and not just because those exact
words are engraved on the plaque bolted to the formal entrance

doors. Or because the building's four wings and central entertaining area form an "H" when viewed from above.

Simply because everything about the property reflects my husband's minimalist aesthetic. Everything but my private rooms.

Passing the public entertainment area requires thirty evenly spaced steps. The King of the Underworld believes in high ceilings and sharp angles. Un-curtained windows offer sweeping views towards the capital, Asphodel City, perpetually entombed within an overcast sky. Hades' single nod to sensuality, at least by my definition, is candles. He hired a "scent-ologist" to create signature blends for every room, like whiskey and cinnamon for the library to encourage reading and conversation, and bergamot, ginger, and oregano for the Club Room and the formal dining room to encourage eating and drinking.

It continues to feel like a snub that he didn't ask for my input; he's aware I have a sensitive nose. I have no idea which scent he chose for his personal suite of rooms, though I suppose I'll find out soon enough. Our annual meeting with our legal and fiduciary advisors is scheduled to take place in three days, and my plan is to pre-empt that session by convincing Hades to meet with me alone. As far as I'm concerned, our marital arrangement is unsalvageable, and we don't need a roomful of besuited advisors to confirm what we already know.

Thing is, I want the two of us to re-negotiate our situation before I leave the Underworld for my mother's house; before I trade my collection of jeweled crowns for wreaths of fresh flowers; before I trade my duties to the dead for those to the living. And I want the discussion to take place between us. Just Hades, and me. No bystanders, no experts, no meddling relatives, no formalities. Surely, he and I owe it to one another. Deep inside, I feel he owes it to me.

If that doesn't work, I'll initiate Plan B and have a third party

I already vetted and put on retainer to serve him with divorce papers.

My breathing grows strained as I mount the free-floating, metal and black-stained wood stairs to the second floor. I've done little to regain muscle tone after my most recent Godsrest, and I'm regretting it now. I hope I can do a credible job of masking my discomfort.

I near the horned guards positioned in front of the double doors to Hades' suite and stop. Relax my hands and jaw. Pressing my fingers to my breastbone, I flip the scrying mirror hanging from the chain round my neck, so the cheery pansies enameled on the backside face outward.

"Is the king here?"

Me asking is merely a formality. If the demons Hades recruited from the Eisochsen Realm are standing legs apart and ceremonial spears in hand, as they are now, rather than lounging in the adjacent reception area, the king is in residence. And as Queen of the Underworld and his wife, I am to be granted passage through any door, at any time.

Or so I've been promised.

"He is," the taller of the two says, making no move to let me pass. Flaring my nostrils, I add his impertinence to a growing list of similar slights.

"I want to see him."

The beefier one lifts his chin slightly. "Hades said he was not to be disturbed."

I lift my chin higher. "I assume that means he has company. Would one of you inform him the queen is here, and that I'm in a hurry."

Which isn't exactly true. I'm not in any more of a hurry than usual to exit this side of the estate, but these two don't need to know that. The guard with the big chin pushes down on the door's gleaming black handle and slips his burly shoulders through the opening. A strong whiff of mint sneaks past him as the other guard closes the door.

Mint, annoyingly bright and sprightly, at least to my nose, seems a peculiar choice for a bedroom. Before I can mull over that information, someone opens the door from inside and Hades steps forward. He's in the middle of drawing a slender, black leather belt through the loops on his black wool dress slacks and his hair is slightly damp. I wonder if I'm seeing the post-coital version of my husband. At least he's showered. How considerate.

"Persephone. I almost didn't believe it when my guard said you were here."

"I have a proposal for you. And no," I say, raising my hands at his attempt to interrupt, "it cannot wait."

"A proposal." Smirking, he fastens the belt without looking. "Must be terribly urgent if it drove you to mount my stairs in the middle of the day."

The guards show no interest in leaving us alone, and Hades seems disinclined to dismiss them. I do what I can to tune out the demons, resisting the persistent urge to wipe my sweaty palms on the apple blossom pink dress I've chosen for its ability to bolster my confidence. The style gives me curves where my own are wasting away, and the color can't be ignored, especially against the estate's unrelieved palette of blacks and grays and whites.

"We are getting a divorce."

I hold my breath as Hades' features go from shocked, to annoyed, to calculating.

"That sounds less like a proposal and more like an ultimatum." One of the guards snorts. Hades shoots him a quelling glance before bending forward and bringing his mouth close to my ear. "Why must we get divorced? What is it about our current arrangement that has you unhappy now?"

Our current arrangement keeps me in-residence in the Underworld six long, contiguous months of the year, from the autumnal equinox to the vernal equinox. I can go anywhere, do anything, see anyone, spend however much I like - and every day I spend under the mansion's hulking mansard roof brings me closer to the death of what little is left alive in my soul.

Hades lowers his voice even more. A lock of still-damp hair hits my cheek. "I have done as we agreed and stayed away from your bed, as you have stayed away from mine."

Stop being so dramatic, Persephone. I don't wait for those to be the next words to leave his lips. "Our arrangement suits you far better than it suits me," I hiss. "I want out."

"But you have duties, Persephone, and—"

"There's no reason I can't do my duties in the Underworld half the day or less and spend the other half in the aboveworld. With my friends. And my mother." I've told no one of my plan to divorce Hades, not even Demeter. Outside of ruling at Hades' side, my duties—are restricted to the Court of Souls. Squaring my shoulders and putting distance between my nose and his mint-infused hair products, I can't help adding a little dig. "You've been gone so much the past six months, even the staff has noticed."

Hades doesn't have the courtesy to blush or apologize. Muscular shoulders strain under his crisply ironed button-down as he draws cufflinks from his pocket and appears to consider my request. "Listen, Seph." He gentles his voice to a more persuasive timbre. "I know you're not happy here, but I'm concerned about how Zeus will react. He really doesn't like it when changes are made to the status quo."

I knew Hades would deliver his reply in that cajoling tone, the one that can turn condescending in the space of a breath. I also knew he would mention the philandering King of the Sky and I've prepared a counterpoint. "I'm not the only one who thinks Zeus is long overdue for his Godsrest and if I were you, I would seek Poseidon's help and double-team him. We know what happens when any of us goes too long without that period of renewal." I drop my gaze to Hades' hands. There was a time when I wished those confident, nimble fingers would touch me, would show me affection. Not anymore. The only thing I want them to do is take up a pen and sign on the dotted line. "He's not well, and you know it."

I continue to avoid seeking Hades' face. He slots a cufflink into one set of holes, and I shove my hands in my dress' side pockets. My fingertips meet the pieces of fulgurite that always seem to find their way onto my person. Energy runs through the fossilized lightning whenever Zeus is in a 'mood', which has helped me avoid face-to-face encounters with him ever since his former shield maiden presented the rocks to me last summer.

Hades shifts his stance and fixes his other cuff. "I'll make time to talk, I promise. Just not—" I hear the distinctive *click-click* of luggage tabs being closed and look up in time to see him signal to whoever's in his suite. "Just not today, okay? Something urgent has come up and I expect to be away for the next week or two. We'll have to reschedule our annual meeting."

I adjust my face to a neutral expression. "I won't be here when you get back. As you know, I leave for the aboveworld soon." Four days, two hours, and twelve minutes. Which Hades likely counts with the same precision. "Just say the word, and we can have the paperwork done and signed by this time tomorrow."

His hands tense into fists, causing the tendons to stand out against his flawless skin. My request bothers him. Score one for me.

"I cannot round up my lawyers and draft a divorce agreement today." And cue the condescension. "As I said, I must get going. I'm already late for my— appointment."

"I'm sure your guest will forgive you."

"My what?" He relaxes his fists and fakes a tight smile. "I

have no guest, Persephone. Say hello to your mother for me. I'll be in touch."

I'll be in touch. My composure cracks. I reach out to grab his wrist, wanting to dig in my nails, the ones I sharpened to points and tipped with gold lacquer, and draw blood. Force him to take me seriously.

"Hades, wait—"

Shame heats my cheeks as the smooth cotton of his sleeve flows beneath my outstretched fingers. Hades slips like smoke into his bedroom without a backward glance, without acknowledging that coming to him and speaking face to face has cost me. I would almost rather we had a relationship fueled by spite or even a common enemy than this lifeless… whatever this is.

The guard with the obtruding chin exits with two carry-ons, while the taller guard makes a point of allowing the door latch to smack the strike plate. I cringe, pressing the back of my hand to my heated cheek. The last of the bravado I mustered drains from my legs; the persuasive words I rehearsed lie like ash on my tongue. There's nothing further I can say to the closed door or to the guards or to whomever is helping Hades ready for his trip; there's no one I can appeal to. In this, as with many other things related to being Queen to Hades' King, I am on my own.

Chapter 2

TURNING my back on the most fractious part of my life, I face the floating staircase. The descent gives me plenty of time to replay what I said, and what I should have said, and to muse on Hades' possible destination. Tossing my head, I firm my grip on the steel railing. I should have utilized one of my tried-and-true tactics, like channeling Demeter's regal bearing or Zeus' implacable mask, before I confronted Hades.

Instead, I remain, as always, Persephone the Compliant.

I step onto the slate floor and nearly break into a run while wearing the precarious heels I paired with my dress. Today, height does not equal might. As soon as I'm out of sight of the guards, I remove the shoes and bolt. Across mirror-polished marble floors. Across a priceless carpet added at my insistence to help mute the noise made when Hades entertains, and his guests are deep into his wine cellar's offerings. Past the doors facing the circular driveway at the front of the mansion and the French doors opening to the gloomy gardens in the back.

I pass the corridor leading to the kitchen and almost - *almost* - make it to my wing.

"Is that you, Persephone?"

The head chef, another recruit from the Eisochsen Realm, is a horn-sized thorn in my side and no matter how much I complain about their cooking - excuse me, their '*art*' - no one on Hades' staff believes me when I say I think the demon is trying to starve me out of existence. That, or they're deliberately plating overwhelmingly beautiful compositions of underwhelming nutritional content as a joke.

I skid to a stop and compose my features in preparation for lying. "Did you need something? I'm late for my afternoon appointments."

"Would you try this combination I just whipped up? The King requested I update our spring menu and I would love to get your thoughts before you leave."

Chef Keldt beckons me to follow, a long-handled silver spoon in one beefy hand, their other cupped beneath to catch spills. I'm unsure whether their mangled smile signals a peace offering, or a taunt. Behind them, the large, round windows in the kitchen's swinging doors provide a view to a stainless-steel prep table and the unfriendly stares of four under-cooks. Or sous chefs. I couldn't care less what they prefer to be called. Every one of them makes food I find inedible.

Wary, I hold back my hair and sniff at the glistening, ruby red sauce. Underneath the raspberries, vinegar, herbs, honey, and lemon, I detect the presence of pomegranates. This is clearly a taunt. Chef Keldt knows how I feel about pomegranates, as does everyone else working for the House of Hades. Yet the fucking fruit keeps popping up in sauces and garnishes, embroidered on table linens, even embossed on bars of soap in the guest bathrooms. I should have fired the insufferable demon, their helpers, and every other staff member who's in on the unkind joke.

But I haven't. Because clearly, they aren't mine to boss around if they can't even bother to call me by my proper title.

"It's a gorgeous color," I say, keeping my voice neutral. I'm not prepared to take up arms against him and his culinary cohorts, not over something as trifling as a scoop of sauce, but one of these days... "Will this become a reduction, perhaps a sauce to go on meat?"

"No, no. This is the base for House of Hades' new signature salad dressing."

Four days, two hours, seven minutes.

"Well, the concept sounds lovely." I manage a brittle smile before I walk away to the accompaniment of Chef Keldt's high-pitched whine.

"But you didn't even taste it!"

By Atalanta's arrow, if I thought I could throw my shoe with enough accuracy to hit Chef's craw, I would hurl one of my stilettos at the demon and call us even. Barely breathing, I double-time it up a curved staircase. The moment I'm through another set of doors, my feet land on a plush, mauve rug. I drop my shoes and sink my aching toes into comforting clumps of shaggy, twisted wool. My fingers fumble for the nearby chair and the soft folds of a cashmere blanket. A rapid-fire *pop-pop-pop* sends me jerking sideways and I fall, landing on one of the shoes.

Ouch. I twitch as more pops, snaps, and crackles spark the air, until it registers that someone has lit a fire.

Oh. I'm in my home, where lamp bulbs glow behind silk shades; where everything is soft and over-stuffed and done up in muted lavenders and blues, where everything is familiar. I tug the shoe out from underneath my sore hip and replace it with the blanket.

Better. I wait for my heart to settle, and for the soft *tap-tap* that will announce my personal assistant's arrival now that I've returned from my failed mission. Gilda eases the door open and shuts it behind her.

"I heard you flying up the stairs, my sweet."

The middle-aged golden salamander and her sister, Tilda, are two of the few employed by the House of Hades who have my complete trust. Like the guards and Chef Keldt, they each draw a salary from the estate's bottomless accounts. Unlike most of the other staff members, they also draw a competitive salary from my aboveworld accounts to keep their ears and eyes open, and to prepare most of my meals in *my* kitchen from ingredients they hand-select or purchase.

"I'll have your lunch ready in a few minutes and I've made a list of supplies we could use to restock the pantry. I'll do the shopping prior to your return in September, and have it delivered."

"Thank you, Gilda. Do you and Tilda have plans to go home?" Most of the sisters' extended family live in the Ukrainian underlands. I know the humans' war has reached the point where it's impacting the Magicals living there.

"We do. We're desperate to see firsthand how everyone's coping, and how we might help."

She and I exchange hugs. I slip my feet into fuzzy slippers a darker shade of pink than my dress and follow her into the kitchen, choosing my usual perch atop one of the padded, low-backed stools at the center island. I find it soothing to watch Gilda and Tilda prepare food, and I appreciate they respect my tastes and never try to force me to eat more than my increasingly finicky stomach can handle.

"Have you spoken with anyone from above?" Gilda faces the cutting board. Shimmery scales on her arms and backside ripple in response to her every action, and I know she hopes I've shared my distress over the Hades situation with my trio of best friends.

"Not recently," I say, confessing, "I'm waiting to talk to

everyone in person. I… I have a hard time baring my soul over the bathroom sink."

Cell phones don't work in the Underworld. Scrying via mirrors or over a bowl of water is a reliably secure method for communicating one-on-one with those living in the aboveworld, but I find that talking at a flat surface isn't exactly conducive to intimate conversation.

"Plus it's not a terribly flattering angle."

Snorting at Gilda's comment, I fold my arms atop the placemat, rest my head, and wait for my sandwich to arrive. "Your mother sent a message," she adds, setting the griddle on the stovetop and turning the knob to ignite the burner flame.

Dread drops like a rock into my head, making it heavier, denser. The situations with Hades has dominated my emotional bandwidth and I've been ignoring Demeter's summons. "I expected she would. Anything new? Or just the usual 'pack this, pack that, remember your jewels,' etcetera, etcetera?"

"She sent a list, yes. She also mentioned she hopes to hire Astrape's company to oversee security for the Lesser Mysteries."

Astrape. The weight inside my head lightens a bit as I mouth her name. I haven't seen her in months, not since that day last summer when I hugged her in thanks for bringing her protective capabilities to a tense situation between me, my mother, and Zeus. The hug we shared woke up something inside me, something lonely and curious and absolutely starved for touch. Whatever I hoped might develop, hadn't been given an instant to take root. Demeter insisted she needed me for some ritual or another, and Astrape had left Scotland to resume working security at outdoor concerts and festivals. By the time my mother released me from her schedule, Astrape was on her way to the Southern Hemisphere. Rather than seek her out, I'd taken an unscheduled Godsrest. The promise of being disconnected from everything and everyone proved too alluring.

I curl the tip of my fingernail under a loose thread in the woven placemat and tug. Unfortunately, that last Godsrest didn't alter a thing. The judges of the Underworld *still* expect my presence during the hours allotted me; Hades *still* wears a titanium marriage band on his left hand; and Demeter *still* expects her malleable sidekick to show up whenever summoned.

"Did my mother specify which site she's settled on for the rites?"

"She may have decided, but she did not share the location with me." Gilda sets a plate on another mat and slides it beside my elbow. "There you are, my sweet."

Leaving the stray thread alone, I raise my head, take a deep sniff, and exchange one placemat for the other. "Grilled cheese on brioche. My favorite." Talk about belly-warming, soul-soothing food. I cut the sandwich on the diagonal, and again, and bite into the first buttery triangle. Gilda stands across from me, cutting her own sandwich.

"Is there anything you want to talk about?" she asks. Concern suffuses her voice. "You seem preoccupied."

I'm still thinking about strong, competent Astrape, and opportunities I've missed or avoided. Another one of the goddess' hugs would feel good right now. Really good. "Is there anything *you* want to talk about?" I counter. The delicate, frilly gills on the sides of Gilda's neck turn rose gold at my question. "Any gossip you want to share? Because when I confronted Hades, it was obvious he either had one of his lovers stashed in his suite or was on his way to meet them."

Gilda's scales make the softest susurration as she shakes her head. "I've heard nothing, which is very, *very* unusual for this meddlesome household. Whether Hades knows it or not, demons love to collect and trade gossip. His staff thrives on seeing who confirms what, first. Did you notice anything at all when you spoke with him?"

"He was in the middle of getting dressed when he came to the door." I finish my second triangle and toy with the third. "Oh, and I picked up a strong scent of mint. Hades is more of a whisky and wood kind of guy."

"Mint. I see." Gilda presses the pad of her clawed finger onto her plate and brings the collected crumbs to her mouth. "Do you want to know who *I* would guess he's been with?"

I picked up the faintest scent of mint. The identity of Hades' lover could not be more obvious and yet somehow, I completely ignored what I already know. I gag on the half-chewed food in my mouth. Gilda presses a paper towel into my hand, and I spit out the offending bite.

"Minthe."

Chapter 3

SOME LIFETIMES AGO, I BANISHED HADES' former lover
from Asphodel City. After I had Minthe escorted to the city's
border - because contrary to the types of punishments usually
meted out by the council on Mount Olympus, I couldn't stomach
the thought of having her killed or sentenced to Tartarus - I
completely wiped her from my mind.

Gilda reaches across the counter and pats my shaking hand.
"She was my first guess too."

"I— I'm not sure I want it confirmed they're seeing each
other again," I continue. "Because honestly, what difference
would it make? Neither Hades nor I are happy with what our
marriage has become, and I'm ready to do whatever it takes to
end this… this sham."

I nibble on the quarter-sandwich in my hand, then set the rest
back on my plate. The bread has cooled, the melted cheese is
hardening, and the constriction in my throat signals I'm not
going to get any more down. But more words force their way up
and out.

"I'm ready to find out who I really am, or could be, if only my life wasn't defined and constrained by actions taken eons ago. Thing is, I don't think Hades remembers why he wanted me to rule at his side in the first place. And if we ever had a contract, those vows are lost to time."

"And to the Godsrests." Gilda's tone is gentle, instructional. "You retire more frequently than most other immortals. And every time any one of you reawakens, you gain more options for shaping the coming chapter of your life. Yes, you lose more of your memories and connections to the origins of your current situation, but that seems a small price to pay for broadening your future possibilities."

"If only the reshaping could take place outside of this mansion-sized cage." I carefully refold my napkin and tuck it under the plate. As much as I appreciate Gilda's caring words, at times her presence feels overly-tutelary. Stifling. Like she's waiting for me to grasp the obvious, and the obvious has absented itself from my understanding. "Thank you for the sandwich."

She shoos me off to my bedroom suite with an empathetic look and the promise of something chocolatey later. I promise her I'll lay out my clothes for packing. Or at least start. I get as far as opening the doors to the walk-in closet containing my spring and summer wardrobes and turning on the lights.

Tilda's organizational expertise glitters along glass shelves laden with shoes, handbags, and other accessories, or hung from racks organized by color and style. Most everything in this closet was ordered for me by my mother during one fashion week or another. She adores having a fuss made over her at couture shows. I do not. Something about spotlights and camera flashes and people touching me, measuring me, judging me— *ugh*. I drop to my hands and knees, crawl across the plush carpet to the free-standing set of drawers in the middle of the room and contemplate the bottom drawer.

If I hug my knees to my chest, I can fit my entire body inside that drawer. I know because I did it after a particularly nasty encounter with one of Hades' groupies. She came into the Club Room when I was there and ordered me to unlock the cigar humidor. I had timed my visit to coincide with Hades being away from the estate. Stunned and startled, I refused. The nymph - I knew she was a nymph because the king has a thing for her kind and she smelled like a woodsy copse redolent with animal rut - yanked my hair, dragged me to the glass-front cabinet, and demanded an Arturo Fuente.

Lucky for me and my hair follicles, a couple of Hades' guards heard me yell. One pulled the nymph off and sent her packing; the other escorted me to my wing with muttered apologies. Neither Gilda nor Tilda were home at the time, so I found solace in the scented embrace of a cedar-lined box.

I ease open the drawer where I hide clothes my mother would relegate to the burn bin and pull out a pair of worn flannel pajama bottoms patterned with floating otters. Emptying my pocket of the fulgurite and removing the necklace with the macaron-sized scrying mirror, I strip out of my dress and undergarments and into the pajamas and an equally worn oversized tee. With my arms and legs tucked in like a pill bug, I find I still fit within the drawer with room to spare. If I could figure out a way to close myself in, I could hide until the voices in my head finish declaiming their familiar litany.

You're weak. You should be stronger.

You bend too easily. You should grow a backbone.

You're a QUEEN. *You should act like one.*

A buzzing sound forces me to surface before I've sunk too far within the labyrinth shaped by my own dark thoughts. I bruise my elbow trying to clamber out of the drawer and flip over the mirror that keeps me connected to my innermost circle.

It's Aušrinė. Another daughter of a powerful goddess mother, and one of my best friends. Pressing my fingertip to the mirror's surface, I swipe a clockwise circle. Rini's sunny smile drops into a frown.

"Persephone! Are you wearing those pajamas again? Dammit, you're supposed to call me when shit gets real."

"I know." I nudge the drawer closed with my foot and tuck my arm under my breasts. "Things just kind of snowballed."

"Are you okay now, or do you need to talk?"

"I'm ready for bubble tea and fuzzy blankets and a sleepover with you and Bé and Ciri."

"You sure that's all you need? Because I can meet you at the portal in, like, half an hour."

"I'm sure."

"Then you got it. One girls' night coming up as soon as you get here. Are you stopping at your mom's place first? Or are we all meeting her at the ritual site? The festival channel is buzzing with rumors about where the Lesser Mysteries are happening this year. Betting's heavy on either Lake Wañaka, or that private island in Finland."

Once Rini gets going, she will not stop until she gets all her questions out. She blames it on being blessed with the immortals' equivalent of ADHD. "My mother hasn't said a word about the location, but everything's frozen in Finland in February, and Lake Wañaka's in New Zealand. You know how conscientious Demeter is about not overstepping into other goddess' territories."

"Hmm, that's true. Then got any hints for your bestie? I could keep that info to myself and make a killing off these suckers." Rini tucks her fingers beneath her chin and bats her lashes.

"Not even a whisper," I say, receiving a fake pout in return for my honesty. Once Magical social media got wind of the rites my mother performs twice yearly, the Greek authorities closed off access to Eleusis, forcing her to search for other sites capable of hosting multi-day initiatory events. I won't know the identity of our destination until we arrive, and the only hints my mother gives before we leave are frustratingly generic, such as, "Bring an extra sweater" or, "Pack plenty of sunscreen."

"Well, my phone is charged, my bag is ready to roll, and I'll make sure Bé and Ciri head for the portals as soon as you say go. All joking aside, we're honored Demeter is allowing us to assist. My own mother even hinted she's proud I was chosen again."

"Saulė should be proud, and I'm glad you'll be there." I lean back against the chest and prop the mirror on my bent knees. "Rini? Can I tell you something?"

"Always."

"Can you promise you won't get mad at me or threaten to cut off anyone's balls?" Aušrinė snorts and draws a big X across her chest. "I told Hades we're getting divorced."

The disconnect I experience daily expands the space between me, and Rini's incredulous face. I'm ready to hightail it back to the site of my Godsrest and implore whatever magic infuses the ground there to not release me until my mind and body are once again *tabula rasa*.

Rini's features rearrange into a radiant smile. Slender beams of her light reach forward until I'm anchored in her warmth. I can't go as far as forgetting everything, because then I wouldn't have her. "Babe. I am so proud of you. How did he react?"

"He did his usual not-now-I'm-busy thing, but I'm not taking that, not anymore." My voice drops to a whisper. "I found someone willing to serve him papers."

"Noooo! Seph, that's so brave of you!"

"It is brave. And expensive." I snort softly. Plan B includes the services of a succubus I found online. She assured me she could track anyone, anywhere, any time. All I had to provide was a piece of clothing or jewelry that had been in contact with Hades' skin for at least twelve hours prior to being removed. The dirtied sock I presented her with at first had her turning up her nose - until she got a sly look in her eyes and congratulated me on making her job even easier.

I didn't ask why. I just paid the deposit she requested out of the funds Hades' financial team funnels into my household account.

"Anything worth having carries a hefty price tag." Rini holds up a squat round jar with a matte gold lid. "Especially my latest beauty serum. Can't wait for you to see the products I've been working on. I've got your swag bag all ready. And don't worry about me and Ciri and Bé. We will be the epitome of helpful, then we'll whisk you away to Bé's estate. Her mom's off doing something Big and Important and the place is ours for as long as we need."

Bé's the daughter of the Welsh goddess, Ceridwen. I've been to her estate before. Its lavish spa and ocean views with endless horizons are exactly what I need.

"Maybe that's a better plan. I'll spend the next few days resting up for the rites, give my mother my undivided attention for twenty-four hours, and then—" And then what? Wait to hear how Hades responds to being served? Follow my mother from one public event to another until crops and orchards throughout her realm are budding and blooming enough, they don't require our combined gifts?

"Seph."

I wedge my finger under the bottom of the drawer beside me and start to slide it open.

"*Seph!* What're you thinking? You just kind of imploded in on yourself."

Lowering my hand, I smooth the carpet's soft pile. Waiting. Following. Obeying. "I need a break, Rini."

"You said the same thing this time last year and—"

"And the moment I entered my mother's estate, she swept me

up into her life, even though I swore I was going to work on setting better boundaries with her and with Hades."

Persephone the Capitulator surfaces again. Just like she did last summer at the end of the gathering of goddesses, when I thought I might have a few days with Astrape, and my mother thought differently.

"It sounds like you're making progress with Hades though, right?"

I don't have the energy to shrug or get up and find a tissue to blow my runny nose. "We'll see."

"Sephie?"

"What?" I whisper.

"Pack. Your. Bags. You have only what, four days more until you're up here, in the light?"

"Four days, and forty-nine minutes," I say, sniffling again.

"You can handle four days and forty-nine minutes. In fact, I promise you that the girls and I will meet you at Demeter's."

"You'd give up Carnival for me?"

"Oh, sweetie, you need your squad more than any of us need to go to Rio or Venice for a random hook-up."

"Okay." Relieved to know I won't be facing Demeter on my own, I waggle my fingers at the cookie-sized mirror. "I gotta go. There are shades at the gate, and I don't like to keep the dead waiting."

____

Chapter 4

____

TECHNICALLY, THERE IS NO "GATE." Hermes and/or their assistants escort the dead to the Underworld's entrance. There, they're met by Charon and/or *their* assistants. One single coin per soul ceremoniously changes hands, whether the coin is carried by the dead or plucked from an ever-filling bowl, thereby allowing the shades to cross the River Styx. Once on the river's other side, the dead converge in a cavernous waiting room outside the Court of Souls until it is time for their fates to be decided by a panel of judges.

Not every human follows the same journey after death, or even ends up in the Underworld. As with my mother in the aboveworld and her refusal to franchise the Mysteries, those of us with specific roles acknowledge the existence of multiple views on life and death; afterlife and reincarnation; and the possibility of forgiveness versus eternal damnation, torture, and other punishments.

I like to arrive around eight in the evening and stay until four the next morning. On occasion, I'm asked to listen in on difficult cases. I usually suggest the dead ask for forgiveness and offer reparations. When needed, I inform the more recalcitrant to prepare themselves to suffer more than those they wronged or hurt.

As I go to slide my thumbs under my pajama's elastic waistband, I pause.

A week ago, maybe more, Hekate stopped me in the hall outside the Court. Though the Goddess of the Crossroads and I both pass comfortably between the realms of the living and the dead, I hadn't spoken with her much since last summer, when we both attended the hastily arranged gathering for goddesses in the Northern Scottish Highlands, the one where I shared that hug with Astrape.

"I've received multiple reports one of the river nymphs has been shirking her duties," Hekate said, handing me a sheaf of papers, "and when I went to investigate, this is what I found. She completely absented herself from the roster for the past six months."

"Which nymph are you talking about?" I asked.

Hekate searched my face before answering, "Minthe."

"Why are you sharing this with me?" Even though I'd been in a state of ferocious hurt when I banished Minthe from Asphodel City, I expected her to continue upholding her duties at the River Kokytus. And while I counted Hekate as an ally, I wondered what compelled her to drop this information on me so long after the banishment. Aside from my lingering aversion to the taste and smell of mint, I'd effectively wiped Minthe from my mind.

"Ask Hades."

I recall that Hekate's dogs started baying. She excused herself to see what they were going on about, and I rolled the papers and tucked them into a pocket of the long, hooded robe I wear in my role as arbitrator.

Hekate had said, "Ask Hades."

I *would* ask Hades about Minthe, only he isn't here, and I'm disinclined to chase him down. His loyal guards won't give up his current location if he even let them know where he's slunk off to. Shaking my head - because Hades' whereabouts are not my concern - I regain my bearings. One task at a time, or I'll get overwhelmed and start shutting down. I paid the succubus to see the divorce papers are served before I arrive at my mother's. The succubus has a muddied sock, and I have her assurances she can track Hades no matter where he is in the Above or the Below; even if he's on Mount Olympus. I just have to trust she'll get the job done.

If she can't, then I'll approach obtaining the divorce from some other angle I haven't yet thought of. Right now, I should choose what I want to wear for the next six months and this time, pack enough I can leave half of my clothes in the aboveworld. Which would be easier if I had my own place. Which circles me around to another problem. I invariably end up staying with my mother at her estates in Greece and Italy for the months I am Goddess of Spring. Demeter's places are beautiful, with acres and acres of olive trees, and potted lemon trees. Her staff see to my every need, yet even with wide open blue skies above me and the Aegean Sea stretching to the horizon, I feel caged in.

I decide to make a date with Aušrinė and the others to go house hunting.

Better. On to packing. I shake out my arms and start with the basics. Pulling stretchy pants from one drawer, tops from another, and assorted hoodies from their hangers, I imagine where in the aboveworld I might buy a house. Or a condo. Or an entire building, with apartments for all my friends. It's a comforting fantasy and before I know it, I've designed the house of my dreams. Hades will hate it, from the pastel color palette to the indoor plants, and Demeter will accuse me of not thinking big enough or placing myself too high above the ground and weakening my connection to soil and seed.

If I can manifest Spring, I can manifest a home of my own. *With* a rooftop garden.

Hours later, neat piles of clothes cover every available surface inside the closet. I'll work on choosing footwear and accessories tomorrow. Satisfied, I traverse my bedroom to my autumn and winter walk-in closet, stripping as I go. I feel February's cold more than usual, so I locate thick cashmere leggings in a luscious claret red and a long-sleeved top in the same color that hits mid-thigh. I choose a fitted trench coat, high-heeled boots, and snug gloves, all in supple black leather.

Before zipping my feet into the boots, I brush my hair, fasten it away from my face, and apply light makeup. Just because I'm heading to my job early doesn't mean I intend to excuse myself from shirking the steps it takes to transform myself from whichever version of Persephone I'm dealing with, into Persephone, Queen of the Underworld.

Supporting her mission to raise my calorie intake, Gilda has left a covered mug of cocoa on the round table in the foyer. I savor a few sips, blot my lips with a tissue, and lean in toward the vase of flowers the gardeners refresh daily. Stems of pale pink tulips arch over the vase's rim, with a few branches of white lilac tucked in to add scent. I brush my cheeks against the tulip petals and close my eyes. Though I'm armoring myself as Queen of the Underworld, soon—*soon!*—I'll be on my way to the aboveworld. The tulips offer a hopeful hint of what's to come.

I give myself another moment with the flowers, then cross the room to the glass-fronted cases holding my crown collection. One per shelf, each protected by a spell keyed only to me. Which will I wear tonight? I scan them all, top left to bottom right. My gaze settles on a circlet set with diamonds and pink tourmalines.

Too delicate for a day when I need to project a commanding presence. Not for the dead's sake. For mine.

There. A yellow gold crown composed of seven ragged

points, each topped with an old mine cut red beryl. The center peak holds a spray of druzy quartz. I don't wear this crown very often - I'm simultaneously drawn to and repelled by its brutal, mountainous beauty - but the red stones seem the perfect accessory. Their cracks and inclusions echo my own flaws, even as the blood red color projects strength and courage.

I breathe against the clear glass, then draw my sigil across the fogged surface. The panel swings open, and I remove the crown and place myself in front of the floor length mirror hanging between the narrow cases. Chin raised, black leather jacket collar framing my neck and jaw, I carefully set the heavy piece atop my head. Magic molds the metal to me and backlights the stones. Satisfied, I wiggle my fingers into my gloves and make my way down the stairs to the estate's main entrance.

Low sounds filter from the kitchen corridor. Mercifully, there's no Chef Keldt in sight, only the ancient butler. My unexpected appearance startles him, and he hurries to rise from his wingback chair.

"Off to Asphodel City, my Queen?" he asks, his upper-crust Bostonian accent as clear as ever.

"Off to work early this evening, Owen."

"Very good. Do you require an escort?"

"Are you in need of a walk?"

"My legs would see me to the gate and back."

Our ritual banter anchors this part of my nightly routine. During the estate's construction, I discovered a decidedly not-dead Owen wandering the shore of the River Styx. He seemed deeply agitated, and I asked if he needed help. Dressed in a formal morning suit lined with peacock-patterned silk, his white hair sticking out in wild clumps, he confessed he was at a loss as to what he was doing in the Underworld. Though he absolutely loomed over me, I offered to take him back to the land of the living, which confused him even more.

"I'm nothing without my job, my lady," he admitted, "and the family I serve has crossed the river and left me behind."

Inspired by his serendipitous appearance, I asked if he would consider coming to work for me at House of Hades. He's been my loyal door-opener and coat-collector in the year since, and I appreciate the man's no-nonsense approach to Hades' gossipy demons more than he'll ever know.

Owen shrugs into his camelhair overcoat and closes the door behind us. I wait as he tugs brown leather gloves over his gnarled fingers before offering me his elbow. I take it, mostly because he gets flustered if I don't. A light dusting of snow covers the gravel drive, and the stuff still falling muffles the steady *crunch-crunch* of our steps. We pause at the massive wrought iron gates, Owen unlocks and opens the inset door, and bows again as I wave goodbye.

Cold air stings my face. The lights of Asphodel City glow in the distance. This nightly walk does me good, and tonight is no exception. By the time I've followed the path down the sloping hill to the edge of the lake and around to the hut, my mind is free of clutter.

"Lights."

Torches ring the hut's circular interior, flaring to life at my command. Bluish light infuses the trio of shades fluttering forward to take my coat and gloves before helping me into my robes. I pat the garment's front and sides, hoping to feel the lumpy roll of papers Hekate gave me in one of the pockets. Nothing, and when I straighten, the shades have already turned their backs and are floating off to wherever it is they wait.

"Papers."

I speak in the confident, assertive voice that wells up within me whenever I'm crowned and robed. The shades jostle to a stop, turning slowly as though they're conjoined triplets forced to move as a unit. The one to my left reaches through the stone wall, extracts the bundle, and holds it out to me.

"Thank you. That is all."

I wait until the trio has completely disappeared before pressing my right hand to a different section of the wall. Flecks of mica shimmer in the torchlight as granite bricks slide aside, revealing the second phase of my nightly descent.

Even now, after so much time and so many repetitions, my legs never tire of this journey - whether I'm going down or walking back up - and I wonder if it's the crown I wear, or the torch I bear, that provides the needed stamina. Or if it's simply that this nightly ritual allows me to fully inhabit a role that by its very name infuses me with the physical strength and emotional capacity to do things I cannot otherwise do.

Ugh, why didn't I stage a confrontation with Hades here, on *my* territory? Being Queen of the Underworld suits me, makes me feel grounded, purposeful, and I wish I could feel this way for more than a handful of hours at a time. But that would entail expanding my duties, and every immortal in charge of some aspect of the Underworld protects their role. Everyone, it seems, except Minthe.

Would I want to assume her duties? Halfway down, I hear paper crackle and realize I'm squeezing the roll in my hand. I set my torch into one of the iron rings hanging from the stone wall, loosen my hold enough for the papers to unfurl, and smooth the top sheet.

Columns titled 'Date', 'Location', and 'Proxy' have been filled in by hand. I recognize the locations, all of them along the River Kokytus, and none of the names, though the use of the term proxy confuses me. At last July's meeting of goddesses, we gave unanimous support to the hearth goddess, Habonde Barleywine, and her inspired idea to open a school for training interested Magicals in becoming proxies for goddesses in need of a break.

Prior to Habonde's raising the issue, I don't know that any of us ever thought about things like taking regular vacations, mental health breaks, or even maternity leave. The school opened barely a month ago, on Imbolc, which is far too fast to properly train a proxy in the ways of the Underworld, no matter how talented the trainee or minimal the duties.

Scanning the neat columns again, all I can surmise is that Minthe has, for reasons not immediately apparent to me, handed over her duties in the Underworld to others. I did not sign off on this change, which means Hades must have, for the temporary personnel to cause as little disruption as possible.

In that moment, I put two and two together - Minthe's apparent extended break, Hades' frequent absences coupled with his sudden need to be away for a week or more - and conclude they must have rekindled their relationship.

Chapter 5

MY HEARTBEAT ECHOES in my ears, counting out the seconds. Slowly, I re-roll the papers and slide them into one of the robe's deep pockets. I can accept Hades and Minthe getting back together, can't I? I close my eyes, search within my body for resistance, for… for any feeling of possessiveness or ownership around Hades. Human society tells me I should be furious for being placed in this awkward position, and most of the immortals I've known my entire life would echo that sentiment. Hells bells, they'd amplify their reactions. Indulge themselves in a public rampage. Burn down a city or two.

That's not me, though.

When the King and I gave each other permission to seek intimate relationships outside of our marriage, we promised we would be discrete. To my knowledge, Hades has kept his promise, while I haven't really had the opportunity or even the desire to test mine. At least, not until Astrape came along. During that same conversation, Hades and I agreed we would maintain our roles and obligations within the Underworld while we figured out how to undo our marital union in the most modern way possible.

Divorce is one area where immortals - with their affinity for banishment, dismemberment, and death - could mirror humans' more compassionate responses.

Questions hammer at the inside of my head. Why is Hades facilitating Minthe working less? Is he looking to take my crown from me, and place it on her head? I massage my temples, sliding a couple fingers between my crown and my scalp to ease the metal's tight grip. Does Minthe know the title "Queen of the Underworld" could never be hers? Do I know for certain the title is non-transferable?

Who would I even ask?

I lean into the wall's cool, steadfast presence for support. My heart's not the least bit hurt Hades found a lover. It's my gut that's in knots, the constant hunger I live with now accompanied by the fear that my place in the Underworld may be challenged.

Touching the chunk of quartz at the front of my crown, I tell myself I will not jump to conclusions, I will stay the course. I will wait for the succubus to tell me she served Hades; I will push for the dissolution of our marriage contract; and I will fortify the bonds I have with those in the Underworld who know I am their Queen and who treat me accordingly.

Pushing off the cool, rough stone, I smooth my robes, release any lingering concerns into the dark, and retake the torch before continuing downward. By the time I near the hall's cavernous waiting area, I'm breathing calmly, steadily. I pause beneath the arched entryway, surrounding myself with the scents and sounds of my workplace. Some days this place is loud, smelly, boisterous; other days it is filled with slumberous silence as the dead mill about as though waiting for the return of some remnant of who they once were.

Tonight, is somewhere in the middle, and more crowded than usual. Which should have prevented me from noticing the figure in a tattered cloak wending their way through the thickest part of the throng. The bits of fulgurite dancing in my tunic's pocket confirm it's Zeus, his leonine presence hidden by one of his countless disguises for a night of slumming in the Underworld.

Curious, I set my torch into a bracket, draw my ample hood up and over my crown, and join the shadows hugging the carved wall. A horn bellows, turning everyone's attention to the dais and the imminent appearance of the three judges. Zeus doesn't acknowledge the sound; instead, he veers towards the same wall I'm using as camouflage and disappears. Rising higher on my toes, I see the sloping tunnel that leads down to Tartarus looming in the distance. I track Zeus's progress and, when I'm sure I won't be seen, I follow.

The crowds moving upward through the tunnel thin to a trickle. Grateful for my boots' cushiony soles, I wrap myself in shadows for the long walk to the lowest level of the Underworld. Why Zeus has chosen to visit a place populated by prisoners he himself sentenced is a mystery worth exploring, as long as I remain undetected. The last thing I need is the King of the Sky picking a fight in a place I long ago claimed as my domain.

A reproachful voice reminds me I never actually *claimed* Tartarus. I wait for that voice to continue, and I'm met with silence. With Zeus on the move, there's no time to delve further. I reset my sights on my target. If I can stay close, discover who he's here to see, perhaps listen in on any conversations, who knows what ammunition I can pick up.

Snorting softly, I correct myself: *information*, not ammunition. Zeus and I are not at war, and I'll revisit the question of Tartarus… later.

Around me, the noisy mélange of voices, metal-on-metal, and stone-on-stone, increases in volume. Smells of hot metal and sweaty bodies intensify. The cashmere top I chose for its warmth clings to my clammy skin. I don't descend all the way to Tartarus very often, and when I do, it's usually with enough notice I can wear lighter layers under my official robes, as well as a less weighty crown.

Zeus is now the only figure ahead of me. He's tucked a gnarled wooden staff under one arm and leans on it heavily. As he moves forward, he favors his right leg. His performance is remarkably believable. Then again, he's a master of disguise. Any number of gods, goddesses, and mortals will testify to that - if given immunity.

Cumbersome chains and the weighty pull of ancient edicts, curses, and spells keep the prisoners confined to Tartarus' three levels from escaping. And that marks the full extent of my knowledge about this place. Gray shapes pass in front of Zeus and though I can't make out who or what they are from this distance, I assume some are immortals and some are guards. Reaching upward, I push back the wide hood covering my head, carefully remove my crown, and tuck it within the front halves of my robe.

"Kronos!" Zeus yells.

"Fuck off!"

Stifling a snort, I cover my mouth and nose at the shouted exchange between Zeus and his godsfather, whom I can't see through the gloom. Shuffling feet, giant ones, if the echoes bouncing off the carved stone walls are any indication, approach from beyond where Zeus waits. Every few steps, the ground beneath my boots reverberates from whatever Kronos drags along with him.

"You're looking well."

"I said, 'Fuck. Off'."

I see where Zeus gets his surliness.

"I will, once you answer my question."

Something heavy and stone-like lands near Zeus and the thick mist in front of him separates, revealing Kronos' hunched, human form, and a wood-handled mace. "What's in it for me?" he growls.

"The company of a fine nymph? More palatable food? A better selection of wine?" Kronos chuffs out an unintelligible response. Moments later, fetid fumes fill the space around me. I pull the side of my hood across my face and force myself to stay put. Zeus adds, "A good teeth-cleaning?"

Kronos harrumphs. "What is wrong with you? Or is this another of your fancy disguises, and you've come to mock my circumstances?"

"I lost my foot."

"Well, I haven't seen it." Kronos bats at the air and starts to turn. "You too lazy to grow it back?"

"I can't grow it back, which is why I'm here."

Outrageous laughter fills the space. Kronos' entire body shakes. Stretching his arms wide, he repeats Zeus' confession to whomever passes behind him within the embrace of the opaque mists. "Fine turn of events, the pup wanting my help."

"I do."

"Come see me in seven days. And bring your foot."

"And what if I can't find it?"

"Bring a block of wood and your carving tools."

Kronos disappears into the thickening mist. I press my back against the uneven wall and drop my chin toward my chest, allowing my hood to conceal my face. I'm a couple hours early to sit in with the court of judgement, which makes it fine to wait until Zeus' shuffling gait fades before I retrace my steps.

The fact that Zeus cannot regenerate his own foot is startling news. I view his confession as another indication that his powers are fading, which underlines my theory he's beyond due for his Godsrest and begs the question, has he passed the point of no return?

Normally, I would have no interest in manipulating the game

board where Zeus reigns as King and Hera as Queen - she *terrifies* me - but this information is too startling to ignore. Can I get his predicament to work in my favor? And if so, how?

Kronos' laugh continues to rumble in the background.

Kronos. I replace my crown atop my head and fluff out my robes. Time to make nice with the relatives.

Chapter 6

POTENT WAFTS of sweat and rot fill my nostrils and set my
stomach churning. It doesn't help that Tartarus' stench is held in
place by a dense, cloying fog. I hear movement all around me,
and see vague, body-like shadows of what I assume are prisoners,
but I'm quickly losing my bearings.

This is a bad idea, and I find myself wondering if getting
divorced is worth never getting this smell out of my nose or these
clothes. I almost abandon my plan to speak with the ancient
Titan.

"Queen Persephone."

A demon emerges from the fog, drops to one knee in front of
me, and bows their head. Another appears, and another, and
soon I am surrounded by kneeling beings, uniformed in a motley
assortment of ancient breastplates, gauntlets, greaves, and other
bits of armor I don't recall the terms for. While the guards
continue to avert their eyes, I adjust my crown and quietly clear
my throat.

"You may rise," I say, in my queenliest voice. The sextet
pushes off the floor as one and stands, their horned heads

towering above the tips of my crown. Though I'm discovering there are things to like about Tartarus, I dislike feeling crowded. I lift my arm and signal for the demons to take a step back.

"How may we be of service, my Queen?" one asks. My first thought is to inquire if they would like to work at House of Hades, replacing the disrespectful, thick-horned guards Hades favors.

"You may bring Kronos to me."

The lead guard nods curtly. Another positions themselves at Tartarus' arched entrance, facing outward. The remaining four peel away and disappear into the gloom. "This could take some time. Kronos can be very stubborn."

I give the remaining guard a regal nod and run through possible conversation starters. Small talk has never been a strength of mine. "Are you happy with your job?"

They look as though I've asked them to rip out one of their kidneys. "My Queen?"

"Are you happy with your job, your— your position here in Tartarus?"

They swallow so hard I can see their throat move. "It has its plusses."

"Which it infers it has its minuses," I comment. "Would you care to elaborate?"

"Will I— Are there—?"

"I would not have asked if I did not desire the truth, Guard. Please, tell me what it's like to work in Tartarus. Hold nothing back."

They lick their lips nervously. "The prisoners are a handful, but we have ways to keep them under control. It's the hours. They're never-ending. I'm new here, but those who have been here longer would tell you we've been short-staffed since last July."

"Short-staffed? Why is that?"

"The King pulled eight of the youngest guards out of rotation."

"Did he offer an explanation?"

"He said they were needed elsewhere in the Underworld, that he was having staffing issues along the rivers, and the nymph in charge couldn't manage on her own."

"Did the King explain why?"

"No, ma'am."

"Was that nymph Minthe?"

Sweat beaded along the guard's forehead. "Yes, my Queen. She's not been seen since the guards left their posts."

Minthe, Minthe, Minthe. After not hearing her name for ages, suddenly, it's everywhere.

"And what is your name?" I place a hand on his forearm. "I want to reassure you your job is secure. Anything you say to me will be kept in the strictest confidence."

"Köhler. Captain Joachim Köhler."

"And where are you from, Captain Köhler?"

"Aurora."

The city he names lies within the demons' Reformed Realm. "Do you get home regularly?"

"No, my Queen." His slick, black wings, which signal he's a mated demon and which he holds tightly behind him, quiver. "Not for many, many weeks."

"I shall have to rectify that. Would you please make a list of what you and your staff require to make your work here more tolerable and forward it to me at House of Hades by tomorrow?"

His response is interrupted by grumbling and I recognize Kronos' intense odor. Joachim thrusts a small jar into my hand. "Rub this under your nose. It's the only thing we've found to combat the smell."

I unscrew the lid and swipe menthol-infused balm inside each nostril. He's right; it helps, and I glance at the label before I return the jar, thinking this could be something I might convince Rini to add to her product line. "Thank you."

Four guards herd Kronos forward and stop, forming a tight half-circle behind him. The aged Titan looks around, confused. I don't expect him to recognize me, nor do I expect to see one renowned for his brutality to appear so shockingly bedraggled. His waist-length beard is matted into a solid mass, his chlamys is ripped and filthy, and layers of peeling duct tape are all that keep his sandals attached to his feet.

"Kronos, I'm Persephone."

"I know who you are," he mutters, looking me up and down with wavering, slightly unfocused eyes. "First Zeus. Now you. What have I done to deserve all this attention?"

Chapter 7

I ANSWER Kronos with the first thing that pops into my head. "As Queen of the Underworld, seeing to the health of those imprisoned here is one of my duties."

"Why is this the first I am seeing you this far down?" The Titan's fingers play along the tattered edge of cloth crossing his chest. I pray the awful thing doesn't disintegrate before my eyes and realize my distaste must be obvious. I relax my features and conjure a friendlier face.

"Earlier, I noticed Zeus had arrived in one of his disguises and I was curious to know who he came to visit."

Kronos snorts, blowing snot into his equally overgrown moustache. "He tells me he has lost his foot and thinks to find it here."

If this is some strange game the Titans and Olympians play amongst themselves, it's one I've never heard of. "And is his missing foot here in Tartarus?"

"No. But the answer to growing it back is." Kronos taps a finger against his temple. Interesting.

"Could I ask you a favor?"

"You may ask, Queen Persephone. I may answer if the reward fits."

The best reward I can offer is a pressure washer and industrial strength cleaning products. I tailor my wording to appeal to his ego. "What would you say to a feast fit for an elder god? And a hot bath beforehand?"

He leans toward me. Though the demon's menthol salve almost covers Kronos' smell, I pre-empt an olfactory disaster and breathe through my mouth. "Meat. I want meat," he grunts "And don't overcook it. Just stun the beast and bring it to me. I shall do the rest."

One of the guards coughs into their fist. "He's not allowed a knife, my Queen."

"Your bath will come first, then the meal. I will specify your preferences to the chef."

"And in return?"

"In return, I ask that you swear you will not tell Zeus how to regenerate his foot, or any other body part. Or that we had this conversation." Kronos extends his arm. He expects me to shake his hand, and so I do, clenching my teeth to keep myself from involuntarily grimacing at the sensation. I release his grip at the earliest opportunity. "I will have a guard escort you to House of Hades tomorrow afternoon."

The milky clouds muting Kronos' eyes dissipate. The sclera shines white and both irises twinkle with summer sky blue. "And will there be dessert?" he wheedles.

Spying a wily clarity behind his grimy, off-putting façade, I assure him there will be dessert. He dips forward in awkward acknowledgment before allowing two of the guards to turn and lead him away. The other two look to Joachim for orders.

"The queen we are here to serve has made a promise to us as well," he begins, checking for my approval before continuing. I give it. "We are to return to our regular shifts, including time at our homes."

"Suitable replacements for the staff you have lost will be here by the end of the week," I add. I will personally contact Queen Violetta of the Reformed Realm to clarify what the arrangement is for subjects of hers working in the Underworld, and the location of the portal I assume the demons use to travel back and forth. "I thank you for your service, and I apologize for the burden added to your already strenuous workload." They again drop to one knee and bow their heads. I stifle the urge to stop them. I am the Queen of the Underworld, after all, and they are mine to care for and to command. After an appropriate amount of time, I ask the guards to stand.

"Remember your list, Captain Köhler." I gather my robes in my hands and make my way toward the hallway's gaping entrance. A sly smile curls my lips, because I'm certain Kronos is exactly the type of guest Chef Keldt desires to wow. Though I enjoy the sensation for a fleeting moment, if asked, I would say I'm not the conniving type. But as I leave Kronos and Tartarus behind, a part of me is pleased with how the evening unfolded. Pleased, and perturbed. Hades is covering for Minthe and it's starting to feel a bit crowded in my marriage, and in my role as queen.

Which has me wondering what lies at the root of these incidents. Is it purely coincidental? Is Minthe doing more than staking her claim on Hades? If that's so, then I would think he would be the one chasing me to sign divorce papers.

I ponder all this and more throughout my shift; on my way back up the underground stairs to the hut; as the shades help me out of my robe and into my long winter coat; and on the walk to the wrought iron gates fronting House of Hades. Ever-faithful Owen is there waiting, silvery gray snowflakes dusting his bare head and the shoulders of his overcoat.

"And how was your night, my Queen?" he asks, tucking his elbow close to his side once I take hold of his arm.

"Everything is in its proper place, Owen," I reply, sharing no details. Much as I adore this lovely man and his constancy, he is not my confidante. At least, not yet. By the time we say goodnight and I return the red beryl crown to its shelf, I realize what it is that most bothers me about what I learned, and it's not the information in the rolled-up papers, or what Joachim the guard shared.

It's my reactions. They feel… delayed, and my emotions… my emotions are muted. I know there are those who would say I'm a woman scorned by a powerful husband, and that a healthy response would be to rant and rave and exact a painful revenge.

But Hades hasn't scorned me; if anything, I withdrew from our marriage first and we scorned one another in tandem. And if my goal is my own happiness, my… my independence and autonomy, then why would I think it's a good move to build my future on a foundation fashioned from someone else's unhappiness? That tack might satisfy some. To me, it's abhorrent.

There is more to these insights than I can fathom in a few short hours - to say nothing of the apparent claim I staked on Tartarus. It has gone from being a concept, to a place with living, breathing beings in need of better working, and living, conditions. My musings follow me to bed, and a restless sleep.

CAPTAIN KÖHLER'S handwritten list waits on the dining room table, alongside a tray set with a small pot for brewing tea. I choose rose pouchong to start my day, and portion out two teaspoons of loose-leaf tea to steep. Seeing the guard's neat writing reminds me I said I would find replacement staff suitable for guard duty in the demanding environs of Tartarus and see to the Captain's other requests before I leave for the aboveworld. I jot a note below his last notation to contact Queen Violetta and ask about hiring more of her demons.

There are now three days left before I'm due at my mother's and I have more on my plate, not less, including contacting the succubus to see if she's served Hades, and having a conversation with Chef Keldt about a meal for Kronos. And who should I speak with about arranging a bath for the rancid Titan I invited to dinner?

I smother a laugh at the idea of Kronos dining here, with me, rather than choosing the easier route and having the food sent to him.

"What's so funny?" Gilda asks, sliding onto the chair opposite me and setting two plates of toast in front us. Toast is about the only food I can handle when I first wake up. Though I eye her scrambled eggs with longing.

"I've invited a guest to have dinner with me tonight," I explain, adding, "in the formal dining room."

"And who's the lucky invitee?"

"A guest worthy of the best House of Hades has to offer, someone I think Chef Keldt will turn themselves inside out to accommodate."

"Now that is something I'd like to see." Gilda tilts her head to the side and searches my face. I pinch my lips to keep from blurting out any more. "You are up to something."

"Yes, I am." I pour the rose tea, Gilda serves herself from her own pot, and we lift delicate porcelain cups to our mouths. I can see she's dying to pry and I'm dying to share my uncharacteristically wicked deed. "I invited Kronos."

Her eyes widen and the feathery gills alongside her elegant neck flare before settling against her skin. "He'll need a bath first, and clothes," I continue, drawing my notepad and fountain pen toward me. I can trust Owen to handle dressing Kronos with the attentiveness the old god likely thinks he deserves.

"Are you initiating a rehabilitation program for the prisoners?" Gilda asks.

I stop mid-motion, re-cap my pen, and place it beside the notepad. Though my immediate impulse is to brush her question aside with a joke, I can't. What I witnessed in Tartarus was disturbing. Guards brought in from other realms being overworked and underappreciated. Prisoners coated in their own filth, everyone breathing in polluted air. Given that Hades pulled staff from Tartarus, I assume he has some knowledge of what's going on. But does he ever wander farther than the reception area, or wonder what lies beyond the mists?

"Persephone?"

The golden salamander's vocal nudge pushes me out of my musing. I sip my tea, set the cup down, and look across the table. Gilda is my closest advisor when I'm in the underworld and she knows she's set my mind to churning.

"Perhaps?"

"Maybe that's exactly what the Underworld needs." She lifts her cup, sips her tea, and lowers it halfway to the table.

"Maybe it is," I concede. "But first, *I* need a fresh start, which can only happen with Hades' signature on the divorce papers."

The tiniest sigh exits my assistant's neck gills, followed by the sharp clink of her cup hitting the saucer. "May I speak frankly, Persephone?"

"Don't you always?" My response comes out sounding much snippier than I meant. "I'm sorry, that was rude of me. Yes, please, continue."

"It occurs to me that if you were to pay more attention to Tartarus and its inhabitants, it might be exactly the thing you need to make the months you spend in the Underworld more palatable."

____

Chapter 8

____

I MULL OVER Gilda's challenge, and the string of thoughts set off by seeing Zeus. He may employ trickery for the occasional foray into Tartarus - I would disguise myself, too, if I chose to walk amongst beings I had sentenced to eternal lockup - but he rules from a throne set high above the clouds, and I am Queen of *this* plane.

Descending the staircase in my wing of the house, it dawns on me that nothing I ever read, or was told, prohibits me from interacting with Tartarus' prisoners, or asking them to dinner, or even re-hearing their case and releasing them if I feel they have served their time.

"Owen?" I reach the main foyer to find the butler's not in his usual spot in his corner chair. The muffled rattle of a drawer handle alerts me he's nearby.

"In here, my Queen."

His voice sounds from deep within the coat closet, which opens onto a spacious, wood-paneled room with stations for mending clothes, and polishing boots and shoes. Soon after arriving, the dear man confessed he couldn't fathom an estate without a room dedicated to the art of sartorial repairs. I had the guest coat closet expanded, remodeled, and equipped to his specifications.

"Stay put," I say, raising my voice. "I'll come to you."

"As you wish."

I pass racks for footwear, hats, and umbrellas, and rods to hang jackets, overcoats, and capes. Owen sits at a workbench situated below a window, looking very nineteenth century in a canvas apron and matching sleeve protectors. The scents of beeswax and something sharper, earthier, rise from an uncapped tin of shoe polish and fill my nose.

"What brings you into the closet today, my Queen?" he asks, looking up. Golden light from the lamp at his elbow washes his patrician features, and I'm reminded how grateful I am our paths crossed when they did.

"We're going to have a special guest at dinner, someone I met when I visited Tartarus last night. Unfortunately, he has no clothes."

"No clothes at all?" Owen lowers his shoe brush to the bench and wipes his hands on a rag.

"Nothing I want anywhere near my food," I confide, adding "The problem is, he's taller than Hades and broad across the shoulders. Like you. Which means I can't go pilfering from the king's closet."

"I haven't much in the way of spare pants and shirts, but I can alter anything."

"I wasn't thinking of asking to borrow your things," I reassure him. Owen continues to feel personally responsible when he can't immediately provide me with what I ask for. I may have to learn to rephrase my questions. "Don't we have a, a lost and found box or something?"

There, that gets him thinking. Owen scans the room, then peers past me, to the coat closet. "No, though I do have a collection of clean uniforms for use in the kitchen when Chef brings in extra help for parties. Give me a couple of hours to dye a coat and a pair of pants blue, or brown," he says as he stands purposefully. "I can also cut and sew a pair of boxers out of the used sheets the housekeeping staff gives me to use for polishing rags."

I cover my smile with my hand and attempt to maintain my composure. This whim of mine has the potential to turn comedic - or tragic. Hopefully, Kronos won't ask about the provenance of his new clothes, and Chef Keldt won't notice our esteemed guest is wearing a once-white chef's jacket.

"Owen, your solution sounds like it will address the problem beautifully. And I would go with blue over brown," I add, remembering the true color of Kronos' eyes.

"Excellent. I shall change out the buttons on the chef's coat, too, perhaps add a silk cravat." He tugs off his sleeve protectors and washes his hands at the soapstone sink, the embodiment of a man on a mission. "Reminds me of the days when I would help the children gather costumes for school plays."

At that, the corners of Owen's mouth droop. "I miss them," he whispers, steadying himself on the sink's front edge and shaking his head. "Such a tragedy."

I open my arms and offer him a hug, welcoming the combined scents of pine soap and shoe polish that accompany my butler's embrace. This gentle giant might be the only male I know who comes close to embodying the father figure I wish I'd had.

NEXT UP IS a conversation with Chef Keldt. I consider summoning Joachim and borrowing the guards' armor, motley as it is, to add a layer of protection, and decide the nails I sharpened before my too-brief meeting with Hades are still capable of drawing blood.

Stepping from the wood-paneled warmth of Owen's domain into the mansion's chilly foyer, I admit I'm much braver and more vocal inside my head than in real life situations. I enter the side corridor leading to the kitchen and square my shoulders before pushing on the swinging door.

It's quiet as I enter the chef's lair, which could have something to do with Hades being away. Chef Keldt's formidable bulk lurks behind the large window in his office. I tap the glass; he does me the discourtesy of rolling his chair and leaning back enough his head pokes through the doorway, forcing me to step out of his way. This demon simply does not understand he's digging his own grave.

"What are you doing in my kitchen?"

I cross my arms and arch one eyebrow. I've been practicing the look; it's one of Demeter's signature expressions and she uses it to great effect. Turns out it works for me too. Chef Keldt scrambles to smooth the front of his starched white chef's coat as he stands.

"I have invited a guest to dinner tonight and I want the meal served in the formal dining room."

Chef begins to sputter. I barrel right through his protestations, even as my eyebrow twitches. "My guest has requested beef, as close to raw as you can prepare it. I trust you can devise a menu on short notice that is worthy of House of Hades' reputation?"

"May I know the name of this guest?"

"No, you may not. Have appetizers for two readied by seven. My guest and I will start in the Club Room. And consult with the sommelier about wines." I turn on my heel. Kronos will like the Club Room, with its boxy leather chairs and soaring central fireplace. I'll even fetch him a cigar if he asks for one. Before I leave the kitchen, I add, "My guest will be accompanied by two guards. See that there is a meal for them, too."

Returning to my office, I send a message to Joachim, asking him, along with another guard of his choosing, to accompany Kronos to House of Hades at four. I assume three hours will be enough time for the ancient god to bathe, groom, and dress, which means I need to speak with Hades' personal servant and make sure the demon clears his schedule.

Or I could ask Gilda to do that for me. She often chides me for not delegating enough and assures me it's very queenly to utilize the skills and services of those I employ. She's not in the kitchen, but now that I'm here, I realize I'm hungry for more than cold toast. Single-serving sized cut glass bowls of fruit salad tempt me from behind the refrigerator's glass door. I take a bowl, and a spoon, and pop my head into Gilda's office.

"There's something I'd like you do to," I begin, moving the fruit around with the spoon, "and it entails informing Hades' personal staff that we have a VIP guest coming to dinner tonight." She glances at me over the top of her mother of pearl-rimmed eyeglasses, grins wickedly, and flutters her neck frills.

"Those Eisochsen demons he hires think way too highly of themselves. They'll balk at your request, you know." Gilda's grin grows more devilish and I'm almost sorry for what I'm about to unleash on those arrogant, unsuspecting beasts.

"Then maybe you should hang around and supervise once the Tartarian guards deliver Kronos."

"Maybe I should."

"They'll be here at four. I told the guards to come to the front door."

"The front door?" Gilda pivots her chair and slaps her palms on her knees. "Oh, Persephone, thank Goddess and Spirit for your conniving side. I promise to make sure the other side of the house is ready."

Chapter 9

I PUT the finishing touches on my makeup and survey my work. I might have gone a little heavy on the kohl eyeliner, while lipstick the rich purple shade of a dusty plum enhances the slightly gothic look I'm emulating. But when I stand and smooth down the three-quarter length sleeves of my black lace-over-silk cocktail dress, I feel youthfully elegant. Self-assured. Ready to choose a fitting final touch, something that doesn't scream "Underworld".

I have a few headpieces set with purple gemstones; tonight, I'm drawn to a silver circlet adorned with teardrops of sugilite, the holding stone of life's dreams. Each deep lavender stone is framed by handmade silver dots. As the spells embedded within the metal snug the piece to my head, I stand taller, lengthening my neck as though Demeter's voice is echoing inside my head. Which makes sense. She gave me this crown - and she's a stickler for good posture.

My mother's words fade, and I can't stop questions about my life's greater purpose from rising to the surface. What am I hoping to accomplish tonight? Am I just filling the hours until I depart for the aboveworld, or will drilling Kronos about Zeus and other topics give my seasons in the Underworld that sense of purpose I've been missing?

Noise filters in from beyond my doors. I table my questions, counting Owen's steady steps as he makes his way from the lobby to my wing of the house and knocks.

"Enter."

He gives me a quick bow, a habit I can't seem to convince him to relinquish, and holds the pose for a beat. Once he straightens, his implacable features offer me no clues about the past few hours. "Your guest is ready, my queen. I situated him in the Club Room."

"And how did everything go?" I'm dying to know what Kronos thought of the royal treatment I arranged. I'll get fuller details out of Gilda later. No matter how the Eisochsen demons feel about me, they'll spill to Gilda if the gossip's juicy enough.

Owen's eyes twinkle. I take the elbow he offers, grateful for the escort. He clears his throat as he closes the door behind us. "Kronos is clean, shaved, and dressed. I found appropriate footwear, and the king's assistant provided unworn underclothing and socks."

"And everyone lived to tell the tale?"

Suppressed laughter rumbles through Owen's barrel chest. "Everyone lived. Though the demon assigned to hosing Kronos the first time might be wishing he'd chosen a different career path." I hide a laugh behind my hand, then thank Owen again. He pats the fingers I curl around his forearm. "You've given me reason to live, my queen. 'Twas a pleasure to rise to the challenge your task presented."

We stop in the common area's wide hall. Heavy sliding doors open onto the Club Room, revealing crackling flames in the floating fireplace centered within the right side of the room. Kronos lounges in one of the leather chairs facing the fire, a snifter of amber liquid in one hand. His other hand rests on his knee and he looks elegant, refined, like he's the rightful master of the house.

"Where did he get that ring?" I whisper, pressing my hand to my belly to calm the sudden and unexpected nervous flutter. Have I taken on more than I can manage? Is Kronos going to be another burdensome male?

"He brought it with him. In his beard." My eyes widen in disbelief as I look up at Owen. "That was not all we found," he adds, drawing me across the threshold and leaving me wondering.

"May I present Persephone, Queen of the Underworld." My steadfast helper releases me, then makes his way to the bar.

"Persephone!" Kronos leans forward to set his glass on the slate shelf surrounding the fireplace and pushes himself up to standing. His movements are fluid, elegant even, and I wonder if I've been played, if Zeus is not the only one employing ratty costumes to disguise his intentions.

"Kronos."

The Titan solves my question of what to do next by skirting his chair and taking both my hands. He lifts them to his lips and kisses my knuckles. "Thank you for your hospitality, my dear."

I quickly hide my shock, because he smells clean, he looks dashing, and though I know the provenance of his cotton jacket and pants, he wears them as though they were bespoke. Owen steps up to us at the perfect moment, bearing a round silver tray with a flute of the vintage champagne he knows I adore. I raise my glass to Kronos.

"Thank you for coming."

He bows slightly. "May I call you Persephone, or would you prefer Queen or some epithet of which I am not aware? Granddaughter doesn't seem quite right."

"My friends call me Persephone." I sweep my glass toward the chairs. I don't trust my knees to not buckle. "Shall we sit?"

"After you."

I lower myself onto an armless, upholstered chair, one with a solid pillow to cushion my lower back. Crossing my ankles, I tuck my legs to the side. Owen returns with a larger tray, places it on the small table positioned between our two chairs, and adds two plates bearing the House of Hades' crest. Kronos and I stare at the tray of offerings, at the empty plates and the pale gray linen cocktail napkins. A solid minute ticks by.

"May I fix you a plate?" I ask. Though I'm slightly nervous and surprisingly hungry, I'm unsure what I'm even looking at. The hors d'oeuvres Chef Keldt sent in look like he raided the garden's dormant bushes, came out with abandoned bird's nests, and decided to call it edible art.

"What in the bowels of Tartarus is this stuff?"

Kronos waves a manicured hand back and forth over the tray. I stifle a giggle and confide I'm thinking the same thing. He glances at me from under his bushy, albeit newly trimmed and shaped, eyebrows. "You did tell your cook I wanted meat, didn't you?" he asks, in a conspiratorial whisper.

"I made your request crystal clear to Chef Keldt." I take up a fork and poke at a nest fashioned from strips of… of mushrooms, maybe, and those clear vermicelli noodles? I'm not sure. "Perhaps he just wants to make sure you get your vegetables in before he drags a steer to the table."

I manage to jettison the tension I'm holding and at the same time endear myself to Kronos. He takes his fork and jabs at a cluster of jellied eggs mounded atop a nest of purple-stemmed sprouts, which sends the glistening blobs rolling onto the tray.

"Ready for a refill?"

Kronos' fork lands with a clatter as he trades stabbing hors d'oeuvres for handing up his tumbler to Owen for more of whatever he's drinking. "I would kill for a cheeseball."

"I have a nicely aged cheddar left over from my lunch. Would that do?"

At the Titan's grunt, Owen excuses himself. It dawns on me that Chef Keldt's plan is to embarrass me in front of my guest. "I'm sorry," I begin. "I really was very clear about your request."

Kronos watches me closely as he takes another sip. His gaze shifts from thoughtful to conniving. "I could eat him," he offers, waggling his eyebrows. "Though Zeus might be tempted to add more years to my eternal sentence. He does love to go for the overkill."

"I didn't invite you here to eat my staff."

He sucks on his teeth. "Why did you invite me into your grand estate, dear Persephone?"

"I told you why. To thank you for not sharing your secrets with Zeus."

"In exchange for a feast befitting an elder god. This," he growled, flicking his wrist at the deconstructed terrarium sitting on the silver tray, "is no feast."

"It's because of me."

"Go on."

"Hades hires most of the staff from the Eisochsen Realm. Chef Keldt prefers to answer directly to my— to the King."

"And him?" Kronos asks, gesturing to Owen as the butler exchanges the offending tray for a wooden cutting board piled with slices of pungent cheese, clusters of green and dusky purple grapes, and a heel of whole grain bread.

"I assume you mean me?" Owen sets a small pair of scissors near the fruit. "I was but a lost and lonely soul wandering the banks of an unfamiliar river. Queen Persephone saw me, recognized my distress, and made me welcome in her home."

Kronos tears apart the bread, loads a piece of cheese on a bite, and hands it over to me before serving himself. "And would you lay down your life for your queen, humble servant?"

"Without hesitation."

"Then I suggest the three of us visit the kitchen."

Chapter 10

MY BELLY QUIETS once I've had a few bites of dairy and carbs. Though I'm not sure what Kronos has in mind, I lead the way out of the Club Room and into the hall bisecting the center portion of the House. Kronos tells a joke, Owen chortles, and as I turn into the short corridor leading to the kitchen, I can't stop myself from thinking this is *not* what I should be doing this close to partaking in the Lesser Mysteries.

I should be sequestered, cleansing my mind, body, and soul in preparation for assisting my mother - not orchestrating an encounter between a human who stumbled into the Underworld, an elder god who did terrible things to his offspring, and a conniving chef.

Or maybe this is exactly the diversion I need to wash away the pain of the situation with Hades and Minthe; the doldrums of being here, in the gray days between winter and spring before arriving in the aboveworld, where the skies are blue and the clouds are white, not hundreds of shades of gray. Before I can change my mind and leave these two to make their own entertainment, Owen lengthens his stride to slip around me and push on the service door.

"Persephone, Queen of the Underworld," he booms, "and her guest, Kronos, King of the Titans."

Chef Keldt's gaze sweeps past me as though my presence is inconsequential, and latches onto Kronos. Swiping his knife-wielding arm through the air, he bends from the waist in an exaggerated bow. "King Kronos, welcome to my humble kitchen. I trust the delicacies delivered to the Club Room met with your satisfaction?"

Kronos crosses his arms and ignores Chef's simpering. "Where's the meat?"

"I… I…" Simpering turns to sputtering which leads to a puffed-up chest and a switch into a different language. "I designed this meal as a journey for sophisticated palates, starting with appetizers constructed from vegetables to reflect the humble origins of the young steer."

House of Hades' chef lapses into the Eisochsen's Germanic dialect when he's upset. Owen, who's familiar with these tirades, keeps the service door open with his back. Kronos ignores the rising tide of distress and Chef's glowing horns, and proceeds to move through the kitchen, elbowing aside the other cooks on his way to the glass-fronted refrigerators.

"Chef," I start, raising my voice and calling forth Persephone the Placater. "I think what my guest is trying to say is he came here this evening expecting one thing and was served another. I assume a meat course is coming, and soon?"

The sputtering stops. Chef Keldt stomps toward the back of the kitchen, which opens onto the herb and vegetable gardens and greenhouses that supply the House with fresh produce. A metal door slams against a wall, a waft of barnyard enters the kitchen, and another round of yelling commences. I follow Chef, grabbing Kronos' jacket sleeve as I pass him nosily lifting pot lids, and drag him with me.

"*This* is the meat course," Chef Keldt announces, shaking the thick rope attaching a massive, living beast to a ring embedded in the mansion's granite facade. "I believe your guest's exact words were, 'bring the animal to the table and stun it' and that is what I plan to do."

I fight to hold back my laughter. Kronos, who must have reiterated his request to the demons wielding the hoses and hedge trimmers, appears to feel no compunction toward politeness or propriety. He howls with laughter, the chef tosses up his arms and storms back inside, and the steer makes a plaintive, lowing sound.

"Does he not understand metaphor?" the Titan asks, wiping his eyes and patting the innocent animal's broad forehead.

"Apparently not."

"Come."

I follow Kronos inside. Passing Chef Keldt's office, I note both his starched coat and tall, pleated hat lie piled atop his desk. Scattered throughout the kitchen, the handful of assistants look to Kronos, then to me, then back to Kronos. Joachim and the other Tartarian guard enter through the door Owen continues to keep open.

I have seconds to salvage this situation. Luckily, I also have the heels and crown to give me height. "Since it appears Chef Keldt has abandoned his station, it is up to all of you to provide a meal worthy of the King of the Titans." Clapping my hands, I give directions as they come to me. "Fire up the grill. Find the best cuts of steak. Gather red peppers and whole onions. Someone get baking sourdough rolls.

"Kronos, can you take charge of cooking the meat?" He's already rolling up his jacket sleeves. I take that as a yes. "Everyone, let Kronos know how you like your steak. Make mine medium rare. Owen?"

"My Queen."

"Set Kronos up with an apron, then come help me with the table. And where's the sommelier?"

One of the assistant cooks raises their hand. "Chef gave her the night off."

I had asked specifically for Hades' resident expert's input into wine pairings for this meal. Fuming, I lean my hip against the stainless-steel prep table and address the six assistants left behind.

"As of this moment, Chef Keldt is out of a job. If any of you find that you cannot, or will not, take orders from me, you are welcome to follow him out the door." I drum my fingers on the table's cool, polished surface. "You must decide now. My guests are hungry, as am I."

The one who raised their hand before, raises it again. "Ma'am, uh, I mean, Queen Persephone?"

"Yes."

"I'm the sommelier's understudy and I would very much like to stay."

"You're hired. Anyone else?"

One other, a female demon by the shape of her horns, also raises their hand. "I would like to stay. I have no problem taking orders from you. Ma'am. I mean, Your Highness." Her cheeks go bright red.

"You're hired. The rest of you, gather your personal belongings and leave. You have twenty minutes to be off the estate." The remaining four grumble as they split off. The two who elected to stay appear shell-shocked. "What are your names?" I ask, now that my irritation has dispersed.

"Torsten."

"Jutta."

"Torsten, go with Owen to the wine cellar. Choose something that pairs well with seared beef and roasted vegetables. Owen will know which glasses to set out. Jutta, assist Kronos." I clap my hands again, hoping it will get the reduced staff moving. "Captain Köhler, you two prep the vegetables. Kronos, may I assume you know how to work a grill?"

"I know how to cook over a fire," he says, "so if Jutta can show me to the fire and hand over the meat, I can give us a meal."

As if I've thrown a switch, the kitchen bursts to life. Flames leap from the top of the grill, to Kronos' obvious delight. Wide-eyed Jutta leaves him to load up a platter with steaks, and Joachim and the other guard gather the vegetables I specified. Satisfied everything is as under control as the Fates allow, I leave the kitchen for the wine cellar to discover Owen has an adoring fan in Torsten. The two are deep in consultation, and my presence isn't needed.

Back upstairs, I open the double doors to the formal dining room, pausing to re-orient myself. I'm here to set the table, not to be seated, and it takes me a minute to locate the butler's pantry, then decide which sets of dishes and flatware I want to use. Counting out a stack of linen dinner napkins, I shake my head. Rini, Ciri, and Bé will think I'm making this up. Me, Persephone, taking the literal bull by the horns to get her guest of honor the meal he was promised.

I decide the table's far too large for just me and one guest. At one end, I add place settings for Owen, Joachim, the other Tartarian guard, and two more for Torsten and Jutta - because why not have the staff join us? I return to the butler's pantry to search for candlesticks and candles, of which there are many, thanks to Hades' obsession. I choose simple beeswax tapers and set them in cubes of brushed stainless steel.

Banging resounds from the front of the house. I step into the hallway, intending to call for Owen to answer the door, when I remember he's off procuring wine. And because I've just fired three-quarters of the kitchen staff, that means I'm on door duty. I hurry as best I can on platform heels meant more for show, than go, and must stop myself from gasping when I see who's waiting on the other side of the sand-blasted glass panels.

"Dionysus?" I swallow my shock. Snowflakes and the ever-present gray mist swirl around the god's silhouette.

"Persephone! You're home! What a delightful coincidence."

Chapter 11

COINCIDENCE? I'm not so sure. I open the door wider and beckon him inside. More snowy swirls follow the sweep of his overcoat. He hands me a bottle of wine, shucks his coat, and hands it to—

"Where's your butler?" he asks, holding the velvet-lined collar while executing a matador's tight circle. Dionysus' flare for dramatic gestures has not waned.

"Owen's in the wine room with the under-sommelier."

"And where is your uber-sommelier?"

I'd forgotten this god, with his appreciation for a good meal and exquisite wine, is very attuned to how House of Hades is staffed. "Chef Keldt gave her the night off."

"And Chef Keldt?"

"I fired him."

Dionysus grimaces. "You fired him? For what, not enough eggs in his quiche?"

"Insubordination. Again."

"Please don't tell me you banished Hades before he could tell me where he procures his cigars." His eyes flash with humor.

"No, I did not banish the King." I lead my guest into the closet and hand him a sturdy wooden hanger. "Hades left the Underworld yesterday. He said he'd be away for a while."

Acknowledging Hades takes some of the wind out of my sails. Dionysus harrumphs as he shoves other coats aside to make room for his. He emerges with a long-handled brush and begins to swipe his jacket sleeves, explaining, "My cat's shedding."

In this moment, I'm convinced someone is trying to turn my life into a sitcom. "Did you and Hades have a dinner date tonight?"

"No, no. Kronos invited me."

"Kronos?"

"Did he not tell you?" Dionysus changes hands and swipes at his other coat sleeve.

"He neglected to mention you would be joining us. But there's plenty of food, and you're welcome to help me finish setting the table or assist Kronos at the grill. Or pour yourself a drink and wait for us in the Club Room."

"I think I'll grab a Scotch," he says, handing me the brush and gesturing to his back, "and see if an extra set of hands is needed in the kitchen."

"You know your way around. Help yourself." I swipe at his coat, hand back the wine, then watch Dionysus leave the foyer in the direction of the Club Room. Graced with killer looks and a Fifth Avenue fashion sense, he's always acted like a doting uncle. A complicated, multi-faceted doting uncle, someone I should probably know more about.

A swell of excited voices announces food is on its way. I drop the clothes brush in the umbrella stand, hurrying to the dining room to arrive in time to applaud Kronos holding aloft a platter of mouth-watering, perfectly grilled meat. He's followed by Dionysus balancing a teak salad bowl on his fingers and carrying a cruet in his other hand. Joachim's next, bearing two plates of grilled vegetables. Behind him, the other guard carries a bowl of fresh-baked rolls. Torsten rolls in the wine cart and parks it near Own, watching keenly as the butler lights a candle and decants a second bottle of red. Jutta tends to the candles on the table, lighting them with the flick of her fingers. I watch, an unfamiliar happiness fluttering within my ribcage, as everyone finishes their task, or sets their offering on the table, and looks to me expectantly.

Owen whispers to Torsten, then moves to the head of the table and withdraws the chair. "My Queen?"

I take my place and once I'm seated, Kronos and Dionysus seat themselves to my right and left. Owen and the rest make to leave the room.

"Wait!" I gesture to the other place settings. "Please, everyone, join us. This meal could not have happened without you, and it would please me if we could all dine at the same table."

Tempting smells waft off the meat and the bread, underlining my invitation. Twenty chair legs slide across the granite flooring; five bodies settle in. Once napkins have been placed on laps, I nod to Kronos and ask him to serve the meat. The platter looks heavy enough to give me a hernia if I try to lift it.

"May I pour the wine?" Dionysus is seated to my left, and if anyone knows wine, it's him. At my nod, he rises, raises the carafe, and speaks a blessing before pouring a small amount in my glass. I sniff, swirl, and sip. "Is it to the Queen's liking?" he asks.

"It's perfect." I raise my glass to Owen and to Torsten. "Excellent choice." The young demon and older human blush the same shade of pink. Once plates have been filled with food, I rise and offer a blessing to the Great Beneath and the Great Beyond, to my mother's gifts, and to the laborers who tend to the earth.

"Let us eat."

The first bite of thinly sliced steak melts on my tongue. My groan startles both Kronos and Dionysus and they look at me like I'm in need of medical attention.

"What's wrong?"

I swallow the bite and take a sip of wine before answering. "I'm fine. It's just so good and I didn't realize I was so hungry."

"Do you not eat, my dear?" Kronos asks in a whisper. "Does your husband not take care of you?"

I spear another bite and shake my head. "It's not that Hades doesn't take care of me, it's just that Hades and I rarely spend time together."

"And why is that?"

I add a bit of grilled red pepper to what's already on my fork before feeding myself. Chewing slowly, I take another sip of wine and contemplate how to answer Kronos' question. Persephone the Compliant and Persephone the Capitulator have been replaced by Persephone the Starved for Attention - and perfectly cooked steak - along with Persephone, Speaker of Her Truth and who knows who else.

"Hades and I are divorcing. I believe he has already taken another lover and I am—" I pause to pat my lips, replace my napkin in my lap, and pull up the truth. "And I am fine with that."

Kronos and Dionysus lean back in their chairs and lock gazes. Some silent communication passes between them before they snap forward, their eyes boring into mine, and ask in one voice, "Does Zeus know?"

Persephone, Speaker of Her Truth's palms go clammy. I want to duck under the table. "No?"

Dionysus removes the knife and fork from my hands and takes hold of my fingers. His skin is warm and dry and his eyes radiate kindness. And concern. Definitely concern, because he uses my napkin to wipe my hands and slides my knife out of reach.

"Then you have a problem, my dear. Because any change in marital status amongst those connected with the primary families of Mount Olympus must be sanctioned by Zeus, and Zeus only."

It's a good thing my steak knife is out of reach. "Would you say that again?"

Dionysus repeats himself. A shudder passes up my spine, through my shoulders, down my arms. Kronos scoots his chair closer and takes hold of my wrists, steadying me as Dionysus adds, "And there is no way in Tartarus he will allow you and Hades to divorce."

Inside, muscles, organs, and bones shrink back from my skin. "Would Hades know this?" I ask in a whisper. I don't want to call attention to myself by alarming Owen and the rest of the table, who are loudly enjoying the food and the leeway offered by the night's unusual circumstances. "Would he?" I repeat, when the silence from both sides drags on.

Dionysus slides a knuckle under my chin and lifts my head. For the first time, I notice his irises are a deep bluish-purple. "I was on Mount Olympus at the conclave when Zeus dictated the decree and signed it."

I would rather think about matching Dionysus' eye color with grape varietals, than know who else attended a meeting I was not invited to. "When did this conclave take place?"

"Last September. Around the equinox."

Last September, beginning on the equinox and continuing for five days after, I was in my Godsrest.

"All fourteen of the Inner Circle were there," he continues, "as Hestia and I both attended. Zeus had several items he wanted clarified and requested everyone's presence."

A calling of the Inner Circle would also include Hera,

Aphrodite, Athena, Artemis, Apollo, Poseidon, Hephaestus, Hermes, and Demeter.

"That means my mother was there too."

Dionysus does not hesitate to answer. "Demeter was present, yes."

The internal shrinkage stops. Blood pounds along my veins, flushing out the cold and building a heat inside my belly I have not felt… ever. Blistering anger bursts through its fragile membrane and splatters against the inside of my ribs.

I am mad. I am *furious*. And I am so fucking hungry. I raise my gaze from the watery blood congealing on my plate to see both Kronos and Dionysus staring at me, concern on their faces and my forearms in their grasps.

"Let. Me. Go."

They do, though they remain huddled in close. I reclaim my knife and slice another bite of steak. Propping the blade on the rim of my plate, I reach for the stem of my cut-crystal wine glass. I savor a mouthful of the grape's gift, its earthy flavor combining with the juicy meat as it washes over my tongue and down my throat, on its way to fortifying my bones and blood. I'm on my third serving of steak and my second glass of wine before I can look any of my fellow diners in the eye. And when I do, my face is composed. Persephone the Royally Pissed and Regally Restrained's anger is safely stored away.

"Was there anything else on Zeus' agenda that I should know?" I ask. It takes consuming a slab of beef and twice the wine I normally drink to recognize that me not knowing about Zeus' latest regulations is my own damn fault. I treat my time in the Underworld as a sentence to be suffered, rather than something I can consciously shape - if I choose to.

"Not that I can recall," Dionysus assures me. "And you have my promise that I shall keep you in the loop if I hear of any further developments."

Part Two

Chapter 12
DEMETER'S ESTATE. THREE DAYS LATER.

MY LUGGAGE and I arrive at my mother's seaside estate on Greece's Pelion peninsula, within the quarter-hour leeway Demeter allots all visiting family members. Close friends get a ten minute leeway. New visitors better plan their portal stops accordingly and arrive five minutes early or risk never receiving another social invitation. Behind me, crushed marble gravel crunches beneath sandaled feet. I have a handful of seconds to whip out my mirror and affix my "Nothing Is Wrong" face.

"You're here!"

Aušrinė squeals and launches herself at my back. Thank Goddess and Spirit my best bestie is first to greet me, not my mother. She's followed quickly by Ciri and Bé, and I realize they're all my best besties, only in different ways. Happily squished by arms, bellies, and breasts, I close my eyes and take in the familiar *clink-clink* of Ciri's many bracelets; the smooth, soothing velvet Rini wears no matter the season or weather; and Bé's woodsy scent. She spends so much time with trees and shrubbery that a symphony of resins and barks permeates her skin and hair.

The three release me, our arms sliding familiarly around each other's waists, and I spy my mother approaching through a break in the rows of olive trees. She's dressed to travel in navy blue slacks, a matching jacket, and low-heeled boots, and she's reflecting my smile back at me. The placid face I've been perfecting since the dinner with Kronos is doing its job. My friends peel away as Demeter nears and I give myself over to my mother's more reserved greeting.

"I see you've put some forethought into your preparations this year," she says, patting the back of my head and stroking my hair. She must have noticed the three matching trunks stacked behind me. Usually, I arrive with one. "Did you pack in triplicate? Because you know we can always stop in Paris or Milan and shop if you're lacking anything."

"I packed everything you suggested." Barreling ahead - because me taking control starts with plotting an alternative itinerary - I indicate my friends and add, "We're heading to Bé's family's castle in Ireland after we finish with the Lesser Mysteries. I needed clothes for that climate, too."

"So Flidais has informed me." My mother releases me and takes a step back. Her darkened eyebrows arch over mirthful eyes. "I guess this is as good a time as any to tell you we're *all* heading to Scotland tomorrow. Habonde has graciously offered to host the rites on Bone Fire Croft and the initiates will come from the proxy training program."

I like this idea. It's… practical. Plus, the last time I visited Bone Fire Croft I took a stab at public speaking and survived. Zeus blew in on one of his winged horses during that same visit and tried to bluster his way into the gathering. If he tries anything like that at the Lesser Mysteries, I'll be ready. I hope. "Will anyone else join us," I ask, crossing my fingers behind my back, "or are we going old school and sticking to thirteen initiates?"

"Just the thirteen, which happens to be the exact number of trainees enrolled in the program. Baubo is already there to help supervise preparations, and Astrape has agreed to provide security."

The confirmation that the Goddess of Lightning, with her wild hair and artful weaponry, will be nearby sends my insides ping-ponging. "That's a good idea, for us and the initiates."

"I agree. I do *not* want a repeat of what happened that year *you* three" —my mother turns to Rini and the others and glares— "talked me into holding the rites on Ibiza and proceeded to splatter the location all over FlittR."

A coordinated chorus of, "Sorry, Demeter" appeases her and she dips her regal head. "You're forgiven. The house is yours. Most of the staff has the night off. Just promise you'll be ready to leave tomorrow morning."

"Are you going somewhere?" The night before departing for the Mysteries, my mother usually drives her staff into a flurry, checking and rechecking every last detail.

"I have last minute things to see to on Mount Olympus." She turns away from me, which is just as well. Mention of Mount Olympus reminds me of Zeus' ridiculous edict, and her silence on the matter. Now is not the time to get into it in front of my friends. "The robes you will wear for the rituals are in a trunk in Persephone's suite. Go through everything and see what fits."

My mother lifts her hand as if to wave. "Oh, I forgot to mention I separated out the headpieces and stored them in their own box inside the trunk. Ciri, they could use some freshening up."

Demeter turns on her heel and makes her way toward the rear courtyard. We wave as she enters the small, marble-columned folly built for her exclusive use and disappears with a *pop*.

"The cat's away and the mice will play." Ciri hefts a toolbox in one hand and a beat up leather portmanteau in the other. Two of the estate's remaining staff, likely culled from the orchards and gardens, load my trunks onto a cart. "What do we want to do? Throw a party? Go out for dinner? Pack a picnic, hit the beach, skinny dip in the Aegean?"

"Ooh, too cold for that." Rini hugs herself and mock-shivers. Shielding my eyes from the sun's light, I agree. It's not quite warm enough for me to consider a saltwater plunge. Besides, adjusting to the aboveworld's brighter light always takes a couple of days, as does acclimating to the general hustle and bustle and accelerated pace. Though I'm eager to party with my friends, to drink and laugh and enjoy a few hours of forgetting the news Dionysus shared, I could just as easily take a dinner tray in my room before for my nightly stint in the Underworld. Unlike Minthe, I'm not about to hand off my duties.

"I vote we stay here," Bé says. "This section of the peninsula's not exactly known for its bar scene, and we've got all spring and summer to party. I mean, I'll be able to hang with you when I'm not working. I'm coming into the busiest seasons of the year."

"I brought a few of my tools and some findings and" —Ciri barks out a laugh and rolls her eyes— "Who am I kidding? You know I haul my kit wherever I go. Let's get settled and after we eat, I can get a head start on the pieces Demeter wants fixed."

Bé adjusts her bag's shoulder strap and takes the handle of her rolling suitcase. "I want to see my room, have a shower, and soak in that glorious hot tub."

As in years past, once we enter the guest wing my friends drop off their larger pieces of luggage before piling into my bedroom. Everyone claims their favorite couch or chaise with a bag or a scarf, and heads for the balcony.

The Aegean Sea lies below us. The balcony follows the curves of the villa's stucco-ed walls. It's large enough to hold a sunken hot tub, with seating built in along the wide railing. The long farmer's table under the portico is set with vases of carefully arranged vines, and unlit candles in wide glass tubes of varying heights. Mesh domes protect trays of food and drinks.

"I know I say this every time I visit, but it's frikkin' beautiful." Bé sighs as she stares out over the water. She spreads her arms, inviting us in for another group hug, and we stand there gawking at the view like we're tourists fresh off the bus. "Let's unpack and meet back here. I bet we have a lot to catch up on."

I chew on my lower lip, a new habit I seriously need to stop, and search the glimmering horizon for guidance. I *do* have a lot to catch my friends up on, it's just that if I share more than the bit about serving Hades with divorce papers, I run the risk of releasing thoughts and emotions I've been avoiding examining, and I don't want to overshadow our duties to the trainees and the rituals.

I decide I'll wait until after the rites when we're safely ensconced behind rugged castle walls.

Chapter 13

AFTERNOON FLOWS into evening with the four of us relaxing
on the balcony, alternately soaking in the hot tub, chatting, and
dozing. My bones feel bendy, pliable. My senses approach
overwhelm as we watch the sky change colors, sip lemony drinks,
and nibble on breads and cheeses I can never find in the
Underworld.

The temperature drops noticeably, and the breeze coming off
the Aegean begins to strengthen. We take the party inside to my
suite's spacious living room, and I close the casement windows
against the gusting wind as best I can. The frames are warped by
sea air and sun, and the hinges and latches resist. I empathize
with their reluctance.

Ciri claims the heavy round table as her workspace. Bé opens
the trunk of ritual wear my mother packed for us, sets aside the
herbal sachets meant to keep out moths, and starts passing folded
garments to me and Rini. We shake them open, arranging the
mostly long sleeved, ankle length garments over the furniture.

Rini huffs, proclaiming everything's either too "matchy-
matchy" or too "been there, worn that" for her taste. I think the

dresses look funereal, and a vague hesitancy rises at the thought of the cloth touching my skin.

"This *is* a lot of white," Bé notes. "Is Demeter going for the virginal look? Or is this just how it's always been done?" She bends over the trunk, lifts the removable insert, and gasps. "Darlings, lookie-lookie what I found."

While I mull Bé's questions about virgins and traditions, she quickly sets the trunk insert on the floor and gathers up a fluffy armful of sheer cottons and silks, laces and ribbons, and dumps it at my feet. I spy an intriguing sleeve and tug on it until I'm holding up a bat-winged mini-dress. This is not ritual wear, this is something else entirely. Draping one sleeve over my arm, I twirl side to side. "I swear I've seen this exact dress on an album cover from the '60's or '70's."

Rini snorts. "Let me see if anything in here fits us fuller-figured gals." She crawls over to the pile, discarding tops and skirts and scarves one garment after the other until she echoes Bé's gasp. Rolling up to standing, she gently, reverently shakes out a triangular swath of embroidered chiffon edged with beaded tassels and wraps it around her shoulders.

"Stevie Nicks. Early '80's."

We all *ooh*. Ciri lays down her tools and drops to her hands and knees and starts rummaging. It's all I can do to keep myself from nudging her aside and attacking the pile. There isn't a goddess in our age range who hasn't coveted the Fleetwood Mac singer/songwriter's wardrobe, especially in its white phase, and if we're not careful we could rip this treasure trove to shreds.

Bé drags the emptied trunk to the side of the rug and plops down beside the pile. "Let's be organized about this," she suggests, playfully swatting Ciri's arm. "We go through the pieces one at a time and if you love it, speak up."

"Finders, keepers. I'll go first and claim this shawl. Anybody want a refill before we start?" Rini drops her treasure atop her bucket bag on her way to the drink tray. We all answer yes, and once she finishes bartending, she carefully places our glasses close enough to reach, yet far enough not to damage the clothes should they spill.

"Ready?" Bé asks. Raised glasses affirm our commitment to fairness. Bé shows off each piece, adding spontaneous commentary, and our collective awe grows. "Does your mother actually *know* Stevie Nicks?" she asks at one point.

"I have no idea." I really don't. My mother rarely talks about anything unrelated to crop management and the importance of maintaining tradition. "Maybe she was a groupie? Or, I dunno, maybe she did some fashion design?" I might be upset with Demeter over what she chooses to not share with me, but I can admire her taste in clothes and the good sense she had to squirrel these treasures away.

Stroking her growing pile of fine cotton, chiffon, and lace, Ciri leans forward and whisper sings, "Listen to the wind blow." Bé, who rarely sings, adds a melodic, "Watch the sun ri-i-ise." Feeling the vibe, I add, "Watch the shadows," and we all rise on our knees and chime in with, "Damn your love, damn your lies," only to fall apart, giggling like little girls. The giggles morph into actions and next thing I know we're all stripping and carefully shoving arms and legs into tops and skirts and dancing around the room singing "The Chain" at the top of our lungs.

Movement is cathartic. I glom onto one of Ciri's repoussé hammers and clutch it in both hands like a microphone. Belting out the line about breaking the silence, my voice cracks like I've burst a sorcerer's spell, freeing the chains wrapped around my heart, *snap snap snap*. More emotion than I've ever felt at one time floods my veins and overflows my reinforced embankments.

My knees buckle, folding me toward the carpet as I drown. I end up spread-eagled on the floor, gulping for air, gulping for *space. Screaming.*

"Persephone. *Persephone!*"

What is happening to me? I roll onto my belly and try to curl into a ball, but I can't. I'm caught. The seam at one elbow tears. Windows rattle like someone's trying to get in. My foot hits a glass and knocks it over, and I'm so frightened, I can't locate my lungs, let alone catch my breath. The rug's pile abrades my cheek and my knees. Bé gets an arm underneath my tender belly. She stands, hauling me up with her, and hands me over to Rini. Soft, soft Rini. Ciri presses a cool cloth over my forehead and eyes, murmuring soothing words as I search without sight for a quiet spot within the maelstrom.

My palm is molded to the hammer's wooden handle. Someone pries apart my fingers and takes the tool from me. No one asks me to explain. No one hurries me through these moments. This is my crew. They know. They *know*.

Thank Goddess and Spirit I'm not alone when I crack.

GAUZY CURTAINS lift with the gusts coming in through the old French doors. My room is dark, my nose is clogged, and the area around both eyes is swollen. Someone moved the candles from the outdoor table to the lip of the hot tub. Little flames reflect off the heated water and I can see steam rising in coils from the surface.

Ciri and Bé sit between the candle holders, blankets around their shoulders, dangling their legs in the water and making circles with their feet. The mattress beneath me dips. A warm, solid body snugs against my back.

"You awake?"

"I'm awake," I croak.

"You scared us, Seph."

"I know."

Rini switches positions, leaning the side of her hip against my lower back and propping one hand in front of my chest. With her other hand, she rubs slow, comforting circles between my shoulder blades, a low hum vibrating in her chest. "I'm glad we were here."

I grip her wrist. Stroke her pulse with my thumb. I want to talk, and I don't want to talk. "Your skin's so soft," I whisper. Rini snorts.

"How else do you think I sell so much product? It's that cream I told you about, the one I brought to share. It's supposed to be for faces only, but I use it all over."

"Think it'll soften what's broken?" I know she'll know I'm talking about my shattered insides. She takes her time answering.

"I think you need more than product, babe. More than glue or duct tape. I think you need to talk."

"Yeah, I guess I do." Sniffling, I change the topic. "What time is it?"

"Almost two. You were out for a while."

Oof, I have to pull myself together. "I'm overdue at the Hall of Judgement. I've got to at least put in an appearance."

Rini smooths back the sticky hairs on my forehead. "You're so damn consistent, Seph. Isn't there someone who could sub for you for one night? Can't you, like, take a sick day?"

"No, I can't. At least not until Habonde's proxies are ready to begin specialized training." I roll onto my back, nudging my bestie off the covers enough I can stretch my legs. "I'll fill all of you in on what's been happening while you work on my face."

"'K. I'll be right back. Got to get my magic creams and something for those puffy eyes."

Rini moves to the sheer curtains and motions to Bé and Ciri. Those two grab towels, dry off their legs, and hurry toward me as I sit up. Bé pours a glass of water and brings it over. Ciri perches on the edge of the bed. Rini returns before I finish drinking.

"Look up," she says, unscrewing a large, squat jar. "Gonna stick these under your eyes first."

"Wait a sec." Bé shoos Ciri off, moves the pillow out from under my head, and scoots in behind me. "I know a great massage for headaches."

"Ooh, good idea. And I've got a salve that'll help." I hear another lid being unscrewed. An amazing scent manages to make its way past my swollen nose. Tears leak out the corners of my eyes and I feel the inside of my nose swelling even more. I can't stop the shudder that passes through my chest.

"You are the best," I blubber. Bé's fingertips move in firm circles. Ciri wipes my nose - I can tell it's her by her bracelets - which makes me giggle.

"You ready to talk?" she asks, pressing a clean tissue into my hand.

I take a breath, and another. "Rini knows I asked Hades for a — I *told* Hades we're getting a divorce. But what I didn't know is that Zeus declared he's the only one with the power to sanction a major change like that." Another shudder passes through me. My whole body quivers.

"That's news to me," Ciri says, adding an appropriate amount of sisterly indignation to her voice.

"Me too," add Rini and Bé.

"You haven't heard about it because Zeus' proclamations aren't meant to for you." I can't blow my nose lying flat, so I roll to the side and try to relieve my clogged nasal passages. "They only affect the families attached to Mount Olympus. And the only reason *I* know is because I had dinner with Dionysus a couple days ago, and he told me after I explained my *brilliant* plan."

Fresh tears form beneath my eyelids. So much for my brilliance. Patting the covers, I find the box of tissues, pull out a handful, and try again to clear my nose. Which doesn't work. My sinuses are stuffier than ever. "My mother has known for *months* that I've been miserable. And Hades has known too, and we've even talked about it, about our marriage, made… made agreements about living separate lives as much as possible for the sake of, of keeping the Underworld running smoothly. But what kills me, what… what pisses me off, is that they *knew* I was stuck, they *knew* I needed a way out, and they didn't tell me.

"They did not tell me," I repeat, twisting the soggy tissues until they tear apart. "Which must mean they think Zeus will say no. Which means I'm chained to Hades *forever*."

Chapter 14

MY FRIENDS HAVE the good sense to not accuse me of being overly melodramatic. They tend to me lovingly, handing me dry tissues, rubbing my back, making soft noises meant to soothe. When Rini mutters that we could have avoided all this by picking one of Fleetwood Mac's more upbeat songs, a giggle burbles up from my belly.

"Feel better?" Ciri asks.

"Much." I roll up to sitting, blow my nose, and reach for the jar of healing balm Rini offers. Sharing my frustration about Hades and Zeus helps, yet something else, some nebulous thing sits even deeper within my bones, waiting. Working the lid off the jar keeps my gaze downward. I don't want to hold back anything from these three, but I don't know what this… this *thing* is.

I dip my fingertips into the jar and rub the balm into my temples, hoping to further ease the headache. Ciri beams and claps her hands. "I've got an idea! I think our theme for the rites should be 'Goddesses Go Retro'."

"Have Demeter's assistants always had to come up with a

theme?" Bé folds her legs under her as she leans back against my bed's headboard.

"Not unless 'Boring' and 'Uniformity' could be considered conscious fashion choices," I offer, aware I'm being snarky. "Though I understand the thinking behind having everyone wear the same style of garment. It acts as a kind of equalizer."

Three heads nod in unison. Rini holds up a second fringed shawl, pouting as she pets the exquisite ivory-on-ivory embroidery. "Are you saying we should *not* dress up?"

"We do both," I suggest. "Days one through four, we dress the same as the thirteen trainees, perhaps differentiating ourselves with a headpiece?" I circle my head with my hand to suggest a crown. "You know, so the trainees can easily see who's there to assist Demeter."

"I can make us simple circlets," Ciri says.

Rini interrupts with, "And on the *fifth* day, for the procession and celebration, we dress in these gorgeous clothes, communicating our individuality and our commonality."

"Commonality, as in a shared love for frou-frou?" Bé's teasing us. Though she's the least frou-frou amongst us, I notice the way she's stretching a pearly white, crushed velvet mini-dress across her tanned, muscular thighs.

"That would be perfect with boots," I suggest, drawing a line just below my kneecaps. "Fringed, deerskin boots."

"And opals, Bé. Lots and lots of opals. In fact—" Ciri stops mid-sentence and hurries to the case of accessories left us by my mother. She lifts the lid, removes two of the trays within and sets them on the table, then hefts a drawstring bag from the box's interior. Teasing apart the knot, she peers in and coos. "I *thought* I remembered seeing these the last time your mom asked for my help. Look!"

We gather around the opened pouch. Polished opals gleam in the candlelight, in pastel shades of pinks, greens, and blues.

"Those are Andean opals. Very calming. Helpful for easing heartache and fostering a sense of peace about whatever the future holds," Bé observes, stirring the bag's contents with her finger. "Do you have time to make something for each of us?"

"Not tonight. But I'll bring that whole box with me and when we're not assisting, I'll make… stuff. I know the urisk-folk on Bone Fire Croft have a metalworking shop and I'm willing to pay for bench time, or trade lessons." Ciri wiggles in her chair. "Gaah, I'm already getting ideas. Can you three put the clothes back in the trunk?" At our nods, she snugs the drawstring on the bag of opals, stuffs everything back into the wooden case, and gathers her backpack.

Ciri tosses a wave over her shoulder as she dances out of my room with her armful of treasures. Bé, Rini, and I stare at the piles before settling in to re-fold each piece - and occasionally claim one for future use - and return the vintage garments to the lower section of the trunk. We fold the more pedestrian pieces with equal care, though none of us rushes to claim any of the plain cotton dresses. Rini lifts an apron-like thing. Frowning, she examines the front and back halves, the gaps at the sides, and shakes her head.

"No one needs to see any of us in *that*," she mutters, shoving the offending piece to the bottom of the pile. "And we are done. You sure you're okay to go to the Underworld alone, Seph? Or do you want one of us to go with you?"

"I'm good."

I've never brought anyone with me to the Court of Souls. Given that I've just had an emotional breakthrough, I should probably stick with my routine. Hugging Rini and Bé, I watch as they pick up their bags and purses and leave, easing the door closed behind them. I remember what Bé said about opal's calming properties and open the trunk containing my personal jewelry. In the box of rings, I locate two set with opals, slip them onto my fingers, and ready myself for a brief commute to and from the Underworld.

HOURS LATER, I wake with the birds, only to sink back into my pillows when I notice the sky is barely lit. My nightly trip had felt strange. Jarring. As though my skin was thin enough to tear; my bones brittle enough to splinter. As sleep reclaims my body, my mind forms an image of a heavy chain lying like a sleeping snake across Tartarus' dank stone floor, both ends disappearing into the cloying gray mist endemic to the lower levels. The chain's weight settles into my chest and belly, and when I go to move my arms and legs, my spine becomes the chain. I cannot move, I can only stare up at the light gray mist and the mottled gray stone and listen to the sounds of life going on outside the prison I am now part of.

Next thing I know, I'm fighting off sheets and flying out of bed. Someone decided banging on my door is a good way to wake me up. Demeter's serious about a morning departure, but that much noise is just rude. When I open my door to complain, I see a breakfast tray laden with my morning staples: toast, and a pot of black tea.

Shaking, because the tile beneath my feet is cold and because I just dreamt about being imprisoned, and being the thing that keeps me imprisoned, I forgive the knocker and carry the tray back to bed. And because my best friends know the routine, they nudge open my door one after the other and enter carrying their own trays.

"How does Demeter remember what foods we like?" Rini's the early riser amongst us. Her face is radiant, like she's lit from within, and my shivers ease. A healthy-smelling fruit smoothie in a tall glass and a French press of coffee grace her tray, along with a glass straw and a porcelain cup and saucer.

"It's her housekeepers," I confide, stifling a yawn. "Demeter sends the head of each household to Mnemosyne for training when she first hires them. As far as I know, my mother still refuses to have internet or computers at any of her properties."

"Thank Goddess and Spirit for hotspots," Ciri mutters. Curling into the oversized and overstuffed armchair beside my bed, she lifts a large mug to her mouth and inhales. Her eyes are half closed and she's slouching. I reach out to tap her wrist. She'll burn herself if she falls back asleep.

"Did you and the opals pull an all-nighter?" I ask.

Blowing across the steaming coffee's surface, she shakes her head. "I stayed up way past midnight re-making the basic circlets we'll wear for most of the rituals. The metal used in the old ones had gotten too brittle in spots. I copied the design." Ciri's lips curl into a self-confident smile. "Made a few improvements."

"As in spells?" Bé opens the tall glass doors to the balcony and settles herself on the floor, resting her tray across her thighs. She closes her eyes and lifts her face to the sun. Sea breezes send ripples through the sheer curtains, bringing in the scent of salt and fish and stone. I slide my legs out from underneath the sheet and blanket and pull a sweater from one of my trunks. The sun may be out and shining, but it's still February and acting like it's short-sleeve shirt weather is just magical thinking.

"Aren't you cold?" I offer Bé one of the folded blankets. She takes it and settles it under her butt.

"Nope."

"Bé's a hottie," Ciri giggles. "And yes, I added *a* spell, as in *one*, that'll let us communicate with each other if we're wearing the circlets. Y'know, in case we want to wow the trainees with the power of our collective woo."

"Our 'collective woo'?" I snort-laugh and spread strawberry jam on a triangle of toast. "My mother might not forgive us if she finds out we're plotting to go off script. The Mysteries are *Serious Business.*"

"We'll just have to make sure she doesn't suspect a thing. And who knows, between Bone Fire Croft's inherent magic and the power Demeter invokes, we might not need to use the spell."

The four of us finish our breakfasts in cozy silence. Or mostly silence. Rini mutters "collective woo" between draws on her straw, and each time she does, one of us giggles.

Chapter 15

BONE CROFT FARM'S welcoming committee includes Habonde, our hostess; Bailoch and Bodhi, the satyr couple who run her barn; and Baubo, Goddess of Mirth whom I've known all my life. Her hugs are among the best and my anxiety drains away as she gathers me into her embrace.

"I've missed you," I whisper into her curly hair. She smells like she's been handling beeswax. I also detect crushed comfrey leaves and… olive oil? Pulling away, I sniff Baubo's green-tinged fingertips. "You making comfrey salve?"

She squeezes my hands and holds tight to my fingers, her gaze darting from my right eye to my left, back and forth. This should be an easy question for her to answer with a simple "Yes" or "No", and maybe a qualifier, but before she does, Rini squeezes my elbow.

"Seph. Look at that gorgeous horse."

I release Baubo's hands and follow the direction of Rini's outstretched arm through the bare trees dotting Habonde's orchard, to the glorious, black-winged beast strolling our way. The horse *is* gorgeous, but my eyes are drawn immediately to the graceful rider atop its back. Galena shakes her head, tossing her long, wavy mane, and Astrape swings one leg over her broad back and lands on the ground. Her own wild mane is pulled away from her face and she's smiling at me. I smile back. The goddess of lightning isn't in my innermost circle, but she could be. Should be. Maybe. If her services weren't always in demand and if I wasn't—

I put a stop to that train of thought. I am tied to the Underworld, and to Hades and the Court of Souls; to the aboveworld, and Demeter. And though I might wonder if the peripatetic security consultant has a home base, or if she lives out of suitcases and saddlebags, always on the go from one job to the next, imagining myself in Astrape's world is just *more* magical thinking.

"Hello!" she calls, waving as she walks closer and casts her gaze around our loose circle. I return the wave and though I want to stay right where I am, I already hear my mother issuing orders that concern me and my friends.

"Demeter. Leave the luggage to us." Astrape's tone says she's here, and she's taking charge. "Bodhi and Bailoch and I will bring the trunks and suitcases to the house. Habonde, could you show everyone to their rooms?"

By the time she's close enough that I can see the fine lines at the corners of her hazel eyes, Astrape's reaching for one of our trunks and hefting it onto the flat cart the satyrs brought with them. The bottoms of her jeans are tucked into worn leather boots, and she's wearing a canvas jacket roomy enough to hide the weapons I know she carries. She lifts the heavy item with ease. I readjust my shoulder bag and offer to carry the box containing the opals.

"Sure," Ciri says, placing it in my outstretched arms. She doesn't let go until I have a good grip on the handles. "C'mon, let's go see the house. It'll take them awhile to load the rest of our stuff and I want to get settled."

I follow Habonde, Ciri, and the others, glancing behind as I duck under a drooping branch. Astrape's back is to me, her attention on other matters, but what I see in her grounded stance inspires confidence. Assuredness. My knees and elbows waver, an unfamiliar physical reaction moving through me like a sudden change in the weather.

Snapping my gaze forward, I hustle to catch up with the others. I've never been inside either of the two mansion-sized additions to Habonde's modest home. Already, the tan, fieldstone exterior feels warmer and more inviting than House of Hades' gray granite blocks. Inside, doors of quarter-sawn oak open off a wide central hallway, offering glimpses of bedroom suites and offices for guests. My feet sink into a thick, wool runner woven in soothing shades of sage green and cream, with coral accents.

"Astrape and her staff are staying down here," Habonde begins. "My rooms are in the other house. There's one other suite besides mine on the second floor. That one has accommodations for larger guests, like big cat shifters, and for those who travel accompanied by more than one partner. The layout of *this* house," she continues, "gives us four single bedrooms upstairs, along with two shared en suites. Want to see all the rooms, then decide where you'd like to stay?"

If I know my friends, they're eager to snoop. I pipe in with, "We'd love a tour of both houses."

"Great! Follow me." Habonde leads us down the hall, in the direction of the oldest part of her home. We end up in a low-ceilinged kitchen that takes up the ancient building's entire footprint, and she explains lovingly that this is the site of her original stone hearth. "And through that back door is my private garden and a covered terrace. I - *we* - spend a lot of time there in the warmer months."

She looks giddy. I assume the "we" she refers to includes her lover, Rhys the Woodsman. I'd like to look that giddy one of these days, blessed with a partner who prioritized being with me.

We follow our hostess out of the kitchen and back down the hall. She points out the tiny rooms that used to be her bedroom and bathroom, and the room Baubo prefers to stay in. Passing into the first of the newer houses, she gestures to the library and issues a blanket invitation to explore its resources. I pause to admire the floor to ceiling shelves - which are also oak - a rolling ladder, and a long study table set with low lamps. Across the hall is the office for Astrape and her staff. It's furnished in a more modern style, complete with computers, multiple monitors, maps, and a whiteboard. Dorm-like bedrooms connected by a shared bathroom lie behind the next two doors.

"My rooms are through here." Habonde waves us into the open-air walkway connecting the two structures and closes the glass-paneled door to the first house. Overhead, leafless vines twine through horizontal trellises, their slender trunks rooted in ceramic pots at the base of each support column.

"Welcome to my home," she says. A matching front door opens onto a circular foyer. She's beaming, and the reason is immediately apparent. On the curved walls hang large, black and white photographs of her and Rhys and a smattering of spots on the croft. I break from the group and head toward a photo of a massive oak tree. Its weathered branches are devoid of leaves, but there's something alive and luminous emanating from the center of its trunk.

"Is this image enhanced, or does this tree really glow?"

Habonde comes up beside me, reaching out as if to caress the image. "That's Darragh." Wonder infuses her voice, and her fingers stop just shy of the glass. "Darragh was— *is*— one of Rhys' brethren, a Woodsman and a hero. His tree still stands and the glow you see is his heartwood regenerating."

"Will you tell us Darragh's story sometime?" Bé asks, adding, "I know of the Woodsmen, and I would be honored to assist with his healing in any way I can."

Habonde's gaze meets my friend's reflection in the glass covering the photograph. "Bé Chuille. We met last summer. You're the enchantress who—"

"Who transforms rocks and trees into monsters." Bé grins softly, keeping her eyes on the image of the tree. "I left that life many moons ago. I prefer to use my gifts to foster and encourage life. Which is why I call myself a landscape architect. Humans accept that more readily than sorceress, or Lugh's witch."

"Rhys and I would love to get your opinion on what we've been doing, and what more could be done. Perhaps once the Lesser Mysteries conclude? He expects to return the day after."

"I would be honored."

We move through the foyer, with its rich, red-glazed walls and gleaming parquet floor, and up the grand staircase. Another runner cushions our footsteps. Habonde opens the door to their private rooms first, apologizes for the clothes heaped on the bench at the foot of the bed, and we *ooh* and *ahh* at the furnishings and the massive bathroom. The other suite is the same size, with a similarly grand four-poster bed.

"Go check out the tub," the hearth goddess urges. "It's to *die* for."

Rini passes through the doorway to the bathroom and squeals. "All four of us could fit in here!"

And all four of us do, which our hostess finds entertaining. Downstairs, we each claim one of the bedrooms. They're furnished similarly to the guest rooms in the first house, with queen-sized beds, and coverings in soft blues and creams. My stomach rumbles, and when I ask about lunch, Habonde directs me to the end of the hall. "Baubo stocked the kitchen with basic ingredients. There's soup heating on the stove, and fresh bread in the basket. If there is something specific you'd like, let Jillian know. She left a pad of paper on the counter and will stop by this afternoon to check in on you and explain our new portal system. She'll also give you directions to the caves with the hotsprings. Enjoy!"

Habonde excuses herself and leaves. Rini, Bé, and Ciri duck into their rooms, and I'm left staring down the empty hallway. The sensory overload that began the moment I stepped out of the portal at my mother's estate, is reaching critical mass. The edges of my vision feel a bit stretched, my skin feels pulled tight over my bones, and the small, empty closet in the bedroom I claimed is calling my name.

Hiding is not an option, not here and not now. I propel myself toward the kitchen. Glass front cabinets allow me to quickly gather what I need, and once the tea has steeped, I add sugar and milk and bring the mug to my room, where trunks await unpacking.

Chapter 16

LATER, as we're eating, Jillian stops in to check on us. The briskly efficient urisk demonstrates how to use the intra-croft portal system, which requires holding pebbles inscribed with specific destinations while touching the portal tree. Jillian also provides us with paper maps of the croft, and issues verbal directions to the caves with the pools. Bé wants to know where Darragh's tree is located. I listen in, recalling a few spots from last summer's gathering of goddesses as I familiarize myself with the croft's overall layout. My ears perk up when Jillian mentions she's off to assist at a "wee emergency" with the naiads.

She, too, smells of beeswax and comfrey, and when Rini and Ciri decide they want to soak in the natural hotsprings, and Bé opts to visit the great oak, I mention I'm tired from our late night and my trip to the Underworld, and that I'll stay behind to wash the lunch dishes and put the soup away - and to rest. I don't mention I plan to search the library for books on herbal medicine and clues as to the nature of the "wee emergency". And to maybe run into Astrape.

The kitchen duties I volunteered for are more taxing than I

imagine. In the Underworld, I have Gilda and Tilda and other staff to do… well, to do everything. And in the aboveworld, I'm so often with my mother that the mundane tasks associated with being fed and having clean clothes are taken care of by seemingly invisible hands.

If I'm going to follow through with my plan to purchase my own property, it would help if I also knew how to run a household - even if it is a household of one - on my own. I plant myself in front of the open refrigerator, the heavy pot of soup in my hands, eyeing the fully stocked shelves. There's no way I'm going to get the pot into the fridge without moving everything off one of the shelves. Which means I'll have to rearrange the contents of the *other* shelves to make everything fit.

There's got to be a better way. I put the pot on the cutting board and search the cupboards for smaller containers. I settle on glass canning jars, experience a momentary sense of triumph, and realize I need to figure out how to ladle the soup into the jars without losing most of the liquid. And the jars will need lids.

A soft tap sounds at the kitchen door, which opens inward before I can say anything. A curly-headed urisk leans in. "Hello, I'm June Bug. Junie. You're Persephone, right?"

Though her face looks more mature, I recall the teen from last summer. She helped her mother attend to the goddesses and their entourages. She was also the first to raise her hand at the general meeting and ask to be included in Habonde's newly formed proxy program. "That's me," I say, clutching an empty glass jar in each hand. "And I remember you. How're you liking your classes?"

"They are a-*mazing*." Junie clasps her hands and closes her eyes. Bliss floods her features. "But it's hard work," she adds, snapping out of her momentary reverie and closing the door with a brisk *snick*. She wipes the bottoms of her laced up boots on the mat and removes her brown woolen coat. "*An'* I still have regular classes at the croft's school, *an'* my chores. Thank Goddess an' Spirit I like to be busy."

Her grin is infectious, and I find myself smiling back. "If you're in the training program, that means you'll be participating in the Mysteries."

"Yes, it does! I'm so excited, I canna barely sit still. Which is why I popped in to check on you. I wasn't sure if me mum had explained the portals an' such—" Junie notices the empty jars I'm still holding. "Do you need help?"

I nod and wave the jars at the pot. "I want to put away what's left of the soup, but I can't figure out how to get it into these without making a mess."

"You need a wide mouth funnel. Here, let me show you my foolproof method." Junie pulls a small folding ladder from the pantry and opens it in front of the sink. Standing on its top step, she directs me to place the jars in the sink and set the soup pot beside her on the counter. She rifles through a big ceramic jar of utensils, shakes her head, and asks me to open the drawers beside the stovetop until I find what she's looking for.

Swinging the sink faucet to the side, which I didn't know was possible, she positions the funnel in the first jar and ladles out the soup. When the jars are full, she wipes the rims with the corner of a dampened towel and screws on two-part canning lids. "There you have it. I'll just rinse the drips off the jars and dry 'em, and then they're ready to go into the fridge."

"Thank you." I shake open a towel and dry off the first jar Junie hands me. "There's a lot more to storing food than I knew."

"Glad I could help. An' thanks to Habonde an' the other teachers, me 'n the other trainees are learning there's a whole lot more to goddessing than just lookin' beautiful."

"There is," I agree, placing the second jar in the refrigerator with a satisfying sense of accomplishment. "I spend half the year helping Demeter with events like the Lesser Mysteries, attending planting and harvest festivals, and blessing seeds before they're sown and crops as they ripen."

"What do you do the other half of the year? I mean, I know you also tend to dead things, too." Junie folds the stepstool and returns it to the pantry. Taking the breadbasket to the table, she adds the small crock of butter, and a jar of fruit preserves from the fridge. "Oh, would you like a slice of bread? I missed lunch an' I'm *starving*."

"I would love a slice. With butter and jam." I open the cupboard with the plates, set two on the table, and sit. As Junie slices the bread, I give her a condensed overview of my duties in the Underworld.

"Did Hades travel here with you?" she asks, sliding my plate towards me. My mouth waters at the scent of the sweetened fruit, and I'm so focused on raising the treat to my mouth and taking a bite I almost miss Junie's question. And her follow up statement. "Oh, wait. He couldna have. He arrived a few days ago."

Bright, reddish spots bloom across the teen's plump cheeks. "Oops. I wasn't supposed to say anythin'," she whispers, staring at her plate and squeezing her hands between her knees.

"I knew Hades was going to be away from the Underworld for a while. I didn't know he planned to visit the croft." Hiding my shock, I take a small bite, chew, and swallow. Fruit delights my taste buds, but the sweet moment doesn't last. If I want to get any more information out of Junie, I must tread lightly. "I'm surprised Habonde didn't provide him a room in this house. Do you know where he's staying?"

Junie's cheeks grow redder. She fidgets with her jam sandwich, then takes a big breath and lets it out. "Me mum always says I act older than I look. She also says I open my mouth before I understand what I shouldna' say."

"I won't tell anyone about anything you share with me, Junie. How old are you?"

"Sixteen. Almost seventeen."

"And you know that sometimes adult relationships—" I search for the kindest phrase possible. "Fall apart?"

She nods slowly and lifts frightened eyes to mine. "Is your relationship with Hades fallin' apart?"

"It broke a long, long time ago. And though we are still married in the eyes of Mount Olympus, we aren't married in our hearts, which is where it really counts."

"Will you stay this way forever?"

"I hope not."

"Me too," she whispers. "You're too beautiful an' kind to be stuck with someone who doesn'a want to be with you."

"I agree." We both turn our attention to the unfinished bread on our plates. "And I know there's more going on at the croft than five days of rituals. I overheard Habonde say something, and Baubo seems preoccupied. And both she and your mother smell like they've been making healing salves. Is Hades injured?"

Pressing her lips together, Junie shakes her head. "Hades seems well. It's… it's someone else who's not fine."

"Is this someone else a naiad?" I sense I'll get farther with Junie if I take a gentle lead and ask for specific information.

"No."

"Is this someone else staying with the naiads?" And if we're playing Twenty Questions, I've got seventeen left.

"Yes." Junie pushes away from the table and washes her hands at the sink. "I'll be right back."

Minutes later, she places an old, leather-bound book between her plate and mine. Lifting the cover, she scans the table of contents, finds what she's looking for, and opens the book to the herb, Comfrey. Two pages in, after detailed drawings of the plant and its component parts, Junie taps a recipe for a salve.

"Read this."

I learn comfrey has mucilaginous properties, meaning it helps heal wounds by drawing together skin tissue. I learn comfrey leaves are placed on a woman's perineum after childbirth, helping to soothe and heal any tearing.

Childbirth. Water. Naiads. My hand shakes. I'm close to figuring this out - and I get that Junie doesn't want to be the one to tell me directly - but I absolutely need to know what it is she's alluding to.

"Junie, help me understand. Please. Is Hades here to… to attend a birth? Are Habonde and Baubo and your mother helping?" I'm on the verge of tears and I can't hide my rising distress. "I promise you again, I won't say anything to anyone."

Junie takes a deep breath. "It's Minthe," she blurts out. "She requested sanctuary with the naiads last summer an' she's been living here ever since."

Minthe asked for sanctuary, and her need for safety was granted. She sought time off from her duties in the Underworld, and Hades honored her request. Not only that, but he facilitated coverage for the nymph's duties within the Underworld. Though according to Joachim, the helpful demon I met in Tartarus, Hades had not brought in enough temporary staff to cover all of Minthe's responsibilities.

The random bits of information that have been floating in my subconscious gravitate toward each other. Every time one clue connects to another, I flinch. The day I visited Hades to tell him we were divorcing, his room smelled like mint. Even his hair products smelled like mint. And when I asked him to meet with me and our lawyers that same day, he brushed me off, saying he had somewhere to be, an, an appointment, and that he would be away for at least a week or two.

Minthe must have been inside Hades' rooms at some point. Or he had come here, to see her, and brought her scent back with him. He had to have known the nymph was pregnant; had to have known she was here, at Bone Fire Croft; he had to know who the father was.

That Hades could be the father of Minthe's child is too big a betrayal for me to absorb. I fight to unfreeze my ribs and take in a breath.

"Persephone?"

Junie's soft touch and gentle voice rouse me out of my inward spiral. Though I no longer have an appetite, I reach for the bit of bread left on my plate. The crust has hardened. I push the plate away, brush the crumbs I dropped to the side, and splay my fingers on the tabletop.

"Yes?" I finally answer, bringing my gaze to meet the girl's.

"There's one more thing I think you should know."

"And what is that?" I ask. Another clue nestles into place, and I know what Junie's about to say.

"Minthe's in labor."

Chapter 17

I HUG Junie before she leaves. She needs reassuring that she did the right thing, or that what she did wasn't *wrong*, and I need to reassure her I will keep this information to myself and share it with no one, not even Aušrinė.

Because I *can't* share it with anyone, not until I know for certain. If nothing else, living within the ever-churning swirl of Mount Olympian politics, scandals, and gossip has taught me that the core of any truth is not always easy to discern. And being Queen of the Underworld has taught me I do have a spine.

Right now, though, my spine wants to sag. I slide the bread into a cloth bag, cover the butter, and return the jam to the refrigerator. I wipe down the table and wash the knife Junie used, and our two plates. I even find a drying cloth and put the dishes and utensils back where they belong. Go, me, Persephone the Domestic Goddess.

In my room, I turn on my phone out of habit. I have two bars of reception. Anyone I'd want to call is already here. I have three unscheduled hours until dinner, which is being held in the Bone Fire Croft's School for Goddess Training's new dining hall. I could join Rini and Ciri in the hotsprings or walk to the big oak tree and see what Bé is discovering within Darragh's roots and branches. I could go to the stables, ask Bodhi and Bailoch to saddle a horse and bravely embark on a solitary ride.

I could close the window curtains, drop onto my queen-sized bed and take a nap, or soak in the two-person bathtub in the en suite Rini and I share. Or I could slide open the closet's pocket door and make a nest for myself in the corner where it's dark and quiet; where only Rini would think to look for me, and Rini isn't here.

I WAKE when a flurry of footsteps moves along the downstairs hall and throw myself into the shower before Rini discovers I opted for option number six - the closet. Hot water relaxes my tense muscles and a short, cold finish perks up my muggy brain.

Stepping out of the tub onto the heated tile floor, I tell myself I can do this. I can bring Persephone, Goddess of Spring, to the forefront. I can portray rebirth personified, and when I swipe a hand towel across the full-length mirror and wipe away the fog, I expect to see a nubile goddess.

Instead, I see ribs and clavicles and hip bones. I see a body that has not been enfolded within a lover's embrace in… in *years*.

I see Persephone Lost.

And if I don't get a grip on myself, I'm going to disappoint my mother, the proxy program instructors, and Junie and the other twelve trainees. Though I am furious with Habonde and Baubo for protecting Minthe and Hades, I know that compartmentalizing *now* will help me deal with all that *later*.

And so, I push aside the hurt caused by the widening rift between me and Hades. I take the feelings of being abandoned to manage our marriage alone, of being unloved by the very being who is supposed to be my bedrock, and shove them under the sink.

Smoothing Rini's rich moisturizer into my skin, I count my blessings. I have friends who stand by me through thick and thin. Friends who seek to lift me up, not knock me down. I have Gilda, Tilda, my dear Owen, and now, Joachim. I believe I can even count Kronos and Dionysus amongst my supporters.

"Seph, you there?" Beyond the closed door, Rini chuffs as she flops onto her bed. "My bones are like noodles. You've got to try a soak tomorrow."

Bending over, I wind a towel around my damp hair. "I'm here," I call. "Just got out of the shower." I shoot my arms through the guest robe's wide sleeves, tie the belt tight, and knock on the door to my bestie's room.

"Come in, come in." Her legs dangle over the side of the bed and she's unwrapping what smells like a chocolate truffle. "Want one? Bodhi made them. The box is on my bureau."

I shuffle over and lift the lid on the box. Chocolate, the cure for *everything*, seduces my nose and sets my mouth watering in anticipation. I choose one, remove the wrapper, and place the truffle on my tongue. Instant bliss. I lie down beside Rini, both of us slowly sucking on the melting chocolate before biting into the centers.

"Mine's hazelnut," Rini murmurs.

"Mine's orange liqueur." Eyes closed, I focus on the sensation of the melting, boozy truffle caressing my taste buds on its way down my throat.

"I think my next product line is going to be sex treats."

"Hasn't that been done?"

"It has. But not by me. And this is giving me *ideas*. And *feelings*." Rini giggles softly. "The Daughter of the Dawn and the Goddess of the Spring gettin' it on with a box of chocolates, oh yeah."

The main door to the bedroom bursts open as I'm willing the aforementioned box to float over to the bed. Lifting my head, I see Bé's already there, holding a matching box in one hand, a half-eaten truffle in the other, astonishment lighting her face. Ciri's behind her and shoves her way into the room. "Have you two tried these chocolates? Oh. My. *Goddess*, they are good."

I pat the bed beside me. "Join us. I'm thinking of proposing to Bodhi."

Bé snorts. "Bailoch might object."

"Nah," Ciri chimes in. "Satyrs are known for having multiple partners."

For minutes after, the only sounds in the room come from truffles being unwrapped and chocolate-starved goddesses getting their fill of ambrosial treats. "It's a good thing Demeter doesn't expect us to work tonight," Ciri mumbles. "Or does she? Or are we just supposed to show up at dinner and meet the trainees?"

"Tonight's like a meet-and-greet. Beginning at sunrise tomorrow, we're Demeter's to boss around. Until the final night." I roll up to sitting, stumble the few steps to Rini's chocolates, and lower my head so I can sniff the contents. I choose a dried pear dipped in milk chocolate and turn to lean against the bureau. "I wish you three could see yourselves," I add, giggling. I bite into the pear, softening the fruit in my mouth, and I swear I can taste last summer's sun.

"We are the *epitome* of—" Bé raises her arm, gesticulating with chocolate-tipped fingers. "Of responsibility."

"Well, if we were truly responsible, we'd get to the dining hall early and make sure everything's set up to Demeter's liking. You know how my mother gets if her chair isn't the biggest, or if she's been shunted off to a side table."

"True." Ciri sits up, sighs, and studies her cell phone. "Mealtime is at six. Let's plan to leave at five-thirty. Faces on, buttons buttoned."

Ciri's "faces on" reminder is the cue I need. After washin vestiges of chocolate off my hands and mouth, I pull out my makeup bag and put on my business face. Clothes are next. I opt for a pair of dove gray slacks, a cropped sweater in a gray and lavender marled yarn, and black leather flats. As for my hair, I pull it away from my face and secure it in a large barrette at my nape.

"Hey gorgeous, don't forget your crown. And your umbrella. It's raining."

"It's always raining here." My eyes meet Ciri's in the mirror. "You think a crown's appropriate for tonight?"

She hugs me from behind. "I think something simple and sparkly on your head will keep everyone from looking too hard at your eyes, babe. Anything you want to talk about?"

I spin in Ciri's embrace and wrap my arms around her waist. I will not cry. *I will not cry.* "Nothing I can't handle on my own. And thanks for the head's up. I was hoping no one would notice I'm a little stressed out."

"We got your back, Seph. And I've got just the topper for that sweater. Hang on a sec." Ciri ducks out of my bathroom and returns moments later, a grin on her face and something hidden behind her back. "Face the mirror and close your eyes."

"Yes, Sarge."

Ciri's soft snort brushes my neck as she sets something on my head and manually adjusts its fit. "Open your eyes."

"Oh, wow." Affixed to a circlet of braided and hammered silver wire are tiny, enameled purple- and yellow-tinged buds interspersed with silver leaves. The piece is… ethereal.

"Buds and leaves for new growth and the potential for a renewed life."

I pluck a tissue from the box by the sink and dab under my eyes. "You have no idea how perfect this is. Thank you."

"And just so your mother doesn't feel left out, I made this one for her." Ciri holds up a wider, similarly delicate circlet of hammered gold. Instead of flower buds, she's added grains and seeds on dainty stems.

"She will love it," I assure her, sneaking one more peek at my own adornment.

Chapter 18

MY MOTHER *DOES* LOVE her crown. She stops micro-managing seating arrangements long enough for Ciri secure the adornment to her hair, then heads out of the dining hall in search of a mirror. I use her absence to check the place cards. At the rectangular head table, I note Habonde will sit to my mother's right, followed by Jillian, Bé, and Rini. Baubo will sit to my mother's left, followed by me and Ciri.

Hmm. I want to be as present as possible this evening, not stewing or fuming or moping, because my focus should be on meeting the trainees; on answering any questions about the history, meaning, and significance of the Lesser Mysteries and outlining the preparatory activities for each evening's ritual.

"Mother?" I raise my arm and waggle my fingers to get her attention when she re-enters the dining hall. "I have an idea. You have the four of us" —I indicate myself, Rini, Bé, and Ciri— "so rather than cluster us at the head table with you, I think you should seat one of us at each of the four round tables. That will give the trainees the opportunity to ask more questions and for us to get to know them a little better."

"And we could switch tables at other meals," Rini adds.

Demeter scans the room, one finger tapping her chin as she considers my proposal. The moment her face relaxes, I know she approves. "Given that we're working with a smaller group than usual, I can see the merit of more bonding time." She plucks our name cards from her table and distributes one to each of the round tables. Our new spots face the front of the room, which means she wants us to be able to watch for her signals.

One potentially uncomfortable situation averted.

With ten minutes or so until the dinner bell is rung, and the trainees are allowed in, there's one more thing I need to do before I can relax into my role. I slip out a side door and remove my shoes. Shaking out my arms, I step onto bare ground, chuff out a breath, and knead the stubby remnants of damp, winter brown ground cover with my toes. Once I am rooted, I lift my arms and close my eyes, taking in air through my nose and across my tongue like I'm tasting the sky. My sweater's wide sleeves slip toward my shoulders, exposing bare skin. It's cool, and the air is heavy with moisture, but opening myself to the role I play requires me to open as many of my senses as I can, no matter the weather.

Standing, feet planted wide, arms raised, chill bumps rising on my skin, I search for signs of spring. They're there, waiting, and slowly, slowly, I hear and feel and taste and sense birds rustling in the trees, mycelium stretching silky, inquisitive tendrils, buds swelling from sleepy branches filling with slow-moving sap. The soil beneath my feet warms, releasing its distinct perfume.

Awaken, awaken, I whisper, sending word molecules upward, downward, outward. Inhaling, I pull different molecules toward me, green notes and brown notes, fuzzy and nimble. Pale yellow petals layered over white, folded tight until the signal to burst and bloom is received.

Happy tears stream out the corners of my eyes, catch on my ears, evaporate as they slide down the length of my neck.

I missed you.

We missed you.

What do you want me to know?

Images stream in through my fingertips and the soles of my feet, stuttered and hesitant at first. A snapshot of otters nesting near the Lake of Sorrows, and badgers in their burrows. Foxes and stoats and mountain hares. Grouse and falcons. Hen harriers and stonechats. Roots, so many roots. Apple and stone fruit trees. Wood sedge and meadow grass, bracken and beech fern. Liverworts, hornworts, and mosses.

Chill bumps morph into delighted, electric sparks of *life*.

All seems well, I say.

All is well, oh Goddess and Queen, all awaits the green green green.

And because my heart is filling and my power, my gifts, extend to the worlds of humans and Magicals and immortals, I inquire about Minthe.

Naiads attend she who smells of mint, she who labors hard.

I breathe in that news. Breathe in again, stretching the muscles between my ribs, filling my lungs before releasing my hurt as I breathe out, out, out.

Ease her way, Blessed Ones. Her and her baby's. So let it be.

As you speak, so we seek. It is done, it is done, it is done.

Voices warble and chair legs scrape along the wooden floor in the room behind the door at my back. I lower my arms. Soft wool swooshes down my arms to my wrists. Opening my eyes, I drink in the night sky on this Eve of Mysteries and press my hands against my chest. *I can do this,* I assure myself. *I can do this.*

I brush soil and bits of dead plant matter off my feet, slip into my flats, and re-enter the dining hall. The single candle placed in the center of each round table is lit, the flame's mellow glow reflected on the faces of the trainees and my friends. I wave to my mother and the others as I pass their tables and take my place with four young women.

Their excitement-laced conversation stops the moment I pull out my chair and sit. Though I know it's my responsibility to make them comfortable in my presence, I wait a couple of beats before I speak.

"I'm Persephone," I begin, "and I'm honored to meet each and every one of you." Tapping the center of my chest, I smile as I scan their faces. "And just so you know, I'm always a little nervous before the Mysteries begin. Do you think we could we go around the table and introduce ourselves, after my mother speaks?"

Shoulders lower and postures relax. I'm relieved to see my confession has the desired effect, and that I spoke just in time. My mother grips the arms of her special chair and rises to her feet. Habonde rings a silver bell, surveying the room until everyone stops talking.

"Good evening. I am Demeter, host of the Lesser Mysteries along with my daughter, Persephone." She gives a slight nod in my direction and continues. "Before we share a meal created from the bounty of Bone Fire Croft, I would like to thank Habonde Barleywine for offering her lands for this year's rites, and for offering all of you as participants. This is a great honor, one which others with your magics and talents would give up use of a limb to be included." Nervous tittering flutters from one table to the next and stops as my mother arches an eyebrow. "Astrape?"

A figure peels away from a shadowy corner and moves toward my mother. Astrape is costumed in a peplos, a drapey garment folded from a length of natural linen and fastened at her shoulders with gold pins. The fabric falls to her ankles and cinches at her upper waist with the help of a strophion woven with gold threads. Her arms are bare but for the snake bracelet circling her right biceps. The look is classic and her oiled skin glistens in the candlelight.

She takes my breath away. Going to one knee in front of my mother, she bows her head. Her unbound curls fall forward, obscuring her face. "Demeter."

"You will assist me as I bless our food."

My mother pushes her chair back and walks around the table. She, too, wears a peplos, though the fabric is heavier, richer than Astrape's. The gold circlet Ciri made is her only bit of jewelry and I'm again reminded my mother knows how to create a look that speaks volumes. She is elegant, restrained, and in complete command of the room.

Astrape rises, meets the urisk carrying a cutting board and a single loaf of hand-shaped bread, and brings it to Demeter. A sheaf of wheat materializes in her hand, and she holds it over the bread. She places her other hand directly on the crust.

"Gaia, ever-providing Mother of us all, bless this bread. Bless us as we gather tonight. Bless us as we enter time out of time on the morrow. Bless us as we face the dark. Bless us as we face the light. Bless us as we face our innermost Self."

Silence fills the room. As Demeter lifts her hand - because right here, right now, she is Demeter, Mother Goddess to us all, not simply biological mother to me - the bread falls apart. She remains standing in the middle of the circle of tables as Astrape walks the cutting board to each group and one by one, we remove a piece of bread. When she stops beside me, I smell almond oil, sun-warmed leather, metal and fire.

I want to lick her arm. I want her to kneel in front of me and offer *me* her service. Though what service I would ask for isn't clear. Seconds pass. I choose a piece of bread, and the Goddess of Lightning moves to the front table, returning to stand by Demeter when she's done.

The cutting board is empty. I'm not the only one who notes the bread provided exactly enough pieces for everyone at the meal, and I get caught up in the sense of awe my mother often evokes as it rises throughout the room. Next, Astrape retrieves a large jug from a waiting urisk. Demeter lays her hands on the jug's curves, leans over its opening, and blesses the contents. Astrape repeats the process of offering each of us our portion of the wine. By the time she pours a splash into my glass, my stomach is grumbling.

The last drops of wine flow into my mother's goblet. She raises the piece of hand-thrown stoneware, indicates she expects us to follow, and once everyone has caught on, she toasts us and drinks the wine. Her smile, wide and warm, radiates from her lips and eyes, broadcasting her magnanimous nature.

"Eat!"

Chapter 19

THE NEXT AFTERNOON, standing on ground barely warmed by the weak sun, I face the Lake of Sorrows. Shallow breaths flow in and out through my nose. One of the shapeless muslin dresses Bé pulled from the trunk covers me to my neck, wrists, and ankles. Like the other nightgown-like dresses my friends wear, this one's been freshly washed and ironed and smells faintly of lemons. Rini stands to my right, about ten feet away and slightly behind. Bé and Ciri are to my left, at the same distance. As we were getting ready, Ciri commented we looked like sacrificial members of the same cult. Recalling her comment elicits a brief smile no one sees.

A breeze off the lake presses the dress' thin fabric against the fronts of my body and legs. Fine hairs on the back of my neck lift, alerting me my mother is coming closer, bringing with her the thirteen trainees. Deliberate, measured footsteps signal the first part of the rites has begun. I shake out my fingers and soften my gaze, pulling the me I am now deep into my bones.

Once I am gone, the earliest version of Persephone awakens.

Once the sensation of emptiness, of being a vessel waiting to be filled permeates these legs and arms and torso, Primordial Persephone expands outward from the marrow in which she sleeps, pushing her way to the under-surface of this body's skin; to the roots of this body's hair and eyelashes; to the beds of this body's finger and toenails.

And when this body becomes Daughter, Persephone turns to face Demeter. The Goddess of Agriculture, the Mother Goddess, sends her power into Persephone's body - into my body - and the rites begin.

MY FRIENDS *and I join hands, lean away from each other and twirl in a circle. Slow at first, then faster and faster as I find these legs, my legs. Until the winterdead grass under our feet glows emerald green with life and clusters of white and yellow wildflowers burst through the ground, here, and there, all the way to the shore of the lake.*

We slow. Diffuse, pink light surrounds the four of us. Between me and the lake, a clump of unfamiliar flowers calls for my attention. I release my friends' hands and wander away, toward the flowers, and as I bend to take in their scent, the earth behind me erupts. Clods of soil and grass hit the backside of my body. I land on my hands and knees, only for a steely arm to circle my waist and lift me off the ground. Breathe whooshes out of me, once, and again as the body attached to the arm now binding me to a chest lands atop a horse. The beast rears up, faces my shocked friends, and leaps into the nightdark chasm from which it came.

FEAR WRAPS cold fingers around my throat, choking me. No, no, no, not this again, not this abduction, this terror, this… this *darkness*. I know I haven't really been taken from the Lake of Secrets. I know the shore is nearby. And though I can't see them,

I know my three closest friends stand a few yards behind me. Their voices echo my mother's as Demeter repeats the secret phrases I know by heart, and every year force myself to forget.

But something is wrong. Wrong, wrong, wrong. This is not my story, this tale of abduction and violation. This is one story layered on top of an older, more ancient story, and as I claw at the arm caging my chest, I fight, I... I rebel.

Because I know I can't do this again, even as the spell of my mother's words wends its way around my body, creating a story I cannot edit, a cage I cannot get free of.

Not yet. Not today. But soon, soon.

HERMES FINDS ME, *tells me they are returning me to my mother. As I leave, Hades - the one who abducted me - hands me pomegranate seeds. I am hungry, my throat is dry, and I bite down on the seeds, releasing their tart juice. Hermes wraps an arm around my waist. My feet barely touch the ground as they whisk me through a dimly lit tunnel that spirals upward. Exhausted, I fall asleep, and when I awaken, when I feel the warmth of the sun on my chilled skin, I open my eyes.*

ASTRAPE CRADLES me in her arms. She is warm, strong, solid, much like Hermes. Her back is to the Lake of Sorrows and my head nestles in the side of her neck.

My mother's silhouette sharpens into view. She's speaking to the thirteen trainees sitting on the ground in front of her. They appear to be listening intently to her every word.

I know what my mother is saying. She is using my story to begin a teaching about archetypes and over the course of what is left of today, and the next four days, I will re-live a journey I have taken most every year of my life.

In response to my sudden shiver, Astrape whispers, "Are you okay?"

"No, I'm not. But I will be." I like that her arms tighten slightly; that she shifts her weight in such a way I feel more secure. "When did you find out you'd be playing the role of Hermes in this year's rites?"

"This morning."

I snort. "Demeter doesn't like to broadcast her intentions."

"I didn't know that about her. I do now."

"Did she tell you what comes next?"

"I'm to put you down. Wait until I know you're okay, that you can walk, and then I am to head back to Habonde's house and change."

I lean my head away, giving me a better angle to see what Astrape's wearing. Her long, curly black hair is drawn back from her face and mostly hidden beneath a golden helmet. I see the tips of wings sweeping up and away from the helmet's narrow brim. "Wow, she made you go full-on Hermes."

Astrape shoots me a fast glance, before returning her gaze to Demeter. "Doesn't she make every Hermes wear this?"

"No."

"Then why—"

"She likes gold. A lot." Before Astrape can respond, my mother signals the day's lesson is over. "You can put me down now."

Hermes' understudy sets me down gently. Her hands sit at my waist until I tap one of her wrists. "I'm good," I assure her. "Thank you for taking care of me."

"Any time, Persephone. Any time."

Though my mother has called an end to this first scenario, I know she expects me to remain in character. And so, I walk away from Astrape, to finish part one of this farce. I reunite with my distraught mother, even as I swear to myself I will never, ever again act the victim.

I don't look back at Astrape, though I am desperate to ground myself in her quiet strength. Before I can consider this longing, and what it means, I have to come up with a survival plan that includes reworking my role in the Lesser Mysteries and uncovering the truth behind Hades' visit to Bone Fire Croft.

Chapter 20

THE FIRST FULL night of the rites, the participants are given an herbal concoction to drink before going to bed, formulated to make them more receptive to dreaming. After a subdued dinner, we file silently through the night to the school's main building. I find a seat in the cozy lecture hall along with my friends and the thirteen trainees, and as I listen to my mother explain why dreaming is important, I wonder why Astrape's not here too.

She has dreams, I know she does, and she has - and had - the inner strength to act on those dreams. She broke away from Zeus' hold and lived. I don't know if she ever talks about what happened between her, and him, and her sister, Bronte. I make a note to mention to my mother that I think Astrape would be a good choice to speak to the trainees about the power of actions, versus reactions. I'm feeling self-satisfied with my insight when I realize Demeter has been trying to get my attention.

"Coming!" I stand a little too suddenly and I'm forced to scramble to keep my basket from spilling its contents. I'm excited for this next part, because there was a time in my own history when dreamtime and awake time were equally interesting, and I was always a sensitive, curious girl.

I still am, it's just those aspects of who I am at my core are wrapped in layers and layers of anxiety, and stories that have strayed too far from their origins.

Before I can right the wrongs done to me, other tasks take precedence. I take two steps down to where a lectern is situated in front of a wall-mounted chalkboard, moveable whiteboards, and a pulldown screen. I set the basket on the long table, move the lectern aside, and place myself in the center of the teaching space. I may have played the role of Persephone, innocent girl snatched from her loving mother's embrace earlier in the day, but tonight I draw on Persephone, Queen of the Underworld, she who cares for the souls of the newly departed.

This is my court, and I wear the crown.

"Creirwy and Bé Chuille? Will the two of you show the basket to each of the trainees and help them choose a figurine?" Earlier, I made my friends aware I planned to ask for their help at this point, and they are ready. They approach the table, and each takes one basket handle.

"Demeter has spoken to you about the importance of your dreams. And Airmid Herself came up with the combination of herbs used in the concoction you will sip before bed should you choose. Both Demeter and I will say to you, again and again, until you hear it and know it in your bones, that you are here with us, by choice.

"That said, we cannot control what you dream or think or feel during our time with you, which is why we have safeguards in place, and which is why you hold the power to say yes, or no. Aušrinė, Bé Chuille, and Creirwy are here as your support team and to assist me when asked.

"Bé Chuille knows the souls of trees and rocks, and Creirwy is a skilled jeweler who can hold metals and gemstones in her hands and read their intrinsic properties. Together these two have created talismans and trinkets meant to facilitate and support dreamtime."

All heads turn toward Bé and Ciri and the basket sitting between them. "I invite everyone to gather in a circle. We'll pass each object around so everyone has a chance to hold it at least once, and then I would like you to choose one."

"Or be chosen by one, in which case we suggest you keep it," Ciri adds. "Neither Bé Chuille nor I placed spells on any of these objects. All we did was to respond to the raw materials' intrinsic qualities, then use our tools and skills to shape and refine that power."

Bé crouches behind two of the trainees and reaches her arm between them. "There's a good chance one of these will seek you out or speak to you." She chuckles as a stubby length of wood, polished at both ends and with its bark intact, releases a slender stem, then a tiny green leaf, and another, as it coils through the air toward a specific student. "And I swear I did *nothing* to make that happen."

The object of the wood's desire, a self-professed earth witch, nods. She leans forward, reaches into the basket for the piece of wood, and scoots back to make room for others. "This is mine to keep?" she asks.

"If you accept the wood's invitation, yes."

The girl strokes the branchling and studies its bark. "What type of tree did this come from?"

"Try to figure that out on your own," Bé counsels, "and if you need help, let me know."

While my friend speaks, the other trainees pass around the rest of the basket's contents. Ciri and Bé made at least twice as many objects as there are students - I know, because I paid the invoices - and I'm glad they thought to do that. I take a step back, in part to resist my own urge to examine the objects, mostly so I can watch the trainees' reactions to this exercise in sensing and connecting.

This group has been here one month. Scanning their faces and bodies, I perceive that they're genuinely curious and open to new experiences. Some exude a bit of fear: of the exercise, of learning something about themselves and their magic, of disappointing their instructors/family/other students. I also catch spikes of excitement, disappointment, anger.

I'm here to facilitate, not judge, and I speak to that, offering my encouragement to what they might have thought was going to be a simple grab-and-go. A good thirty minutes pass before everyone holds at least one object in their hand. One trainee holds two. Another holds three objects - one wood, one stone, and one metal - and when I channel my mother and raise an eyebrow, they extend their arms and turn their palms to face the floor. Nothing falls.

Interesting.

"They chose me, I swear it."

"Perhaps you have affinities to more magics than you know," I offer. "It might be good to speak to your instructors."

"I will do that," she promises.

"Now that you each have your object, or objects, please take a seat, with at least one empty chair between you and the person next to you."

I wait until the trainees are ready and continue. "Make yourselves comfortable. Place your feet flat on the floor, hold your object in your hand softly. And when you feel centered, close your eyes."

I wait until I see everyone follows my instructions. "Connect to your breath. Exhale any mental clutter, any internal commentary, and as you inhale, connect to your power center. Connect to your magic, to the magic that you might share among family members, and to the magic that is uniquely *yours*."

. . .

"I FORGOT how much the rites tire me out." Rini and I stand at our bathroom's side-by-side sinks, brushing our teeth. My legs can barely keep me upright. "And this is a much smaller group than usual."

Rini pauses, her toothbrush wedged between the side of her mouth and her teeth. "For sure. I think it's because the trainees are so attentive. No wine and dancing for me tonight."

"We get to dance on the last night and drink wine when we're at Bé's castle, recovering."

I hold back my hair, spit into my sink, and rinse my mouth. "G'night, Rini."

"G'night, Seph."

Chapter 21

DAYS two and three of the Lesser Mysteries continue in the same pattern, without the early two-hour session Demeter added to the first day and without me having to re-experience any more trauma. It's clear the trainees are relieved at the reprieve. They've been given a lot to absorb.

And Goddess and Spirit, *I've* been given a lot to absorb, as have Rini, Bé, and Ciri. My mother neglected to mention beforehand that she was taking a new tack with this group by providing much, *much* more in the way of theory and lecture and lengthy Q and A sessions.

Over our fourth communal breakfast in the dining hall, I ask why all the classwork. My tone conveys irritation, not curiosity, because I've continued my nightly sojourn to the Underworld and I'm running on fumes. My mother reminds me that these young woman are in a program that will train them to act as proxies for capitol G goddesses; that these young woman filled out detailed applications and went through vetting processes that made sure they were physically strong and emotionally stable enough to handle the rigorous program.

"The trainees must understand how to locate the source of their personal power, their personal magic; how to rein in that power, channeling and adapting it to match the power and magic of whichever goddess they are taking the place of. We're breaking new ground here, Persephone, by asking others to subvert the natural flow their own magic seeks to make it follow, to make it *serve*, another's.

"And not by using bribery, or trickery, or coercive spells. By acting voluntarily and knowingly as a conduit." My mother chuckles, and adds, "Well, they're not exactly volunteering. Once they're trained and through their apprenticeship year, they will be generously compensated during their tenure as proxies."

"Do you think these Magicals *really* understand what they've signed up for?"

"No. Nor did any of us who were here last summer, and during the ensuing planning session, understand what we were creating." Demeter chuckles again, which is two times more than I've heard that sound coming from her in recent memory. "Even now, I don't think Habonde understands all the implications. But after our time with these students, she'll know more. And maybe we won't get invited back next year."

"Or maybe we will," I offer. "Ending all the lectures and research and experiential sessions with the Sacred Spiral Dance will finish our time here on a high note."

"My daughter is wise in the ways of the youthful." My mother leans toward me and kisses my cheek. I keep the shock off my face - barely - by lifting my mug of tea to my mouth and swallowing until there's not a drop left. She adds, "Did you happen to check out what's in the bottom of that trunk I left you?"

"You mean the Stevie Nicks knockoffs?" I ask, licking the corners of my mouth.

"Those are not knock-offs," she whispers. "I had friends in high places."

"You mean high friends in high places?" My comment makes my mother snort - *snort!* - which she covers up by coughing into her napkin. I look around the room, challenging anyone to comment on Demeter's behavior, and hand her a glass of water. I lower my voice. "Rini, Bé, Ciri and I had a blast going through the trunk and trying things on. We each created an outfit, and we asked Jillian if she could help us get them cleaned and altered in time for the final night. And don't worry, we paid the urisk for their help."

"Was Ciri able to use the bag of gems I tucked in there, and any of the other jewelry?"

"Mom, she was so excited and inspired, I think she's had only like two, three hours of sleep a night. Oh, and she arranged with the urisk to come back and run metalworking and jewelry-making workshops to anyone who wants to learn."

My mother sets down her empty glass and takes my face in her hands. "I'm glad the four of you have each other. And before I get too mushy, may I remind you we have one more day of tedious but necessary tasks before you get to show off?" At my nod, she releases me and stands, smoothing her hands down her dress.

AT THE END of the day, I excuse myself from the dining hall before dinner ends. There's been so much to do, so much that is different about this year's rites, that I've taken barely a moment to think about Hades and Minthe. Tonight, I'm determined to find him, confront him, and demand he gives me what I want. After we clear the air, I'll visit my Underworld court, then return to Bone Fire Croft in time to dance away any residual frustration, anger, grief— dance away everything.

And once Hades and I have settled things between us formally, I'll speak with my mother and come to an agreement with her.

Confident in my plan, I search the ground floor closets in Habonde's house for weather-appropriate outerwear, like boots and a warm, waterproof jacket. I find a pair of worn, green Wellies and one of those green and black plaid overshirts outdoorsy types love. Though I'm not used to wearing something this ungainly, between the wool shirt, the boots, and one of Bé's wool caps I borrow without asking, I'm ready for the task I set myself: follow the path along the river toward the Lake of Secrets until I find the naiads' encampment, and pray I'm not recognized.

Night has fallen. Compared to the Underworld, the sky here is a darker, sharper, bluish black, the air more misty than foggy. I find an assortment of flashlights in a drawer in Habonde's old kitchen. Pocketing one that works, I leave the house via the closest door. Down a couple of steps, my boots hit a pebbled walkway. I make it to the gate, and through, and again shine the light on the paper map. Which wipes out my night vision. I memorize the route as best I can and dim the flashlight.

I can do this. I can traverse an unfamiliar landscape in the dark. Isn't this what people do when they want to make changes in their lives? Face their fears? I'm less afraid of Hades' reaction than Demeter's, but the situation between him and me is more easily solved.

I think.

I hope.

Keeping the flashlight trained on the ground, I follow the well-worn path. I even remember to veer to the left when the path forks. The scent of river water rises, and I realize I'm muttering. At least no one's around to hear or answer me back.

"May I help you, Goddess?"

A rough, rumbly, disembodied voice sounds from the stand of trees to my right. My heart leaps into my chest, I swing the flashlight in the voice's general direction, and stumble on a root. Which I would have seen had I stopped and left the light trained on the ground. A large, strong hand takes my elbow. Luckily for the dryad - I know it's a dryad because I can see the woody fellow in the light's beam and he has human legs, not horse legs, which means he's not a satyr - he doesn't try to move me any closer to him or the trees. As soon as I'm steady on my feet, he releases me and takes a step back.

"Thank you. And yes, you can point me in the direction of the naiads'…. tents?" I'm not sure what kind of dwellings the waterborne live in and I sense by the dryad's reaction I've guessed wrong.

"The naiads' *dens* are clustered closer to the mouth of the river. If you stay on this path, you should be there in about fifteen minutes. Watch for poles hung with fae lights and a large clump of marsh grass. When you get to the grass, you'll see a pathway to the water and a small dock. If there isn't a boat, you'll need to wait for one to be brought over. You might have to wait awhile."

"A boat?" I squeak.

"Yes, a boat. It's a narrow thing, easy enough to pole across. It's just that sometimes all three end up on one side of the river or the other."

Easy enough for waterborne to pole a boat, I think, but I don't tell him that. "Thank you for the directions and for your advice."

"My pleasure, Goddess. Enjoy the rest of your evening." He melts back into the leafy shadows without making a sound. Inspired by his example, I sweep the trail ahead with my flashlight and place my feet consciously. Quietly.

Stealth works to my advantage. As does *not* talking to myself aloud. Voices carry across the water before I see the lights the dryad mentioned. I can't make out what anyone is saying, only that conversations fill the air in muted bursts. The grass I was told to keep an eye out for looms above my shoulders, temporarily blocking my view. I locate the path and follow its gentle slope to the water. A flat-bottomed vessel bobs on the river's surface - lucky me - and lights on the far shore provide enough illumination I can stash the flashlight in my boot.

I'm ready. I can do this. I fill in for Charon and his nephew, Moros, on the *extremely* rare days when neither is available to ferry souls; I can ferry myself across a river that's a quarter the width of the Kokytos.

The narrow dock shifts the moment my foot meets the first board, dropping me to my hands and knees and pointing out that the whole thing's a pontoon. Relieved there's no one around to witness my less-than-graceful actions, I crawl forward until I come alongside the boat. I reach out with my left leg, remember to keep my weight centered as I grip the gunwale, and settle my other leg.

Not only is this position ridiculously awkward, but I neglected to undo the rope looped between two dock boards. If I don't cast off, I'll get nowhere, and right now, I'm rethinking my strategy. Balancing on my hands and knees in a flimsy boat is not exactly a position of power from which to negotiate, or issue ultimatums.

I laugh - because what else can I do? - work the rope out from where it's stuck, coil it in front of my knees, and prop my butt on the center thwart. Carefully, I guide one end of the long pole into the water until it meets the muck at the bottom, then stops on something solid. Ish. Solid-ish. Solid enough I'm able to stand on my knees, hold the pole with both hands, lean slightly forward, and *push*.

The flashlight slides out of my boot and lands on the floor of the boat with a *thunk*. I quickly work up a sweat and I would remove the plaid shirt layer if I dared take my hands off the pole.

Halfway across the river, wobbling side to side every time I adjust my grip, I feel moderately proud of myself, and only slightly foolish.

A matching dock appears upstream. Maneuvering myself to the right without capsizing is a skill beyond what I'm currently capable of. I keep my eyes on the shore, continue poling, and manage to avoid the clutches of a downed tree. The dryad did say there were three boats available; hopefully I can pull this one onto the embankment and let someone know its location.

The bow scrapes across pebbles and sand, and stops, sending me toppling forward. I manage to not lose the pole, thank Charon and Moros and their constant refrain, and get one leg out of the boat and into the shallow water. Land! Sweet relief. My legs are so wobbly, I'm not sure I'm going to make it back across the river once I've had it out with Hades. Using the rope, I haul the boat out of the water, dodging slippery, mossy rocks, and collapse onto my butt.

I made it.

Flashlight re-secured in my pants pocket, I locate the footpath. Stop. Listen. The voices are much closer, and I think I can make out the rounded tops of the naiads' dens. Squaring my shoulders, I straighten my clothes and head toward the activity.

The path widens and flattens out, almost like a road leading into a village. Ahead, dens line the river side of the path, trees line the other, and at the end is the largest domed building of all. It's small by regular house standards and once I'm closer, I realize it sits on stilts above a looping section of the river.

I'm shaking, and my condition doesn't get any better when the shadow of a broad-shouldered male figure appears behind the cloth hanging in the den's entranceway. Another figure hands him a bundle, and the two of them move closer, their heads nearly touching.

Fury rises from deep in my gut, churning up stomach acid. I

want to throw up. I shouldn't make a snap judgement. I don't know for sure that the figures are Hades and Minthe and her - their - baby. But the pain in my gut branches into my heart and the rest of my chest and I want to turn and run.

I take a deep breath, hold it in, let it out slow. I do that again, and a third time, and a fourth just to make sure I have my emotions under control. Only then do I take one step, and another, continuing without stopping until I've reached the handful of wooden stairs that will bring me face to face with my husband.

Chapter 22

I MAKE A FIST, and instead of sending it through the canvas flap and into the side of Hades' head, I knock on the den's wooden frame. Whoever is with Hades passes the bundle to him and draws aside the canvas. Scents of lavender, motherwort, comfrey, and mint waft out of the candlelit space.

Mint.

"That was fast, Jill— Oh, you're not Jillian." Airmid, Goddess of Herbal Healing, whose earth-soaked magic and grounded presence I always find formidable, stands there, mouth agape. Until she lifts the cover higher and recognition flares in her eyes. "Persephone? What are you doing here?"

Neither of them invite me in. Hades turns on his heel and transfers the bundle of baby to another set of arms.

"I'm looking for *him*," I answer, pointing at my husband. "We have important things to talk about, and a little birdy told me he was here. The birdy also told me Minthe was in labor. Is that her child?" I point past Hades, to the woman garbed in pale green surgical pants and top, with a matching mask strapped across her face. I swing my gaze back to Hades, adding, "Excuse me, I meant *your* child."

Out the corner of my eye, Airmid's face distorts into confusion. She looks from me to the nurse, then to the baby. "I think there's been a misunderstanding. Hades, we have everything under control here. Why don't you—"

"Oh, there's been no 'misunderstanding'," I say, curling my fingers into air quotes. The pain in my body floods my vocal cords, lending a gravelly, sarcastic tone to my words. "I see Hades, and though I don't see Minthe, I *smell* her. I smell her here, and I smelled her in my *house*." I stop to inhale, to unclench my fingers. Hades moves, fast, whipping the canvas out of Airmid's hand and stepping directly in front of me, blocking my view into the room. He grabs my arm. I can't see past his broad shoulders and the heels of my too-large boots are close to the edge of the plank step. If I fight him, I'll fall.

"*You*. Are coming with *me*."

"To where?" I ask, transferring my weight to my front leg as I search for solid footing on the step below. I wrench my elbow out of his grasp, turning so I can see the next few steps. I may feel antagonistic towards Minthe, but I'd rather not make a scene this close to a brand new baby. To Hades' baby.

Goddess, I want to cry. Not because I wish it was my child, but because I wish I was better at confrontation and conflict resolution.

"Persephone, stop. Please." I stop, giving him my back, and he hurries down the steps. "Follow me."

"Where are we going?"

"Across the river. I have something to show you."

"Isn't your baby enough of a show-and-tell for one night?"

Hades again takes my elbow and hurries us forward, down the wide pathway between the dens. He's breathing through his nose, sharp inhales and sharper exhales, and he doesn't stop until we've reached the dock I was aiming for and missed. A bigger boat is moored there. It even has a driver. A poler. A whatever.

"Sit."

He releases me, and because this isn't my first boat trip this night, I get myself into the low-slung boat without tipping it too badly or embarrassing myself. Hades asks the urisk handling the pole to bring us across the river, and we don't say a word to one another. As we draw alongside the dock, I help myself out. Coins clank as Hades pays the fee, and I start on the path without waiting.

There's only one direction I can take at this point, unless I want to turn around and cool off with a midnight swim. I head toward the copse of trees where last summer's gathering of goddesses was held. There's a wide field beyond where the main tent was staged. The tent's no longer there, and the far end of the darkened field is where Zeus landed, intent on disrupting our meeting.

"Do you remember how to get to Hekate's yew tree?"

Hades' voice startles me. I answer, "Yes. Sort of."

"When we come out of the trees, bear right and continue on."

Luckily, the path is flat. I dropped my flashlight at some point, probably at the shock of seeing Airmid, and the moon lends her light sporadically. The yew tree's silhouette is darker than the sky, and I keep its branches in my sights until I'm just under the drip line.

"Now what?"

"Follow me." Hades swerves around a thick, low-hanging branch, and heads for the trunk. The closer we get, the better I can see the portal's gaping entrance. Once inside, the pathway within the heart of the tree narrows. We come to stairs, and Hades starts down.

"We're not taking the portal?"

"Hekate has not given me permission to use it."

Oh. I am both startled and pleased. "Would you like me to get us there? Because if you insist on walking, it'll take hours."

He stops. I can read the tension in his back. "If you wouldn't mind, yes, I would appreciate a lift."

"Follow me," I say, mimicking his imperious tone as I negotiate the tight space. The enclosed pathway is narrow, the inner walls bumpy, and I can't avoid pressing up against Hades' front side. For two seconds, our bodies meet, and it's more touch than we've shared in eons.

I'm unnerved, but I ignore the tingle at the back of my neck and take over the lead. At the portal threshold, I place my hand on the tree's smooth heartwood and call forth my power, my connection to the Underworld, blending it with the magicks coursing within the fibrous wood.

"Hold onto my shirt."

My sleeve tightens under Hades' firm grip. I picture a door opening here, and in the hut in the Underworld where I begin my nightly visitations. Moments later, we arrive at the precise spot I envisioned. The three shades who attend me peel off the walls and stop midway. "Mistress?" one asks.

"I am here for another purpose. You will attend me later." I lead Hades out of the hut. "Okay, we're here. What did you want to show me?"

"It's in Elysium."

"Elysium? That's a… that'll be another hour's walk. We haven't spent an hour with each other in ages and I'm not exactly open to it tonight. Either pick someplace closer, or get us there faster, because you stink of mint."

My hut has a portal to the island of Elysium and its enclave of goddesses and gods and other magical beings, but I want to see what alternative Hades comes up with. He plants his hands on his hips and turns in a circle, staring off as if he can glare an alternate mode of transportation into existence.

Turns out, he can't. "Persephone, is there a portal door within your" —he waves his hand at my hut— "I don't even know what to call this, this heap of rotting boards."

"It's a *hut*, Hades, and it's mine." I don't let on that I pay a fae to maintain the glamour that disguises the hut, protecting it from unwanted visitors. In reality, it's a lovely little round building built from stones gathered from the shores of all the rivers in the Underworld. "And yes, I can take us to Elysium. Follow me."

Once again, our presence startles the trio of shades, and I wave them back to wherever they spend their time when they're not attending me. I find the correct niche in the stone wall, insert my hand, and speak our next destination. One hard lurch later, I open my eyes. This end of the portal gets moved according to who's in charge of beautification in Elysium, and today - tonight - we land in a gazebo in the middle of a park. Smoothing my sleeves, I step down from from the wooden structure and wait for Hades on the manicured lawn.

"Lead on."

The King of the Underworld barrels ahead, his longs legs taking us to a cobbled street with a wide sidewalk. I hurry to stay at his side, and he doesn't slow his pace until we come to a modern, elegant house with windows more suited to a setting with views towards mountains, or an ocean. Last I knew, this home was unoccupied.

Hades presses the bell beside the painted iron gate.

"Hades, is that you? Wait, let me check the camera." The intercom clicks off, and on again. "Oh, thank Hermes it's you. Come in, come in." The gate clanks as it opens, metal squealing against metal. I follow Hades up the drive to the front door, which is open.

"Did you bring the— *Persephone?* What are you doing here?"

Chapter 23

I STEP out from behind Hades to see Achilles garbed in striped pajama bottoms and a sweater so bulky and lumpy I wonder if he's wearing a pet. Purplish half-moons under both eyes mar his otherwise elegant face and he looks just as startled to see me as Airmid.

"Hades brought me. He says he has something to show me."

Achilles looks shocked and slightly off kilter. "I don't understand. I thought Hades was here to—"

"I am. I mean, I was coming here to give you the news, but Persephone—" He looks at me, exhales in exasperation, then goes back to Achilles. "Could we come in? I could use a Scotch."

"Goodness, where are my manners. Of course, you can come in, both of you. Though I must ask you to take those boots off, Per— my queen." Achilles affects a bow. "I'm sorry, we're all a bit off tonight."

"Achy? Who rang the bell?"

The door shuts behind us. Patroclus enters the foyer, takes one look at me, smacks his hands against his cheeks, and opens his mouth in a big "O." His gaze bounces between Achilles and

Hades and me. Achilles gathers him into an embrace. "It's alright, my love. Hades has brought us news and a visit from our queen."

Patroclus gasps, points at my muddied boots, then at my plaid shirt and my knit hat. "*Persephone?* What are you doing here? I mean, I mean, I know you *belong* here, but I've never seen you *here* here." He spins within Achilles' embrace and searches the god's face. "Darling, help me out before she sends me to Tartarus."

I burst out laughing and shrug off the shirt. A servant, or someone I assume is a servant because they're wearing a uniform, appears out of thin air and whisks the shirt and the boots away, returning moments later with two pairs of house slippers, one for me and one for Hades. Another servant comes up beside them, offering warm steamy towels with a pair of tongs. "For your face and hands," they murmur, looking at the floor.

"Thank you." The heat is delicious, and my hands are worse for the wear after all that poling.

"Let's take this to the informal living room." Achilles herds me and Hades out of the foyer, past a kitchen and an office, toward the back of the house. The "informal" living room is a carpeted oasis, set three steps down from the rest of the ground floor, and furnished with sectional couches, two fireplaces, a wet bar, and in the middle of the room, a stack of gift-wrapped boxes and supplies for a—

"Are you expecting a *baby?*" I ask, my legs frozen in place. The three men, all taller than me and all looking the worse for wear, sink into the depths of the nearest couch. Achilles puts his arm around Patroclus' shoulders, and Hades pats his knee. They stare at me like I'm the one who should be providing answers - not them.

"Persephone. The baby is not mine," Hades begins. "Minthe is the mother, but I am not the father."

Tentative, Patroclus raises his arm. Achilles raises the arm not clamping Patroclus to his side. "And we are the fathers," he says.

"*What?*" The nearest piece of furniture to me is a bean bag chair covered in fuzzy faux fur, with a big satin bow pinned to its side. I sit, sinking in until I'm nearly horizontal. I do not feel dignified. Lucky for the three males, not one of them snickers or smirks or makes any sound until I right myself and get most of the stuffing positioned behind my back. "Would one of you please start at the beginning? And could I get something to drink?"

The two servants return, wheel a drink cart out from behind the wet bar, and bring it to me first. Without thinking, I ask for champagne, only it dawns on me it's a beverage for celebrations. If the men are telling the truth, that Hades is *not* the father of Minthe's child, then I do indeed have something to celebrate. And, perhaps, apologize for.

"Champagne for everyone!" Patroclus cheers, scooting to the edge of the couch's broad cushion and passing a glass to Achilles, and one to Hades, before accepting his own. I raise my glass when prompted, though not as high as they raise theirs, and empty it in one long sip. The crystal flute is refilled without my asking.

Hades swipes his face with his free hand and turns to face his couch mates. "Do you want me to start, or—"

Patroclus waves one hand. "No, no, this is our story to tell, so let me." He smooths the fronts of his pajama pants, which match Achilles', and clears his throat. "Once upon a time, a long, long time ago, I fell in love with this man." Batting his lashes at Achilles, he lifts his empty glass for more champagne.

"I think our queen's patience would be better served if you were to begin with our *recent* history, my darling."

Patroclus nods. "You're right." He makes a rolling motion with his hand as though he needs the motion to help move himself along. "By the grace of Zeus, Achilles and I were reunited about five years ago. The deal was, I could join Achilles here in the Underworld, if Achilles would agree to live here, not in the aboveworld."

"Once I had the love of my life back in my arms, choosing him and staying here was easy," Achilles says, picking up their story. "And once we had been together awhile, once we were able to accept that we would never, ever be apart, we began to think about starting a family. Which is where Minthe comes in.

"She agreed to act as our surrogate. And our king" —Achilles leans forward and salutes Hades with his glass— "agreed to assist our endeavor by providing Minthe with help covering her duties here in the Underworld when she began to encounter difficulties in her pregnancy. He facilitated negotiations with the naiads, who agreed to care for her until after she gave birth."

"Why did you do that for her?" I ask, looking directly at Hades. "For… for them?"

"They - these two - are my friends. And Minthe." Pressing his lips together, he scrubs his hair back from his face. "I did it to protect her, to protect her - their - child."

Something inside me deflates. I roll sideways, enough to get my feet under me and stand, and set my champagne flute on the low table in front of the couch. "Hades. I wish you had put a quarter of the effort you give to your friends, into our marriage. Into considering how you might take actions that could be helpful to us, to *me*."

Forcing my arms to hang at my sides, rather than reach for any of their throats, I add, "Patroclus, Achilles, congratulations on the birth of your child. I hope you will invite me to meet them as soon as you are ready to receive visitors." I turn to go, keeping my back to the couch. "Hades, you know what I want. I will find you tomorrow, after I have finished the rites, and you *will* sign those papers.

"Goodnight."

Chapter 24

I MAKE it to the gazebo, and from there, to my hut. The shades hesitate at my appearance, only fully peeling themselves away from the wall when I indicate I'm ready for my robes.

"But you're… dirty," one shade says.

"And what about your crown?" another asks.

I glance at my pants, and the long-sleeved shirt I pulled from the dresser drawer in my room at Habonde's. I have no idea who the shirt belongs to. "Don't I have a change of clothes here? And isn't there a spare crown or two for emergencies?"

One shade darts off, returning with a floaty nightgown similar to the ones my friends and I were just wearing at the rites. "Will this do?"

"Sure." I shuck my pants, pull off the shirt, and slide my arms into the sleeves. The shade pulls the soft gown over my head, and I watch as the hem settles around my dirty toes.

A second shade disappears, then reappears, a crude iron crown in her translucent hand. She places it on my head. The metal smells old, and like it hasn't been handled in ages. Sharp bits poke my scalp.

I don't mind, I think, as the third shade helps me into my robe and draws the generous hood up and over the crown. The physical discomfort will keep me alert, keep me from wallowing in the emotional soup sloshing around inside me.

I'M EXHAUSTED by the time I climb the stairs to the hut, change, portal to Hekate's yew tree, and start the long walk to Habonde's house. Sunrise is four hours away, and I won't get to sleep until I've had a shower. Which I am going to really need, as I'm barefoot and smelly, with a long walk ahead.

I'm bemoaning the lack of a flashlight as I register the ground shaking beneath my feet. The vibrations resolve into the distinctive sound of hooves. Lifting my head toward the darkened horizon, I make out the silhouette of a winged horse and its rider heading my way.

"Persephone, is that you?"

It's Astrape. Relief floods my muscles and I almost collapse. "Hey! Yes, it's me!" I stop stumbling in the dark and wave my arms. Galena slows as she nears and Astrape leans towards me, extends her arm, and scoops me up as they pass. She settles me sideways, between her chest and Galena's neck, and my heart pounds from the combined thrill of watching a massive beast hurtle toward me, and the commanding strength of the woman who swept me off my feet.

"That was exciting," I admit, my voice shaky. Galena slows to a canter.

"I always wanted to do that," Astrape says. "Scoop you—scoop someone up without trampling them."

"You've trampled people before?"

"Nah. I was joking. Sort of. Galena's headstrong to the point where she might have knocked you over. But she likes you."

I wind cold fingers through the horse's slick black mane. "I like her."

"Where are we taking you?"

"Home. I mean, Habonde's." I stare straight ahead.

"That's where we were headed. Except an alarm went off, alerting me someone had used Hekate's portal. Galena and I were on our way to check it out when I saw you."

"You knew it was me?"

"I would know you anywhere, Seph," Astrape says, chuckling softly. "It's my job."

The first part of her confession warms me in unfamiliar ways. I ignore the second part and relax against her chest. Astrape changes her grip on the reins and Galena slows her pace to a rolling walk. I close my eyes for a moment and breathe in through my nose. I smell horse sweat, whatever oil is used to keep the leather gear pliable, and hay. Underneath those stronger scents, is Astrape, all banked fire and heated metal.

"Tomorrow's the last night of the rites."

"Mm-hmm," I answer.

"I have to leave as soon as it's over. Got a job in California." She reaches both arms around me to fiddle with Galena's reins. "But if you don't have other plans, I would love to take you with me."

"Because I'd make such a badass security guard?"

She chuckles again. I decide I like the sound and feel of Astrape's laughter. "No, because the band contracted me to provide security and I think you'd like them. Their music is great for dancing, and I think you deserve a night off."

"Then it's a date," I murmur.

"It's a date," she echoes, drawing her horse to an easy stop. "And we're here. I'm dropping you off before I stable Galena for the rest of the night."

Astrape tucks her hands into my armpits before lifting me up. She lowers me off her horse like I weigh as much as a loaf of bread. "G'night. And thank you for the ride."

"Good night, Persephone. Sleep well."

Galena clip-clops across the paving stones. "You were the best part of my day," I whisper, smiling into the dark that swallows the horse's swishing tail and Astrape's solid back. I'm in no hurry to continue inside Habonde's house; I'm not even sure the building is big enough to hold what I'm feeling. Every emotion connected to Hades lost its momentum, its air, when he explained about the baby and now, I've got all these, these lumpy, deflated shapes littering my internal landscape. I can appreciate he did someone a kindness - but he did it to the detriment of our relationship. And the deal Achilles made with Zeus. Doesn't that indicate Zeus is willing to compromise? Or does the King of the Sky have a short list of preferred Olympians?

Beneath the walkway connecting the two big houses, I lean against a support post and curl my fingers around the vine's twisty trunk. If I want to get any sleep at all, I'm going to have to leave my questions on this side of the door.

THE FIFTH AND final day of the Lesser Mysteries starts with someone sneaking into my room and bringing coffee and tea with them. I stay on my belly, facing the wall, and let the smells coax my brain into accepting that it is, indeed, a new day and I do, indeed, need to get myself vertical.

"Oh, Sephie-ee-ee, time to wake uu-up."

I grin into the mattress, snake an arm out from beneath the warm, cozy covers and waggle my fingers in the air.

"No tea until you're up and at 'em."

I decide I'd better roll over before Rini decides more drastic wake-up measures are needed. I'm rewarded for my efforts with a large mug of Assam. "So," she begins, climbing onto the bed and settling her back against the wall, "where did you go and what did you do after you left the dining hall last night? There's a dryad spreading a rumor he ran into the Goddess of Spring walking alone in the woods, and one of the naiads' boats is missing."

I blow across the top of the mug. Rini knows I like a strong black tea if I've had difficulties sleeping, and she's prepared it just the way I like it, with generous doses of sugar and milk. Rini also knows I'll tell her everything if I'm feeling safe. Loved. Cared for. And right now, I feel all of that.

"The rumor is true, and I'm responsible for the boat. Technically, it's not missing, it's just not parked where it's supposed to be." I sip my tea, swallowing slowly and tracing its path down my throat. "I left dinner early because I heard Hades was on Bone Fire Croft, and that Minthe was in labor. And in my mind, that meant that my husband wanted to be at the birth of his child."

Rini's eye grow wide as I speak. I continue. "I found out that Minthe was with the naiads, and to get to the naiads' dens, I had to cross the river, and the only way to cross this time of year is by boat.

"The dryad gave me directions to one of the docks on this side of the river. When I got there, I untied the boat and poled myself—"

"Wait. Persephone. You wandered off by yourself on a mission of extreme emotional importance and physical danger and you didn't think to invite any of us along?"

I gulp my tea. Like guilt, tea burns going down if you're not careful. "I didn't want to bother you?"

Rini just stares at me. "Go on. I'm sure there's more."

"I made it to the other side of the river, just not to the dock, dragged the boat onto the embankment, and found the path. I had a flashlight," I add.

"Well, that's a relief."

I ignore Rini's sarcasm. "There was a building on stilts at the end of the path, very rustic, and when I got to it, I could see people inside. I thought I saw Hades and Minthe— and a baby, like, all bundled up. So, I confronted them. Only it wasn't Minthe, it was Airmid."

Rini sucks in a loud breath. "You *confronted Airmid*. She scares me."

"Me too," I confess. "She was very surprised to see me. As was Hades."

"No. Shit. Then what happened?"

"I accused him of all sorts of things, which he denied, and then he dragged me to the yew tree and made me portal us to the Underworld. He said he had something to show me." I sip more tea. I'm simultaneously listening to my own storytelling while continuing to absorb and process everything I learned last night.

"And did he? Have something to show you?"

"Long story short is Patroclus and Achilles are the baby's fathers. Minthe offered to be their surrogate."

"I see. And Hades didn't think to share any of this with you *before* the bébé arrived? Not even that he was helping his former lover?"

"Nope. Not. A. Word."

"Your marriage really is fucked up, Seph."

"Tell me something I don't know."

Silence stretches, filling the room, broken only by the sound of us swallowing our respective hot drinks. "Good thing is, Hades now owes me." Rini grunts in agreement. I think. "And you know what else? Astrape's taking me dancing tonight. In California."

"I wanna go with you."

"I'm sure she'd take us both," I offer half-heartedly. "Bé and Ciri, too, if they want."

Rini snorts. "Seph, I'm joking. We'd be the third, fourth, and fifth wheels on a horse built for two. I think Astrape's taking you on a *date*."

Chapter 25

"WHO'S TAKING PERSEPHONE ON A DATE?" Ciri enters from the bathroom connecting my room to Rini's and plonks onto the bed. "And has anyone vetted them yet? And where's my coffee?"

"Astrape's taking her to California. I'll get your coffee." Rini slides off the bed and shuffles out the door. She runs into someone in the hall, probably Bé, and I hear muffled voices.

"It's about bloody time you two got together." Ciri covers her eyes with her arm and groans. "When this is over, I'm sleeping for a week. Two weeks."

"What do you mean, it's about time? And why aren't you sleeping?"

Ciri snorts. "I have eyes, Seph, and I see the way you look at Astrape and the way she looks at you and for Goddess' sake, it makes me want to step in and just mash you two together. And between helping your mother with the rites and repairing those old pieces she let us borrow *and* creating new pieces because I'm constitutionally incapable of not creating when I have an idea," —she lifts her arm off her face and turns her head to me— "I've fallen behind on posting. And because I'm the queen of Magical social media, I can't slack for too long or I'll lose my crown."

"Would that be so bad?"

She rolls her bloodshot eyes at me. "It's the damn algorithms, Seph."

"Are you saying it has nothing to do with your somewhat obsessive attention to detail and need to be at the center of whatever you do?"

"Shut. Up." I catch sight of a grin as she recovers her eyes.

"Hire a VA," I suggest.

"Now there's an idea."

"And here's your coffee." Rini sweeps back into the room. "Bé said to say good morning to your lazy assess."

"She go for a run?" Ciri asks.

"She went for a 'cross-country' something-or-other and said she'll be back in time for lunch. She also said we are not to get dressed in our froufrou without her."

"Bé's been *obsessed* with this long distance running thing ever since she hooked up with Atalanta."

"Speaking of hooking up, guess who has a date with Astrape?"

Rini, whose been inhaling the steam curling off the top of her mug, glances at me, then Ciri. "Can't be you," she says, chortling. "You like cock, and only cock."

"Our *Persephone* has a date with Astrape."

"Good on you, Seph. 'Bout time you swam with the big fishes. Oh, speaking of fishes, she almost landed in the water last night." Rini proceeds to fill Ciri in on my late-night adventure on the river. I decide this is a good time to excuse myself and refresh my tea. They're both ominously quiet when I return.

"What?" I ask, setting my mug on the bedside table so I don't spill as I slip my legs between the flannel sheets.

"How're you going to fix this, Seph, this discord between you and Hades? You're not thinking of giving up your crown, are you?"

"I will *never* give up my crown. Or my wreath." I jam another pillow behind me and pick up my mug. "Maybe I'll have a house in the Underworld and the aboveworld, and a… a special friend to go with each."

"'Special friend'?" Rini asks.

The secrets I've been keeping from my friends were supposed to be shared once we were ensconced in Bé's mother's castle northwest of here. I had it all planned. I did not have this morning's spontaneous confessional planned, but I decide to go with the flow. I take a deep breath and let it out.

"I don't get romantic feelings like you two do. I don't get aroused just because I see someone who's physically beautiful, or who's flirting with me. Not that anyone ever flirts with me. And Hades and I haven't shared a bed since… since forever. I can't even remember when my feelings for him just… I don't know, just withered away. But when I'm around Astrape, something happens. In here," I add, rubbing the middle of my chest. "And lower. Something about her wakes up parts of me that feel pretty damn dormant most of the time."

I cup my mug, soaking the heat into my skin and bones. The room's gone silent again. I lift my gaze to see Rini and Ciri staring at me. "What?"

"We know that about you, Seph. We've known it a long time."

"Why didn't you ever say anything to me?"

"Because that was yours to share when you were ready. And today, you were ready. So, I say cheers to you, and to Astrape, and I hope you can let these feelings you're having just… happen."

"Is the attraction mutual?" Rini asks.

"I think it is. I mean, when Astrape looks at me and talks to me, her face changes. Her voice changes, and I feel this, this energy spark between us. And I've never felt that with either of you. I mean, I feel sparkly with you, but I can differentiate feelings of friendship from feelings of… attraction. Physical attraction."

"Like you want her to kiss you, and you've never wanted any of us to kiss you."

"Exactly." I can't hold back the grin cracking my face. I don't know why I feared coming out to these two, or Bé. Especially Bé. Because she's always been so open about who she is and who she's attracted to. And not attracted to.

Rini leans forward and squeezes my feet. "I don't think your mother knows, because she's always telling people you and Hades are on the outs and are seeing other people."

"I don't tell my mother *anything* having to do with intimate relationships." I swallow hard, like I'm trying to absorb her disappointment in me. "I'm the Goddess of Spring, y'know? Symbol of fertility, the joining of male-female energies for the purpose of procreation, yada yada? She rarely talks about marriage and stuff like that, but when she does it's to tell me it's okay for me to have a lover, that it would even be okay to get pregnant and have a child by someone who wasn't Hades."

"Demeter really likes to stick her nose in your business, doesn't she?"

"I think it's her way of trying to get me to tell her what's really going on." I lift the tee shirt I wore to sleep in, exposing my torso, and arch my back until my ribs stick out. "She already knows I have trouble eating. When it's just the two of us, her solution is to feed me toddler food." Embarrassed at how much I've confessed, I drop the shirt back down and pull the covers to my waist.

"You eat fine when you're with us," Ciri observes.

"That's because I feel safe with you. I feel like I can just be me. Persephone. That your love for me isn't dependent on whether I'm wearing a crown or a wreath. None of you has ever tried to bargain with me to use my power for something you want. And I can't tell you how unusual that is."

Beneath the warm, thick layer of bedcovers, my stomach shrinks. *I* shrink, and my hand's shaking so much I quickly set my mug on the bedside table and tug the covers up and over my shoulders. That awful sensation of shrinking spreads to my depth perception, and the whole room starts to recede. I shut my eyes, grab hold of my thumb, and squeeze until my fingers stiffen.

"Time for cuddling," Ciri says. I sense her crawl up beside me and join me under the covers. "Rini, hand me one of those throw pillows. Sephie's hogging all the ones on the bed." She giggles as I elbow her, and she elbows me back. "And bring me my phone. Please."

"Do I look like a housemaid to you?" Rini asks. As I open my eyes, she's holding the front halves of her peachy velvet robe away from her body and spinning in a circle.

"No, you look like a godsdamn goddess. But I'm cozy and you're standing, and I want to text Demeter and let her know the bags under my eyes have bags and that her troupe of assistants need this entire day to ready themselves for tonight's grand finale."

"'Grand Finale'?" I ask. "Do you know something I don't?"

"Nah. I just know your mother loves a good show, loves it when we raise a lot of power. And tonight, I think she'd like us to bring all the goddessy goodness for the trainees. Give 'em a taste of what to expect once they get their proxy certificates and are trying to decide which goddess they want to apprentice with."

"You don't think we'll scare them off?"

She chuckles. "Forewarned is forearmed. Power is power. And if they want to wield it, that's fine. I just want them to experience *our* power. And the vintage Stevie Nicks pieces will just enhance the whole experience." Ciri's phone chimes with alerts. She types in another message, smiles, and turns her phone to face me. "She says go for it."

Lines of text blur together. "My mother said, 'go for it'?"

Ciri turns her phone to face her and reads, "'You girls have worked very hard this week and you have certainly earned a spa day. Send the bill to me. Please be at the tent by 6:00pm. Signing off now. Demeter.' Not a single emoji. No abbreviations or acronyms. Uppercase letter at the start of each sentence. Your mom's a machine." She drops her phone on her chest, and asks, "Where's the closest spa?"

Chapter 26

Ciri, Rini, Bé, and I stand with our shoulders jammed together, facing what might be the largest mirror in all of Scotland. Mounted on the wall at the foot of the bed in Habonde's largest guest suite, encased in a carved frame, it promises generous views of whatever might be happening on the massive mattress at our backs. We're here now because we gave up on finding a spa with the capability of treating us simultaneously and opted to stay on the croft. Habonde gave us the key to this suite and provided a list of urisk and other Magicals who know their way around a stressed-out body.

One ninety-minute massage, two naps, a delicious lunch, and a facial later, I am feeling—

"Ready!" I lift my arms, taking Bé's and Rini's with me. Ciri joins in and gives her hips a shake. "Can we put on our accessories now?" I add.

"The trays are on the b—" Before Ciri can get the words out, we're spinning in place and tearing toward the behemoth of a mattress. Swaths of black velvet showcase circlets, bracelets, rings for fingers and toes, and other adornments.

"Creirwy Cari, you are fucking amazing." Bé grabs Ciri around the shoulders and enfolds her in an enthusiastic embrace.

Ciri taps Bé's prominent biceps. "Bé Chuille, I *am* fucking amazing and you're a fucking *beast*."

"It's all the outdoor work I do."

"Yeah, yeah, we know you like to impress the girls." Rini elbows them apart and looms over the glittery display. "C'mon, time to armor up. We have a circle dance to lead and wide-eyed trainees to impress."

We transform ourselves into a quartet of winged night moths, sleeves and skirts and scarves fluttering as we proceed from Habonde's back garden and up a gently sloping path. I'm in the lead, and I pause as I reach the hill's crest. Below us, and past a line of trees, lies the croft's largest field. Tonight, its entire ambit is marked by lit torches.

"Ready?" I ask.

"Ready."

We arrive at the bottom of the hill. Other figures make their way toward the field from all directions, and as we pass through the trees, we're met by two of the proxy trainees. Each holds one end of a wide ribbon, which they lift to let one person pass, then lower. When it's my turn to enter the sacred space, I appreciate the symbolism. I stop, wait, and when the ribbon lifts to let me pass, I step over the threshold with a greater sense of awareness than if I had just barreled ahead.

I make my way across the field to the ring of stones at its center. It will take a few minutes for everyone to enter, so I crouch by the stack of tinder, kindling, and split logs and meditate on tonight's dance; on using movement to connect each participant with the Great Beneath, the Great Above, and the Great Within.

Magic is building within me and I'm ready to begin. I move

to stand, and notice Habonde walking toward me. She stops on the other side of the circle. Her wavy red hair flows over her shoulders like strands of captured fire and she gazes straight into my eyes. "I owe you an apology," she says, speaking quietly. "I found out about Minthe's condition last summer, and I knew that the naiads provided her with a safe place to stay."

"I was very angry with you and Baubo," I admit, keeping my voice equally low. "And with Hades. He took me to see Achilles and Patroclus last night, and they explained the whole arrangement. I just wish—" I glance down, gather my thoughts. "I just wish that Hades had been open with me from the very beginning, because I've spent a *lot* of time building scenarios in my head."

"I accept your anger, and I will do better in the future." Habonde hands me a box of wooden matches. "Give it to the fire, lovely Persephone, all of it, and invite something new to rise from the ashes."

Fire is the Goddess of the Hearth's element, not mine. Though I am willing to make it my ally, I accept her apology and her advice, and return the matches. "You honor us all by sharing your hearth and your fire, Habonde. Please, do the honors."

My sister goddess steps closer to the unlit wood and turns her arms to expose her inner wrists. Fiery lines appear beneath her skin, and she feeds thin stream of flames to the dried grass and leaves. The kindling catches quickly, and Habonde dims her power. Satisfied the larger pieces of wood have caught fire, I turn to assess the trainees' readiness. As my eyes adjust, I notice more than thirteen have gathered. I locate my pillars - Bé, Ciri, and Rini - then my mother and Baubo. Jillian. Astrape and the three assistants she brought with her. Airmid, alongside the nurse I'd seen holding Minthe's baby. Atalanta, standing proudly beside Bé. A clutch of naiads, draped in dripping lengths of river weeds, and behind them, many more I do not recognize in the dark.

It is time to begin. Facing the growing flames, I raise my arms out to the sides, elbows slightly bent and palms turned up, and nod at Habonde. Sparks rise from the burning logs, circling her body in a shimmery blessing. As she speaks an invocation, I follow along, connecting through my legs to the center of the earth far below. Connecting through the crown of my head with the stars far above. Connecting with my innermost self at the center of my chest.

The flames quiet, the sparks dim, and my feet begin to take me through familiar steps to one side, and the other: turning in circles, stepping forward, stepping back. Once I feel the dance's rhythm flowing through my blood, through my sistren's blood, I reach for Rini's hand. She reaches for Ciri, who reaches for Bé, who reaches for Atalanta, on and on until every one of us in the field is connected.

I turn to my right, my feet marking an ever-widening spiral that will eventually encompass the entire field, and when I sense the edge of the wild grasses and the beginning of the forest, I turn back again, drawing the spiral of dancers closer to the fire, closer to the center. Hands travel to shoulders, bringing our bodies closer. Feet land in unison, marking a singular beat that echoes in our hearts, and the hearts of every female that ever came before us, and we remember. We remember the fertile times, the barren times, the burning times, and as we fill up with these remembrances, we move from a spiral into a circle, and I join hands with my mother.

I am complete.

THE DANCE ENDS - AT LEAST, the part I'm responsible for ends. The trainees, animated by the magic they connected with, gather by the pile of embers. Once I know I've deposited everything I need to let go of, I head for Habonde's house to change. Only, I don't change. I decide I like the retro look, and Astrape's low whistle of approval tells me she does too. She hustles me into one of the kitchens, pours powdered electrolytes into a glass, and makes me drink the citrusy concoction.

And then we're off, traveling via four portals until we land at the concert site in Los Angeles. Astrape explains she has to check in with crew. Exhilaration zings and zips through my body and I assure her I'm fine. I enter the fray, welcomed in by the singer and her bandmates and the music they make; by the uncensored dancing and the freedom granted by anonymity. Amid the chaos, I thin the skin of the bubble I live in and allow my senses to explore this new experience.

Which, in some ways, isn't so new. Humans have danced for tens of thousands of years; used movement as a form of storytelling; as a way to convey emotions; as a way to release themselves from the mundane and enter the liminal. And while I've let down my guard enough to smell sweat and beer, I'm sharing my power, too, in small doses. I know when the humans closest to me feel the gift I'm giving, the same one I conjured and shared hours ago with all those who danced the Spiral and the Circle at Bone Fire Croft.

The singer finishes one song, and takes a break, wiping her face and the back of her neck with a towel, drinking down a bottle of water, shaking out her arms. When she starts running in place, the crowd seems to know what's coming. Those closest to me hop up and down in place, throw their arms in the air and whoop. I whoop too, just… just because I'm inside whatever magic this is, and I can't stop. Don't want to stop.

Astrape materializes out of the crowd, her face alight with vibrant deep blue lights, her skin sheened with sweat. She grabs my hand and jumps right into the whooping and fist pumping until we're both singing along to the "high-er, high-er, *ooh*" refrain as the band plays an extended version of the song.

I'm sweating. The seams under both arms give, but it's okay. Everything about this is okay, is fine, is more than fine, including the moment I jump into Astrape's arms, wrap my legs around her waist and one arm around her neck. She stops bouncing and suddenly she and I are bubbled in an oasis within a swirl of wild, colorful energies. She snugs an arm around my lower back. Fingers splay between my shoulder blades. Magenta lights flicker across Astrape's face and I want to kiss her full, beautiful lips.

"I want to kiss you too," she says, loud enough for me to hear above the band and the people singing along. She lifts her chin, I tilt my head, and my mouth finds hers.

Sweet Goddess she tastes divine. I am lost in my own curiosity. In the novelty of the sensation, and the knowledge I'm kissing a girl, a woman, an immortal, like me. A wave of voices hurtles towards me, voices telling me I shouldn't, that I can't. I move my power outward to reinforce the invisible container around us and I kiss the Goddess of Lightning until the song ends and whistles erupt all throughout the outdoor arena.

Astrape loosens her grip and lowers me until my feet touch the ground. She glances to one side, and the other. Bringing her mouth close to my ear, she says, "I think a few of those whistles were for us."

All I can do is smile. And I keep smiling as the singer leaves the stage, only to come back for an encore.

I keep smiling as Astrape grabs my hand, leads me through the crowd to the backstage area, and introduces me to everyone, including the singer, who hands me an autographed baseball cap and tells me my name is "tight". Someone hands me a cold beer, and I sip it as Astrape finishes her end-of-show tasks and debriefs with her staff.

"Ready?" she asks, clinking my beer bottle with hers.

"Ready for anything." I am. I really, really am.

"I need to get you back to the croft, to the yew tree. You've got a job to do, and so do I, but we can do this again. Same band and everything."

"I'd like that," I say, and for once I'm wishing I didn't feel obliged to visit the Underworld every single night, especially this night, because I really want to know what comes after a first kiss, after *our* first kiss.

Chapter 27

"PERSEPHONE. *PERSEPHONE.* WAKE *UP.*"

There's no smell of coffee in the air, just Rini and her soap.

"What," I mumble, unwilling to lift my head off the pillow. Maybe I'm having a bad dream. After Astrape dropped me at the yew tree, and I finished my nightly obligation in the Underworld, exhaustion kicked my butt. It was all I could do to stay awake as I portaled back to Bone Fire Croft. I even used the portal to get me to the ancient apple tree behind Habonde's house. My legs had been jelly-like, the house dark inside, and quiet, and I drained the last of my energy stripping, showering, and finding my way to bed. To *this* bed, the one I never, ever want to leave.

"Zeus is here and he's making a *scene.* He's insisting that you and your mother and Astrape and every other goddess on site 'attend him.'" She shakes my shoulder, leans closer and sniffs the back of my head. "Ugh, he is such an ass. And you smell like beer."

"Is he here? In the house?" I pinch the bridge of my nose. I haven't had a dance hangover, ever, and I think I have one now.

"Nope, but he will be if you don't get moving" she says,

getting off the bed. Rini the Meanie flicks on the bathroom lights. "Get dressed. We're due at the field in fifteen minutes. Bé and Ciri are almost ready."

Rini's words finally register. Zeus is here, waiting for us at the field. Probably the same field he used last summer. How predictable. Pushing off the mattress, I force myself to brush my teeth, braid my hop-scented hair, and dress in sweatpants, a tee, and a fleece-lined hoodie.

"Whoa. Who are you and what have you done with Persephone?"

I push back the hood, adjust the cap I got at the concert, and grin. "I left the old Persephone in southern California."

Rini laughs. "C'mon. I hope the 'new' Persephone likes her tea strong with all the fixings, because that's what she's getting." She slaps an insulated cup into my hand. "Don't forget shoes."

Umbrellas in hand, we file through the old part of Habonde's house, out the kitchen door, and down the path. Ciri looks at her phone, swears, and nudges my back. "Pop those umbrellas and hustle up, ladies." Bé starts to run. I'm gasping, because between all the dancing and hopping I did last night, and the lack of sleep and hydration, my legs do not want to cooperate. They complain all the way up an endless hill, and down, and along the path that leads to the dancing field. A mix of sleet and rain is falling, and I struggle to keep my umbrella over my head and my to-go mug from slipping out of my hand.

Clouds hovering above the horizon split, revealing a steel gray sky. A dark object slides through the opening, resolving into Zeus' winged horse leading more winged horses. As they fly closer, I can see the two lines of flying beasts carry a cart between them. No one's riding Zeus' horse; I assume he's in the cart.

The entourage lands at the far end of the field and take their time making their way to those of us assembled and waiting. Hades steps out from the trees bordering the river and stands at the edge of the assembled group of goddesses, his arms crossed and a scowl on his face. I know by the sudden flush at the back of my neck that Astrape is standing behind me.

"Hey," she says softly, touching my lower back. "You got the summons too?"

I close the space between us, until my shoulder nestles into her armpit. "Yeah. Any idea what this is about?"

"No. But we'll know soon enough."

I swear the air has gotten colder as we wait. Small hailstones mix in with the sleety stuff. I sip my tea and wait. This moment will pass, Zeus will enact whatever drama he's come to deliver, then he'll leave, and life will go on.

I feel Astrape stiffen, and I follow the direction of her gaze to see that her estranged sister, Bronte, is riding one of the horses. I don't know who the five other women are, but they're dressed in gold, from their lace up boots, to their leather pants and snug jackets, to their warrior-style headgear. All seven horses stop at once and the riders dismount. I give them points for choreography. They surround the cart carrying Zeus, bend their knees, and lift. Two females adjust the canopy protecting the back half of the palanquin.

The whole thing seems staged, especially as they move closer. At some predetermined distance, they stop, snap down legs that support the palanquin about three feet off the ground, form two lines off to one side, and remove their helmets. As usual, the attendants are stunningly beautiful. Zeus stands on one leg and rests his other knee on the palanquin - which must mean he hasn't been able to regenerate his missing foot. Planting his staff, he gestures with his other arm for us to approach. I'm not the only one swearing under my breath as we leave the protection of the trees. Sleet returns with a vengeance, pelting our umbrellas as we walk out onto the open field.

"Bronte." Zeus' voice booms. "Please step forward." She

does, then continues to the front of the palanquin and begins to kneel. He extends his staff and taps her on the shoulder. "Stand, my loyal servant."

I cringe at his wording.

"Astrape." Zeus' tone is harsher. "Come forward." Astrape stiffens, and I slide my fingers between hers and squeeze. She darts a glance down at me, her expression shuttered, and rolls her shoulders back before moving forward on wooden legs. She does not kneel, or even pretend to want to, nor does she look at her sister. Zeus fixes his gaze on her.

"Unlike you, Bronte, the esteemed Goddess of Thunder and your *sister*, has protected me loyally and without fail." He pauses, as if waiting for Astrape to acknowledge Bronte. She does, eventually, turning slightly and offering an awkward bow.

"Bronte." The goddess lifts her proud face to Zeus. "I have taken your wise counsel to heart." He pauses and shifts to face those of us he summoned. "I come before you to announce that, effective today, I am removing myself from my numerous duties and taking my Godsrest. To assure my holdings remain protected during my absence, I herewith appoint Bronte as my proxy for the duration of thirteen full moons, after which time I shall return to my throne on Mount Olympus."

My jaw slackens. A thirteen-moon Godsrest will provide a *serious* reset. Zeus surveys us with some satisfaction, as he knows he's caught all of us off guard. If he told any others of his decision, that news has not been leaked.

"As she has protected me, my Bronte now requires the same. Unassailable protection provided by someone she trusts, body and mind. It is my duty, and desire, to provide her with such. To that end, I command my former shield-bearer to take her place once again at her sister's side and remain there until I return.

"Astrape. Do you accept?"

I hear a sudden, collective, intake of breath. Zeus's gaze

doesn't waver off Astrape's face. She's not answering, and he whacks his staff, once, twice, against the palanquin's side, setting off a dull *clang, clang.*

"I accept."

Astrape's words come out in a low growl. Zeus leans forward, makes a show of cupping his ear with one hand and asking her to speak louder.

"I said, I. Accept."

"Stand beside your sister."

My heart cracks. Zeus grips his staff with both hands, turns it parallel to the ground, and extends his arms toward Bronte. She grasps the staff with him.

"In full command of my faculties I, Zeus, King of the Sky, do hereby pass the Sky Throne unto the care of Bronte, Goddess of Thunder, for the duration of my Godsrest. Do you accept?"

"I do," Bronte answers, loud and clarion clear. Zeus dips his chin. His power, in the form of pale yellow light, pours through his arms and into Bronte's, slowly infusing her entire being until she glows with ethereal radiance. She looks every inch the female version of Zeus, even as the transfer drains his life force. The golden women who accompanied him gather around, catching Zeus as he begins to fall backward. Carefully, reverently, they lower him to the palanquin and cover his entire body with a cloth embroidered with golden threads.

"It is done," Bronte intones, righting the staff and resting the unadorned end on the ground. "And you, dearest sister, are coming with me."

Murderous gray clouds roar toward the hill. Thunder booms as they meet overhead, shaking the ground. Bronte sweeps her arms skyward, pulling in power from the sky as the other females reattach the palanquin to their horses before remounting. Zeus' horse lowers its head and kneels on its front legs. Bronte takes hold of the golden reins and leaps onto the beast's back. "Ride my horse, sister. I insist."

Astrape seems frozen in place. Behind us, far behind, a mournful whinny pierces the air. Galena. I want to run to Astrape, hold her back from placing her foot in the stirrup, tell her she doesn't have to do this. Tell her that Zeus, who delights in gossip, must have found out about our kiss and is doing this to punish me. But I could be wrong. Zeus could be punishing Astrape for leaving his side in the first place. He's the epitome of petty when he feels wronged.

At Bronte's sharp whistle, the seven horses and their riders move as one, making a tight turn to the right and heading back the way they came. Their hooves leave the ground, drawing the palanquin into the air, into the heart of the storm.

And then they're gone. Just… gone. Warm, horsey breath chuffs against my neck. Galena nudges me between my shoulder blades as lightning dances around the split in the clouds that swallowed the flying cortege. Before I can catch my breath, a single, slender bolt pierces the grass at my feet. I bend to retrieve it, tugging down my sleeve to protect my skin against the metal's sharp edges. I lift the bolt close, study the inscription along its jagged shape.

"*Wait for me.*"

"I will," I whisper. Tears well in my eyes and my newfound sense of rebellion drains out my feet. "I promise."

Part Three

Chapter 28

"WHAT THE *FUCK* WAS THAT?"

Bé, Ciri, and Rini huddle closer to me. My mother hurries off the field. Habonde, Baubo, and Airmid stare at the sky. I'm numb - number than numb - and it's not because of the crappy weather and the dipping temperature. Zeus just took Astrape from me, and any moment now, as soon as I can breathe again, I'm going to scream.

"That was the last gasp of a god who's lived long beyond his time." Airmid stares at the section of sky where the riders and their winged horses and the palanquin disappeared.

"One can only hope," Baubo mutters.

"But he said he'd return in thirteen moons," Bé points out, "a year, more or less."

A year, more or less, for me to wear the face of Persephone the Patient as I wait for Astrape to return to me, and for Zeus to return to Mount Olympus - where I'm *sure* his first act will be to grant my divorce.

Not.

Habonde elbows Baubo. The two friends share a look I can't

translate. "Should we tell them?" Baubo asks. Habonde puts her arms around the other goddess' shoulders. Airmid continues to stare at the sky, shaking her head - until she shoves her hands into the deep pockets of her apron and pulls out fistfuls of dried plant matter. Speaking an incantation, she tosses brittle leaves and flakes into air, and I feel the shredded bits of my joy flying off with them.

"Come back to the house." Habonde's voice is gentle, soothing. "I'm guessing none of you ate breakfast, and we can talk while we eat."

"Meet us in the old kitchen," Baubo adds. "There's plenty of time to change into dry clothes first."

Galena follows those two as they hurry along the path leading back up the hill. "Airmid, did you hear the breakfast invitation?" Rini asks.

"I did. If you wouldn't mind letting Habs and Babs know I appreciate the invitation, but I shan't be joining, not this day. Zeus' appearance has rattled me, and I feel compelled to cleanse these grounds of his presence."

"Thank you for doing that, and if you change your mind, I know the hearth fire will stay lit."

"Thank you, my dears."

I can't make words exit my mouth. Silently, my friends and I follow the same path as Habonde and Baubo. We crest the hill, giving us a view to Habonde's original home, the two additions, her personal gardens, and the extensive orchard. Smoke rises from the kitchen's two chimneys, to be quickly swept away in the wind. We hurry the rest of the way, my leg muscles complaining and my heart still numb.

"WHAT IS THAT DELICIOUS SMELL?" Apparently, my belly, ever a source of distress, now longs for food. My tastebuds, stimulated by the mingling scents of fresh-baked bread, cinnamon, and cloves, chime their agreement. Entering Habonde's ancient kitchen, which constitutes the entirety of her original home, I'm ready to claim my seat at the worn table, pick up my utensils, and dig in.

"There's chai in the pot on the stove. Use the ladle and strainer and pour yourself a mug. We've got a loaf of sourdough, made yesterday, and anadama, fresh out of the oven and too hot to slice. Pots of jams and preserves are on the table, and I'm about to whip up a platter of scrambled eggs.

"Nothing fancy," Baubo adds, "but we don't need fancy this morning, we need calories to feed our bellies and our brains, because Zeus' little surprise visit has given us an opportunity we'd be fools to waste."

"What do you mean?" I ask. Hope pokes its finger against my discouraged heart.

The Goddess of Mirth spins to face me and winks. "I shall share my thoughts once we're all gathered." I've known Baubo forever, and I'm not surprised she's already working on a plan. She's close with my mother, but since Baubo and Habonde met decades ago, I think it's safe to say she and the hearth goddess are better friends, their relationship based on mutual love and admiration, not, What can you do for me?

Within a few minutes, Rini, Bé, and Ciri straggle in from the hall. Habonde opens the back door to let in her dog and tells us she'll be back in a minute. Bruiser snuffles for crumbs and settles on top of the ratty towel underneath the table. Habonde returns, carrying a parcel wrapped with butcher's paper and tied with string. She and Baubo exchange another one of their looks, and Bruiser's tail thumps against the floor.

We eat family style, like we did in the school's dining room, passing the platter of eggs and the cutting boards of sourdough and anadama breads. "What's in this?" I bring the one board closer to my nose so I can get a better sniff of the bread's reddish-brown crust.

"Molasses, honey, cornmeal, and wheat. I found the recipe in an old New England cookbook. Someone must have left it in my library, as I've never traveled there. It should be cool enough to slice."

I accept a bread knife, cut half a dozen slices, and add one to my plate. Mundane tasks keep me from shrinking into myself, as does the bread's wonderful scent. Before we eat, we gather hands and speak a familiar blessing. Next, we each break off a piece of bread and offer it to the goddess, Hestia, and the fire crackling in Habonde's hearthstone. No one speaks until they've finished their eggs and first piece of bread. And then voices flood the air as everyone speaks at once. Habonde raises her arm for quiet, and Baubo offers to refill our mugs with more chai.

"I think we can all agree that Zeus' declaration was long, long, *long* overdue," Habonde begins. "If I hadn't heard it with my own ears and watched him transfer power to Bronte with my own eyes, I'm not sure I would have believed it."

"Same," I agree, rubbing my breastbone. Sensation is returning to my body, and it's all centered in my chest.

"Me too."

"So, the big question is, how do we use his Godsrest to our advantage?"

"Who here knows Bronte?" Rini asks. "And what happened between her and her sister? Do any of you know why she and Astrape don't speak?"

I shake my head. Those questions were just a few of the many I had been planning to ask Astrape on one of our next dates. Baubo taps her water glass with a spoon. "Habs, maybe now would be a good time to show our guests what's in that package." She tilts her head towards the paper-wrapped bundle sitting on the counter by the sink.

"Might be better if I describe the contents. I don't want anyone to lose their breakfast."

"Hah, you're right."

Habonde grins at Baubo, then at the rest of us. "Last summer, after the gathering of goddesses, I was sitting in my garden, enjoying the quiet and minding my own business, when I heard shouting coming from the orchard. I assumed a visitor had arrived. In fact, I assumed it was my darling Rhys, and so I was slow to stand and greet them.

"Well, it wasn't Rhys, it was Zeus, and the reason he was hollering like a banshee was because Bruiser here had bitten off his foot." Bruiser thumps her tail harder and growls. "You might have noticed earlier that Zeus' foot has not regrown."

"Are you thinking that's why he decided to take his Godsrest now?"

I recall the bit about Zeus' foot from the conversation I overheard between him and Kronos. "I know he's concerned about his foot not regenerating." I relay the story of my visit to Tartarus, Zeus' disguise, and Kronos' response to the King of the Sky's request, adding, "I wonder if Kronos was messing with his head?"

"Could be," Baubo agrees. "But what I do know is that if Zeus has not been able to call upon his ability to physically remake himself, then something is definitely wrong with his power."

"But we all saw him give a lot of power to Bronte."

Baubo leans back in her chair. "But did we? Or did we witness a show to make us think that?"

"Say more."

"You'll notice Zeus chose to gift his domain to Bronte, not any of the other immortals he could have chosen. And you will also notice he basically coerced Astrape into returning to Mount Olympus. Though the sisters are estranged, obviously their bond is not completely broken. I suspect Astrape is the only one Bronte fully trusts to have her back, as this would be a prime moment for someone to overtake Zeus' throne."

"Someone like Hera?" Habonde asks.

"Definitely Hera. Also, Aphrodite and Demeter."

I'm stunned at Baubo's observation. "You think my *mother* would go after Zeus' position?"

"Persephone, I *know* she would. She is wise in the ways of Godsrests and politics. Plus, she loathes Zeus."

<hr>

Chapter 29

<hr>

I SIT WITH THIS NEWS, still stuck on the image of Zeus' frozen foot sharing counter space with empty bread pans and mixing bowls. I point to the package. "How does *that* figure into all *this*?"

"It's a bargaining chip. Foot. A bargaining foot." I'm not the only one who snorts. "Zeus thinks the Godsrest will heal his foot. And it won't. If he wants his foot back, someone must give *that*" —Baubo points to the sink— "to Bronte, because she's the only one who'll be able to access Zeus's body. And surely whoever returns Zeus' foot deserves a boon. So, what do we want to ask for?"

"A divorce," I say quickly. "I want a divorce from Hades and my understanding is that won't happen because Zeus decreed he's the only one who can sign off on major changes concerning Olympian families. Hades may be an outlier, but at heart he's one of them. And I can't even get him to stop and read the divorce papers my lawyer drafted."

"Persephone, Bronte holds Zeus' power." Baubo leans toward me. "She also holds his staff, his crown, and his ring. It's that ring you want. Not his signature on a piece of paper. Your task is to find what Bronte most wants and figure out how to give it to her."

Right now, Bronte controls something else I want. Astrape. But the way I see it, my way to Astrape is also blocked by me being married to Hades.

"I say strike while all this is very new," Baubo continues. "Go to Bronte soon, today even, and ask her what it will take to get her to plant Zeus' ring on a wax seal and declare your marriage over. And bring Hades with you when you go."

I swallow hard. After my last interaction with Hades, I can hardly picture him being willing to accompany me to Mount Olympus. "Why now?"

"Because right now, all hell is breaking loose among the Olympians," Habonde says, smacking the side of her hand against the table for emphasis. "You saw your mother's face. She's pissed at Zeus for not choosing one of the elite to stand in for him. She and Hera and others are probably plotting behind Bronte's back while we butter our bread."

Ciri raises her hand. "What about approaching Hera?"

I know the color is draining from my face. Reaching out to Hera would be a last ditch move on my part. Queen of the Olympians and Zeus' wife, she's known for having a short fuse. "I'm having a difficult time imagining pleading my case for divorce in front of the Goddess of Marriage."

"Do you want us to go with you?" Rini asks. "Because you know we will. Bé's got the biceps. We'll overpower Bronte, grab Zeus' ring, and free Astrape."

Rini and I stand at the same time and rush to throw our arms around each other. "Thanks, but I think Baubo's right. It has to be me and Hades together who approach Bronte, and we should go now." I hope Hades is still here, with the naiads and Minthe and the baby, and that he's willing to forgive my paranoia. And I hope Astrape doesn't… I don't know… try to protect me when I show up. Things Baubo and Habonde shared convince me Zeus did not pull this stunt to punish me. I think his actions boil down to fear.

For once, my stomach isn't rebelling against the influx of tension and excitement, and my muscles are telling me they need fuel. "Could someone pass the anadama? If I'm going to Mount Olympus with Hades, I want to pack real food."

"How are we going to keep in touch with you, Seph? You know, in case things go sideways."

"The circlets I made for us," Ciri suggests. "They should work in whichever realm you're in, at least, in theory, especially if we add our blood." She pushes her chair back and stands. "I'll go get them while you pack food. Be right back."

"While Ciri's doing her thing, let's get you properly dressed for Mount Olympus."

"Could one of you go find Hades?" I ask. "He's probably with the naiads, or with Minthe and the baby."

"You know about the baby?" Baubo asks, blanching, as Bé stands to leave.

"I do."

"And you know who fathered the child?"

"I do. I met with Patroclus and Achilles two nights ago." Baubo glances at Habonde, who nods. Now it's my time to clear the air. "I just wish someone had let me in on the big secret. Do you know how painful it's been, thinking that Hades was seeing Minthe again?"

Baubo stands behind me, places her warm hands on my shoulders. "We owe you an apology, my dear, even though Minthe swore us to secrecy. I made the mistake of thinking you were long past having any feelings for Hades."

I reach back and pat her hands before turning in my seat so I can see Baubo's face. "It's not that I don't have feelings for him, it's that our situation is complicated. With every Godsrest, we grow farther apart. I see divorce as being a step in the right direction for both of us, and he's been putting me off and putting me off. Now that I understand why, I can forgive him. Sort of. He may detest Mount Olympus, but he's every bit as political as those who live there. And for far too long, he's put me last on his list of concerns. And that ends now."

"I'm proud of you."

"I'm proud of me too. I just need to make a convincing case to Bronte and hope she's willing to negotiate. And hope her price isn't too high," I add.

Rini takes hold of my wrist and guides me back to our rooms. She starts pulling dresses and wraps and coats from her luggage. Everything is velvet, and most pieces are too generously cut for my scrawny figure. She and I are the same height, though, which helps when she insists I try on a long-sleeved, lightweight opera coat fashioned from pale plum silk velvet.

"All we have to do to make it fit is take it in down the center back seam from neck to waist and create a pleat."

"But I can't sew."

"I can, and I'm sure Habonde has a machine, or at least needles and thread. I'll go ask. While I do that, start fixing your hair. You look like you've been traipsing around the Scottish Highlands in bad weather." Rini laughs on her way out the door, knowing full well that's exactly what I've been doing.

I stand in front of the dresser mirror and start combing through the tangles. My hair has suffered from the stress and anxiety I've been living with; wearing it loose isn't an option. I manage a simple French twist, pulling loose a few wavy hairs to frame my face. With a circlet on my head and makeup, I should present as a passable applicant when I ask for a favor from Bronte.

· · ·

BÉ ARRIVES at the kitchen door with Hades, who greets everyone by name and asks Habonde if he can use a spare bedroom to change in before looking in my direction. "Persephone, thank you. Your desire to act quickly on this may provide us the advantage we need." He nods, then weaves through the crowded space, a suit bag draped over his shoulder.

"That man is the opposite of an open book," Bé observes. "When I told him why I was whisking him away from the nymph and her baby, he listened, nodded, and came without asking for any more details."

"Did he say anything to Minthe?"

"I'm not sure. I spoke to him outside the naiads' communal den. The fewer who know your plan, the better."

"Thanks, Bé."

She refills her mug from the pot of chai on the stove and retakes her seat at the table. Holding the mug between her hands, she turns it slowly as she blows across the top. "In my family, a gathering such as the one you're about to attempt with Bronte would require a great deal of magic. I understand you use portals to access the Underworld, but how do you plan to enter to Mount Olympus?"

The meal I had earlier weighs heavy in my belly. I pull out a chair across from Bé and sit. "I… I've never traveled there on my own, always with my mother, and she—" I wrack my memories for the last time Demeter brought me to Mount Olympus and all I can remember is the arrival part of the trip, of stepping into a circular space ringed by soaring, white marble columns. "There was always someone there to meet us, and another to accompany us to Zeus' court."

"Mount Olympus is protected by obfuscation spells. They are rooted in ancient magic and said to be impossible to break." Hades stands in the doorway, looking every inch the modern royal. "The most direct route is above us, in the sky—"

"Which was how Zeus arrived here this morning, and also last summer," Habonde observes.

"Correct." Hades does that thing with his shirt cuffs, tugging one down and adjusting where the button sits in relation to his wrist bone. "Had I known I would be making a side trip to Zeus' court, I would have brought a horse. I did not, so Persephone and I will take the longer route."

I have one of those lightbulb moments at Hades' mention of a horse. Zeus' entourage flew in, and left, on winged horses, and Astrape was forced to ride one of their mounts, which means Galena should be on the croft. "I'll be right back," I say, nearly knocking my chair over in my excitement. "Don't go anywhere."

I fly out the kitchen door coatless, down the path, and through the gate, all while trying to raise a mental image of the map I'd used two nights ago. The stables are in the opposite direction, and I run through the orchard, past the portal tree, until I find a path wide enough for a single car, or a cart.

Had I seen anything labeled "Barn" on the map? I look left, and right, and left again. There. Arms pumping, feet flying, I run. The pins holding my hair loosen and I sweat through my shirt, but I have a purpose, a mission, a goal, and that goal looms in front of me.

"Bodhi! Bailoch!"

I make it to the sliding door at the front of the barn just as Bodhi slides it open.

"Goddess, what the—"

"I need a horse." Ugh, I can't breathe. I have got to exercise more. Bending forward, I grip my knees and try to catch my breath.

"May I inquire why you need a horse? Not that I won't give you one, it's just—"

"I need Astrape's horse. The big one, you know, the one with wings."

"You mean *Galena?*"

"Yes." I realize I can stand, which is a much better position from which to bargain. Bodhi is skeptical about my request. Or maybe he doubts my ability to ride Astrape's beloved flying horse.

"May I ask why? Did Astrape send you? Because normally, I would never let anyone ride Gally on their own." Now he's kind of glaring at me.

"Bodhi, Zeus came to the croft this morning and ordered all immortals to gather in the field."

"Obviously, B'loch and I did not get the memo," he sniffs, looking not at all put out.

"Lucky you," I say, eliciting a grin from the satyr. "Anyway, he dropped a bombshell, that he was taking his Godsrest, and then he appointed Bronte to take his place and insisted that Astrape protect her."

Worry washes across the satyr's bearded face. "So where is our girl?"

"She had to leave with them, on another horse."

"I still don't know why you need Galena. You're not planning to ride her to the Underworld, are you?"

"No. Not at all. I'm planning to fly her to Mount Olympus."

Chapter 30

IF BODHI WAS SKEPTICAL BEFORE, he is even more so now. And I guess me telling him I plan to fly a horse I've never ridden solo before, does sound crazy, but— "Bodhi, I need to get to Mount Olympus fast and I don't have time to fill you in on the whole story. Nor do Hades and I have time to take the other way to Zeus' court, which is" —I fling my arms out like useless wings — "I don't even know. So, would you please let me borrow Galena? She likes me," I add, in my most cajoling tone. At least, I think she likes me. She was receptive to me riding her when Astrape held the reins, and the magical horse did nuzzle *me* this morning, not anyone else.

"You'll bring her back?" Crossing his arms, he raises one eyebrow.

"I will bring her back."

"Wait here." He shuffles away from the sliding doors and disappears into the barn. Minutes later, the door opens wider, and Bodhi leads out Galena. "You're light," he begins, infusing his words with an instructional tone. "I'm setting you in front of her wings. Just don't sit too far up her neck. She won't like that, and she'll try to shake you off. But if you keep your seat firm and your hands soft, she'll listen."

Firm seat, soft hands. I gulp as I unclench my fists and shake out my fingers. Maybe this isn't such a good idea.

"Hades will sit behind the wings. The only thing he'll have to hold onto, is you. Galena won't pay attention to his signals, which means you're going to have to take charge and stay in charge, understand?"

Take charge. Stay in charge. "I understand."

"Good." Bodhi stands against Galena's side and interlaces his fingers. "Step here with your left foot, and as I lift you, throw your right leg over her withers."

I plant my foot against his hand and go flying upward as he straightens. I land slightly off center. Galena helps me find my seat by shifting her stance. She's a lot taller than I remember, and the ground is very far away.

"Now what?"

"Now you pick up the reins, lean forward a bit, and tell her where you want to go."

"Clicking my heels three times would be so much easier," I mumble.

MY TRIP to the barn to get Galena takes longer than anticipated, and once she and I are through the orchard and approaching Habonde's back gate, I can't figure out how I'm going to get off the horse to open said gate. Plus, there really isn't room for a beast this big in the goddess' plant-packed backyard.

"Hades," I yell.

The door flies open and Rini, Ciri and Bé gather on the tiny stoop, mouths open and eyes wide. "Brilliant," Rini says, clapping. "Just *brilliant*. Oh, and here's your coat." She shakes out the pile of velvet draped over her arm.

"And I've got your circlet, Seph. All I need is a drop of your blood."

"You're going to have to come here to get it," I answer.

Hades follows my friends down the steps. He's added a leather jacket to his ensemble, and his hair is neat. Everything about him is neat, precise, expensive. I'm sure I look like some feral witch conjured from a bog.

"You surprise me," is all Hades offers. He stops at the gate, looks up at Galena, and shows her his palm. She snuffles as if expecting a treat. "You going to let me on board?"

She snorts. Prances. I'm trying to hold on, to not lose my composure. Ciri gestures for me to give her my hand. I lean over, way over, and she pricks my finger, squeezes a drop of blood onto the center stone of each of the four circlets, and whispers. Separating one, she hands it up to me. "Put this on. Bé finished making sandwiches for you. They're in the bag."

She steps away and Bé takes her place. "Wear the strap across your body. That should leave your arms free."

My friends have made food, and their concern makes my eyes water. Hades offers to wear the bag. Rini hands me the velvet coat. I manage to stay atop Galena as I jam the circlet on my head, get my arms through the coat sleeves, and toss the rest of the velvet behind me. "I put something in the inner pocket," she says, pointing to her own to show me which pocket she means. "It was on your dresser."

I feel for the object. It's the bolt Astrape sent me, the one with the message. "Thank you, Rini."

"You're welcome. Goddess-speed and all that. And good luck."

Baubo sets a wooden box on the ground. Hades uses it to mount Galena. I take up the reins, keeping my hands soft, and guide us away from the house and toward the field. Hades' hands rest on my hips, not holding tight, more for balance. At least, that's what I assume. He's touched me more in the past two days than he has in the past two years. Or more. It's not uncomfortable. Just… unusual.

"What do we do when we get to the field?" I arranged our mode of transport. I hope he can do the rest.

"We— Hmm, it's been eons since I rode a horse like this to see Zeus. What's her name?"

"Galena."

"I believe it's up to Galena to get us there, if we ask nicely."

I chuff. We move out from the trees and onto the field. Galena's ears perk, twisting slightly like she's picking up signals. She shakes her head and I think she wants to move faster. I lean forward, keeping my weight as centered as I can. "Galena, please take us to Mount Olympus. Take us to Astrape."

The winged horse gives a soft nicker. Muscles move beneath my thighs as she goes from walking to running - though I know me calling what she's doing "running" is probably an insult to her kind - to thundering her way across the field. My eyes water at the cold and the force of the air and I almost miss the moment she launches us upward.

Hades wraps his arms around my waist, and swears as his chest smashes against my back. I'm wishing I hadn't eaten so much at breakfast. I'm wishing I'd taken riding lessons at some point. I'm wishing I knew what the fuck I'm doing.

Clouds surround us, gray and filled with of rain. Lightning flashes, slender bolts that look more decorative than threatening. We're moving fast, and I'm so out of my element, I realize I'm not breathing. My chest loosens and I inhale, quickly losing my breath as I slam against Galena's neck. Hades lets go of me with one arm, then the other, reaching forward until he's holding the horse's long mane, which means his body is pressed even more tightly against mine. I hope he keeps his legs where they are. I turn my head, intending to remind him to stay seated behind

Galena's wings. The side of his faces bumps mine. Harsh wind whips his words away, though I think he said something that sounds like an apology.

"What?" I yell. Clumps of rain soaked hair, Hades' and mine, whip against my face.

"I'm. Sorry," he repeats, keeping his cold cheek pressed to the side of my head. "For everything."

This is a shitty time for an apology. Curious as I am to hear what else Hades has to say, riding a winged horse through stormy weather is not my first choice for places in which to receive a confessional or hold a therapy session. "Can we talk later?" I feel him nodding, and I add, "What do we do when we get there?"

"I have… Clean up… Take horse…"

I get the gist of what he's saying, and return my attention to the view ahead, which is still clouds, clouds, and more clouds. Shapes take form behind them, vague silhouettes of mountains that sharpen into towers and fortresses. Galena levels out, enabling Hades to sit more upright. It takes a few moments for my arms to unbend enough I can straighten them. My hands are frozen to the reins, and I remember Bodhi's caution to keep my hands "soft".

"We're almost to the council chambers. I don't know if you heard me, but I have an apartment, and staff, and I think we should go there first and freshen up. I can have someone see to Galena."

"Do you trust that someone? Because nothing can happen to this horse." There would be no more kissing Astrape if anything happened to her beloved horse, and I'm counting on there being a lot of kissing Astrape in my future. When Hades says he trusts his staff implicitly, I snort, "They can't be worse than the demons you hired for House of Hades."

"What do you mean?" I'm debating how much I want to tell him, when he squeezes my arm and points to one of the towers.

"There's where Zeus sits and the council gathers. Have Galena maintain her current altitude and take us around the dome, to the back. My quarters are three floors down. We'll land outside, on the balcony."

Maintain her current altitude. Though I don't speak horse, I repeat Hades' instructions. Galena seems to understand and stays within the cover offered by the clouds. She circles to the backside of the massive round building, with its gleaming white columns and golden roof, and dips lower when I point out the balconies stacked in tiers like a wedding cake.

"The largest one at the bottom is mine," Hades says into my ear. I draw on the reins and lean forward. Galena knows exactly what to do and where to go, and as we get closer, my fear of falling rises as she does something with her wings that causes us to hover. She lowers herself slowly, hooves clattering as they meet stone.

"This is it."

Hades disembarks with an *oof.* He appears beside my knee and helps loosen my hold on the reins, before flinging them over Galena's neck and securing them to one of the posts on the curved balustrade. I'm reminded of my mother's homes in Italy and Greece. Maybe the Olympians got a discount on design service. I snort at the thought, and squeal as Hades holds my waist and hoists me into the air. My dismount isn't close to a ten, or even a five, and my legs wobble when I try to stand upright.

"I've got you."

For a moment, Hades does, indeed, have me. But this isn't a second chance romance, and we have a plan to execute. I lock my knees and focus my attention on the horse. "You stay here, girl. We'll be back as soon as we can."

Hades gives me space. I double check to see Galena's reins are securely tied, even though I wouldn't know a good knot from a bad one and follow the King of the Underworld into his apartment.

The first room we enter is every bit as austere as House of Hades, only the floor, walls, and arched ceiling are shades of white and cream stone and tile. Furniture groupings swathed in off-white fabric resemble stiff-armed ghosts. Hades strides to a small table to the side of a pair of soaringly tall doors, pulls a box of matches from a drawer, and lights a fresh candle. He sticks it into the waiting silver candelabra, and lights two more.

"Are you sure you have any staff left? This place looks deserted."

"That's because I'm rarely in residence, Seph, and yes, someone is here. They haven't come to greet us because I didn't have time to let them know we were coming." He raises the candelabra above our heads and opens the right-hand door. Warmer air moves across my face, bringing with it the faint scent of rosemary. "This way."

Hades leads us down a hall with a high, arched ceiling. Glancing up, all I see are shadows. At the end of the hall stands a door limned in pale yellow light, and beyond that, the sound of someone humming. Hades knocks, and waits.

"Master." The door swings inward and Hades looks down. Whoever is there must be quite short. "I… I did not receive your message, I am so sorry, else I would have—"

"Lidia, it's fine. Could you bring Queen Persephone to one of the guest rooms and make sure she has everything she needs? We traveled on very short notice and our flight was cold and wet."

"Yes, Master. I am most honored to serve you, my queen."

Hades steps aside. Lidia's an old woman so stooped and gnarled by time I can't see her face. Gray braids wind round her head like a corona. "Persephone?" Hades grabs my elbow as I turn to follow Lidia. "Will thirty minutes give you enough time to

—" he waves his hand like he's trying to magic away my windswept hair and chapped cheeks.

"An hour would be better, but I'll try." I'm not sure if it would be to our advantage to appear in front of Bronte as bedraggled travelers, or more put-together royalty.

"An hour it is. I'll have Lidia bring you something hot to drink. Oh, and here's your bag."

Once inside what looks like a bedroom, the servant lights a fire in the small fireplace and drags over a coatrack. She shuffles to the armoire, removes a wooden hanger, and helps me out of the velvet cloak.

"Do you think it will dry?" I ask. The rain and wind were not kind to the beautiful fabric, and I hope I haven't ruined Rini's loan.

"I can bring most any garment back from the dead, my queen," Lidia says, chuckling - I assume - at her reference to our connections to the Underworld. She fluffs out the sleeves and the jacket's long panels, and adds, "Toiletries are in the bathroom. Hot water takes a few minutes to come up, though we get it faster than those ninnies above us." She points a bony finger at the ceiling, then indicates the armoire. "More hangers in there if you need. I will make you tea."

With that, she leaves the room, latching the door behind her, and I feel like I'm the one who's been dismissed. Rubbing my stiff, cold hands, I drop the bag on the dressing table on my way to inspecting the bathroom. There's no shower, only an ancient tub, copper buckets, and two pipes, each with a single faucet. It seems I'm to fill my own buckets and haul them to the tub.

This day is turning out to hold one big first after another.

While the bucket fills, I find a bar of paper-wrapped soap and a stack of towels. The towels go on the stool by the tub, and four bucketsful later - three hot, one cold - my bath is ready. I peel off my clothes and run them into the room with the fire. Once I drape them on hangers, I hook the hangers on the coat stand, hustle back to the tub, and lower myself into the water for a soak.

Thawed, soaped, rinsed, and dried, I wrap myself in a worn linen robe and consider my reflection in the mirror above the dressing table. I fashion another French twist using hair clips Rini must have added to the bag. Setting the circlet on the dressing table, I straighten the bent leaves, then apply the makeup Rini also packed. My hand is shaking, and I have to stop for a moment. I'm no longer cold, I'm… I'm overwhelmed with the care and attention my friends show me every opportunity they get. I know I don't always let it all soak in and so I take a moment, close my eyes, and do just that.

When I'm ready to put the finishing touches on my game face, I realize the old mirror and dim lighting aren't offering much help. Satisfied with the basics - sweeps of eyeliner and mascara, dabs of blush, and a strong red lippie - I check to see how my clothes are doing. Finding they are mostly dry, and that Lidia's brought in a pot of tea on a tray, I quickly pour a cup, stir in milk and sugar, and drink it down. As I'm pouring a second cup and considering unwrapping one of Bé's sandwiches, there's a knock on the door.

"Come in."

Lidia enters, wielding a clothes brush like the one Owen uses, and begins to work on the velvet cloak's thick nap. I'm feeling rejuvenated, and the knots in my stomach have loosened enough I breathe with more ease. When Lidia pronounces the coat is ready, I slip it on. The servant takes over buttoning the front down to my knees, whips a polishing cloth out of her apron, and stands with a groan. She gets to the circlet before me, wipes it down, and gestures to the small chair by the fire.

"Allow me to attend you, my queen," she says. "I have never had the honor, and this will give me something to talk about with the other servants."

Sitting tall, I muster a regal demeanor. "Hades' other servants, or the those who work for the other Olympians?"

"'Tis only me serving King Hades, my queen, since my sister passed beyond the Mount. It's a gossipy lot here, and you can be sure there will be much said about you and him should you attend council unannounced."

"Should I be concerned?"

She chuckles. "Oh no, not at all. In fact, we knew of Zeus' plans before the higher ups did."

"Is that so?" I note the satisfied look on Lidia's face.

"And we know where Bronte stays, too," she says, lowering her voice and leaning closer to my ear, "and where she has placed her sister, and so when the King knows you are ready, I shall take you there by the servants' stairs."

"Why the servants' stairs? Why not go directly to the council?"

"Forewarned is forearmed, my queen, and I told Hades 'tis best to surprise Zeus' proxy before the power goes to her head."

Chapter 31

I LIKE Lidia a lot more than the demons Hades hired from the Eisochsen Realms. I can even see bringing her to the Underworld to work at House of Hades. If she wants. She might not want to leave Gossip Central. Grinning to myself, I follow her tiny figure down the hall. She stops before we reach the room at the end and pulls a key ring from her bottomless apron pocket. Hades steps out of another bedroom, smelling of the same soap I used to bathe and no longer looking like he rode in through the rain.

"Are you ready?" He stands beside me, hands clasped, waiting patiently for Lidia to find the correct key from the dozens on her keyring and insert it into the lock. A few seconds of jiggling later, the lock gives, and she tugs the door open. Ahead, a steep set of narrow stairs rises to a small landing. Motes of stone dust tickle my nose.

"Two flights up you will come to three doors. The one on the right leads to rooms for guests and secret rendezvous. The hall beyond the center door takes you to an anteroom behind council chambers. The door to the left is Bronte's apartment. The layout is the same as yours, my king. Hurry. My source says Bronte has used Zeus' golden girdle to bind her sister and the two are dressing for their first meeting with the council members." Lidia lowers her voice to a whisper. "And all the members are here, even Poseidon."

"What does the girdle do?" I ask.

"Prevents the wearer from moving more than the length of an arm, plus the tip of a sword's length, away."

Hades' hand is at my lower back, guiding me to the bottom step. "Thank you, Lidia. Send word if there is anything you need, anything I may send to you."

"Word of my beloved sister's fate would be a kindness, my king."

"You shall have it. Perhaps I can enlist my queen's assistance in the matter?"

I'm not exactly paying attention, but I know Hades is indicating there is something he would like me to do for Lidia. I'll get the details later. "Of course."

"My lady, one more thing." Lidia pulls a narrow cuff bracelet from her apron and gestures for me to give her my hand.

"What is that?" I ask, noting the tiny symbols stamped onto the metal's scratched surface.

"'Tis a means to travel between the aboveworld and Mount Olympus. The King gave one to me, and one to my sister. This was hers."

"I shall use it to visit you, Lidia."

The servant nods, then closes the door behind us. Pale light filters down from the ceiling far overhead. Hades stares up at the many steps ahead of us. My legs ache in anticipation. "What's our plan?"

"Do you have the divorce papers?"

Hades moves his attention from the stairs to me at my

question. He looks slightly amused. "Yes. Your server was quite ingenious. I may hire them myself for future work."

"She's expensive," I warn, starting upward. "Let's plan as we go. Lidia seemed to think we don't have much time."

"Lead on, my queen."

Unlike a recent encounter with Chef Keldt, I don't think Hades is taunting me. Even so, I have no intention of addressing him as my king. "Best outcome would be we make our request, Bronte signs the papers or does the wax and ring thing purely out of the goodness of her heart, and we fly Galena back to the croft."

"Highly unlikely. What's the second best scenario?"

"Bronte asks for something in exchange, something either one or both of us can deliver without too much—" I shrug. Too much blood? Money? I have no idea what the Goddess of Thunder could want now that Zeus has effectively elevated her status. "Worst case would be a flat out no, as in a never kind of no."

"Assuming she'll opt for an exchange, how much negotiating would you want to do?"

"Do you mean, how much do I want this divorce?"

I continue up the stairs, nearing the second landing before I realize Hades isn't moving. He's looking down, one foot on a stair, the other on the stair below, his hand clutching the banister. "Are you sure this is what you want, Seph?" he asks softly.

I'm confused. This is more than Hades and I have talked in *ages*. And it feels oddly comfortable, fraternal, like we're on a mission and we're in it together, us against them, united. But are we really?

"Yes. I'm sure. Neither of us is happy, Hades."

He starts to move toward me. I wait for him to get closer. "When did we stop being happy?" he asks.

"Excuse me?"

"We were happy, weren't we?"

"Hades, I—" I look at how many steps we took to get this far, and the many steps ahead of us. "Maybe we were happy? I don't know. What I do know is that it has been many Godsrests since I felt anything affectionate toward you and while us working together like this is… is *nice*, it's not the life I want. I don't think it's the life you want, either."

"I think I've lost sight of what makes me happy."

He looks forlorn. Dejected. If this was a rom-com I'd either slap him or kiss him. Instead, I cross my arms. "This is neither the time nor the place for you to have a midlife crisis. Snap out of it. Let's get this done and if you want to talk, we can do that later. Let's do what we came here to do and leave. This place gives me the creeps."

Lucky for us both, Hades shakes off whatever doldrums snag his spirits and pretends to shiver. "This place has always given me the creeps. Which is why I mostly avoid it."

We're silent the rest of the way up to the second landing. I survey the door to the right, and the one in front of us, and Bronte's door to the left. "This is it," I whisper. "You ready?"

"You, Persephone, are Queen of the Underworld. Act like it."

"And you, Hades, are King of the Underworld. Kings who have existential crises lose their heads, so *you* snap out of it." Holding back a smile, I raise my hand and prepare to knock on the door to Bronte's apartment. Hades' fist appears next to mine.

"On three," he whispers. Mouthing *one, two,* we knock together on a silent *three*.

Heavy footsteps move toward the door. I have just enough time to lift my chin and affect a confident, imperious look. The door swings open - and Astrape stands before us, agony embedded in her features.

"Persephone, how did you—"

"Astrape, step aside." The figure coming up behind her is decked out in gold armor, from her clamorous feet to the top of her head. "You two, enter and state your names. Bronte, Proxy to Zeus and Goddess in her own right, will see you if she so deigns."

"Persephone, Goddess of Spring and Queen of the Underworld."

"Hades, King of the Underworld and consort to the Queen."

$$\rule{6cm}{0.4pt}$$

Chapter 32

$$\rule{6cm}{0.4pt}$$

I KEEP my face a mask of coolly unflappable imperiousness, even as I register Hades' comment about him being my consort. He has never acted as my consort, never expressed interest in adding the honorary title to his, and why this matters now, I don't know. Astrape's already pale face grows paler, and she recedes into the background. The woman in gold removes her headgear and drops to one knee.

"I beg your pardons. I— we were not expecting you."

"Or anyone like us, I assume," I say, using the velvet cape to its intended effect as I sweep into the room and act every inch the haughty queen I'm not. "Please inform Bronte we are here. We shall not take up much of her time."

There's a fireplace, with two chairs and a small table to one side, and a small couch to the other. I think it's a love seat. I debate sitting and decide it's better that both Hades and I stand. I want to see how Bronte reacts to seeing us.

Her guard prepared her. Though Bronte wavers whether she should bow to us, she chooses not to.

"Persephone. Hades. I am honored by your presence."

"Bronte, congratulations on your appointment and thank you for seeing us. We understand you have a council meeting to attend. Before you go, there is a matter we wish you to solve." I hesitate to use the word *help*. She's got a stoic, implacable look about her and I doubt the concept is in her repertoire.

"I am listening."

Hades speaks next. "We would appreciate you signing off on our divorce papers. Persephone and I have been discussing this for a good long time, and we feel it is the best solution to an intractable problem. In fact, we were making plans to meet with Zeus when he surprised us all by opting to take his Godsrest. As his appointed replacement, you—"

"I have the power to dissolve your union. I am aware of what I can do, Hades. Of what I am expected to do and the policies and procedures I have been entrusted to uphold."

Policies and procedures, I think to myself. Is Bronte already making plans to cross over to the dark side?

"Then we have come to the right person. Would you affix Zeus'—*your* ring to these papers?"

"What do you offer me for this service?"

"Does not such a service come as part of your duties?"

"You know it does not."

"Then what is your fee?"

"My *fee*?" Bronte snorts as if offended, turns her head, and calls one her shoulder. "Iris. Hades and Persephone are here, and they come bearing gifts."

A golden light infuses the dank, depressing room. Within that light walks a female form and as she stops beside Bronte and takes the Goddess of Thunder's hand, the light shifts and settles, attaching to the body. This is Iris, Goddess of Rainbows. "Gifts?" she asks, her voice awe filled.

"Ask for something," Bronte says, interlacing her fingers with Iris' and kissing the side of her head. "Anything."

Iris gazes into Bronte's eyes. I don't know how the latter isn't blinded. Or perhaps she is, metaphorically. "I would like my sister to have her life back, as I have been given mine by Bronte."

"And who is your sister?" I ask, though I vaguely remember Iris has at least one sibling. In the moment I can't recall who it is.

"Arkė," she says, shyly turning her limpid gaze to me. "Her name is Arkė, and she has been imprisoned in Tartarus as long as Zeus has worn his crown."

"And when would you like to see your sister?"

Bronte, whose lips are dusted with gold, responds instead. "Bring Arkė to me before the sun completes another daily cycle, and I shall certify your papers. Astrape, see Hades and Persephone to the door." Bronte wraps her arm around the back of Iris' waist and the two move to exit the room. Iris pauses, turning to address me over her companion's shoulder.

"My sister has been in the dark far too long. Please hurry."

I'm aware that Astrape's hand grips the elaborate doorknob. I half expect her to leave the imprint of her fingers in the metal, or to rip it off. "Wait," I whisper. I need a moment to process Iris and her request, because something about it, about her, feels off. And I need another moment to soak in Astrape's presence, because what I want most is to enfold her in my arms and sweep her out of the room, back down all those stairs to Hades' apartment and the balcony where Galena waits.

"Are you okay?" I ask softly. "Can you leave?"

Shuddering, she shakes her head. "I can't leave, not while I wear this damn belt. Bronte won't talk to me, won't tell me what's going on. And you should hear what's being said upstairs. The servants are taking bets on who's going to challenge Bronte and claim Zeus' crown and right now, Aphrodite's winning and Hera's a close second."

"My mother will be so offended," I blurt. I cover my mouth

with both hands to keep from laughing - because really, what else can I do?

"She will, won't she?" Astrape darts a look at me. She fights to keep her composure and can't, which makes me laugh out loud. Hades hurries us both out of the room and into the hall. Astrape gasps and clutches her hips.

"I can't go any further," she wheezes, backing into Bronte's apartment. "Magic."

Hades, who was heading toward the stairs, stops and returns. "Persephone, can you handle freeing Arkė from Tartarus on your own?"

"Do you know why Zeus imprisoned her there in the first place?"

He dips his chin and moves closer. Lowering his voice, he explains, "In the war between the Titans and the Olympians, Arkė sided with the Titans. She's a messenger goddess, and her talents were desired by both sides. I don't recall the story well enough, but Zeus took her support of the Titans as a betrayal and sentenced her accordingly."

"So why is Iris free?" I asked. "Didn't the sisters stick together?"

"They did not. Iris supported the Olympians, and Zeus rewarded her for her loyalty."

I consider my newfound friends, Joachim and the other Reformed Realm guards who are getting to see their families again, thanks to me. And Kronos, eater of steaks and lover of good Scotch, who wants to spend more time at my table. I can enlist them in the search for the messenger goddess, but I'm torn whether to turn her over to Iris and Bronte or wait to see what she has to say about where she wants to spend her freedom.

"I'm certain I can find her." I make no further promises to Hades. He's already preoccupied with something else and doesn't appear to notice.

"Then go, find Arkė, and while you do that, I'm going to do something I've been avoiding."

"What is that?" Astrape asks.

"Take my rightful seat on the council. We need to know everyone's agendas."

"But you hate politics," I remind him.

"Just because I hate politics doesn't mean I don't know how to play their games," he says, smirking. "Go. Time marches on, Queen Persephone, and you have a mission."

I take a good look at Astrape and Hades, standing shoulder to shoulder. One whose kiss awoke a dormant part of me. The other suddenly acting like an ally, if not a spouse. I hold Astrape's dark-eyed gaze last, waving as I fly out the door and down the stairs.

GALENA MANAGES to understand what it is I want her to do. Though she may never forgive me for my awkward attempts at getting myself astride her back. I retrieve the three-legged stool from the bathroom, place it on the balcony, and use it to give me a boost. With as much grace as I can muster, I settle myself on the great beast, and take up the reins with soft, shaking hands.

"Home, Galena. Home."

Only, I don't specify which home. I don't know where Astrape lives when she's not on the road, and I have no idea how to direct Galena to the Underworld, or if flying there is even possible. I amend my request to "Bone Fire Croft," adding mentions of "Bodhi" and "Bailoch" and she must understand because she extends her wings, pushes off from her hind legs, and gets us airborne.

The entire ride, I'm less mindful of being astride a flying horse, and more concerned with plotting my next steps. As soon as we exit the clouds above Bone Fire Croft, voices crackle and overlap inside my head, like a staticky old radio. "Rini? Ciri?"

"Persephone, oh my goddess, you're back. Are you okay? We lost contact with you once we couldn't see you. Who do we need to hurt?"

"I'm fine," I yell, ducking my head as the wind direction changes and I end up with a mouthful of horse mane. "We're almost back at the barn."

"We'll meet you there."

So much for the circlets and Ciri's communication spell. I see the barn, can feel Galena do something with her wings that shifts the angle of our approach. My stomach lurches, literally moves up inside my body. I have no idea how to steer a flying horse.

"I hope you know what you're doing," I whisper, closing my eyes and drawing more of Galena's mane between my fingers. "Because I don't want to die."

Chapter 33

I DON'T REMEMBER LANDING, or stopping, or how I got off Galena. My mind snaps into the present as Rini holds my face and repeats my name over and over.

"I'm here. I'm here," I hear myself say. "I'm back. And I've got to go."

"You've got to go where? We were scared shitless, Seph. We tried to communicate with you and got nothing. And where's Hades?"

"Rini, hey, give her space." Rini's worried face is replaced by Bé's take-charge presence. She offers me her hands and helps me stand. "Shake out your legs. Good girl."

"You sound like you're talking to one of the horses," I joke, shaking out my legs and my arms. "I'm good. I need a hot shower, and clean clothes, and then I'm off to Tartarus."

"Tell us all about it on the way to Habonde's. She's stress baking and Baubo's got a pot of hot chocolate warming."

Mm, chocolate. I slip my arm around Rini's waist and give her a squeeze to let her know I'm okay. "We flew directly to Hades' apartment, and Galena landed us on a balcony. Hades said he rarely uses his place, but he had a staff person there, someone named Lidia, and she helped me get ready. She also let us know where Bronte was staying, and when we entered her apartment, we saw Astrape." I tug on Bé's arm to slow her down. I'm speaking so fast I'm forgetting to breathe. "You know who else is with Bronte?" I continue.

"Who?"

"Iris."

"Iris, as in Iris the messenger, Iris the rainbow queen, Iris the spoken word poet?"

"Yes, I think that's her."

"Is she *with* with Bronte?"

"I don't—" I pinch my forehead to concentrate, recalling the way Bronte reached for Iris, the way she kissed the side of her head, the promise she made. "Yeah, she definitely is. Turns out Iris has a sister in Tartarus and if I want Bronte to sign the divorce papers, I have to bring this sister to her. On Mount Olympus. In under twenty-four hours." Walking and talking at the same time has given me a stitch in my side and I still can't catch my breath. Nevertheless, I pull ahead of my friends with the excuse the clock is ticking.

I REMOVE Lidia's bracelet before showering and wash then dry my hair in record time. It's cold and rainy here, and it'll be cold and dreary in the Underworld, so I dress in comfy leggings and a brand new hoodie that has that delicious softness on the inside. I add socks, grab a pair of sneakers, and hustle to Habonde's kitchen.

"Do you want any of us to go with you?" Bé asks, once we're all sitting at the ancient, scarred table on the opposite side of Habonde's central hearth.

"I'm good," I say, tightening the laces on one sneaker. "I can get the guards to help me." I accept the mug of cocoa from the tray Baubo walks around the table. Habonde sets a stack of dessert plates, knives, and napkins on the table, and returns with two baskets of muffins.

"I had to do something with the overripe bananas. The lumpy muffins are banana walnut with chocolate chips." She sets down that basket before displaying the second one. "And in here are pumpkin muffins - those're the ones topped with pumpkin seeds - and my 'everything but the kitchen sink' muffins. Today, those feature last summer's frozen berries."

Baubo sets down a butter dish and a crock of cream cheese, and I attack the food. I… I have an appetite. My body is telling me it needs calories, it needs some of everything inside these muffins. I load two onto my plate, cut each one in half, add butter to the one with berries, and cream cheese to the pumpkin muffin, and eat. Inside my head, I walk myself through what I need to do next: get to Hekate's yew tree and portal to the Underworld. From there, take a secondary portal to my hut, which will further confuse the shades.

No, wait. I'm entering Tartarus again, intending to locate and extract a prisoner, which means full Queen of the Underworld regalia. I need a crown. And because the cases where I keep my crowns are keyed to my breath, and my breath only, and my sigil, I can't ask Owen to choose one and bring it to me at the hut.

Wiggling my toes in the sneakers, I envision more running in my immediate future.

"Seph? Persephone? Anybody home?"

I look up. My plate's empty, there's a smear of cream cheese on my fingertip, and going by the curious and concerned faces ringing the table, I haven't shared my plans. "Sorry, I'm a little preoccupied. But there is one thing you can do for me. Bring Galena to the big yew tree and wait for me. I'll scry one of you to let you know I'm on my way."

"Hopefully with Arkė," Ciri says.

"Hopefully with Arkė," I echo. If her physical condition is anything like Kronos', I'll have to bring her to my house first.

MY FOOTWEAR CRUNCHES on the gravel path between House of Hades' front gate and the mansion's entrance. I veer off to the right, following the walkway that leads to my side of the building, and place my hand against the door's security panel.

Beyond the small foyer, the living room lamps are unlit. There's no fire going, and because it's my season to be the aboveworld, Gilda's likely in Ukraine. I jog upstairs to my room bedroom suite and closets, wondering what I can wear that's both queenly, and that won't get ruined if Arkė also needs hosing down. I grab a roomy handbag, and spin in place.

Stop, Persephone. Think.

It would help if I could pull up anything about Arkė from the depths of my memory, but I can't. I tried while riding Galena, and that didn't work. Fear of dying froze my brain while the whipping winds froze my hands.

The library.

I leave the bag on the floor of my spring/summer closet and jog back down the stairs, through my living room, and out the door leading into the central section of the mansion. Past the hallway leading to the kitchen, which feels abandoned. And which makes sense because I fired Chef Keldt and most of his assistants.

Running through the foyer, I dart a glance towards the front entrance. Owen's chair is empty, the door to the coat closet is open, and strains of classical music filter into the air, along with the scents of beeswax and lemon oil. I feel guilty not saying hello, and so I don't stop until I'm at the library.

One of the smooth, black-stained wood doors is partially

open. I slip inside the room and go right to the stand holding the guide to the library's contents. The thing weighs a ton, and I flip thick handfuls of pages to the right until I'm at A.

Arkė's entry is sparse on biographical details, noting only that she's a Titan, and that she's the sister of Iris, which confirms what Hades said. And then I see mention of Arkė's alleged traitorous activities, and Zeus' punishment, and as I read what was done to the messenger goddess, I force myself to step away. Walking to the tall windows, I face the lawn and gardens rolling in gentle waves toward Asphodel City and consider how I'm going to approach someone whose wings were ripped from her body. And then given by Zeus to Thetis and Peleus on their wedding day. And then regifted - if it could be called that - by Thetis to her son at his birth.

Her son being Achilles. Who has just become a father himself and might want to continue the family tradition.

Or he might not.

Given that he and Patroclus already appear to be bucking trends, I add a second visit to them to my list of things to do, because if Achilles still has Arkė's wings, I think he should offer to give them back. But do I see the new fathers before extracting Arkė from Tartarus, or after? I rest my forehead on the cool glass, drawing my gaze back from the distant city to the ghostly white clusters of asphodel flowers rising on their long stalks. Though I don't know either man well enough to predict how they will react, I know what would sway me.

I will approach Achilles and Patroclus later. First, I must find Arkė.

Grateful I didn't trade out my sneakers for the classier boots, I run back to my living room and scan the display cases of crowns. What combination of metal, gems, and artistry conveys peace, tranquility, compassion?

There. Soothing aquamarine. I breathe on the glass, trace my sigil in the fog, and the case containing crowns adorned with clear blue gems opens. I choose the one with a single, emerald cut stone set in a filigreed sterling silver band, as well as the matching ring. Tearing back upstairs, I switch out the hoodie for a mock turtleneck, shove the crown on my head and the ring on my finger, and move out the door as the magic in the crown snugs it to my head.

"Hi, Owen! Bye, Owen!" I yell, passing the coat closet and barreling out House of Hades' main entrance. Oops, he has the key to the gate. I run back inside, grab my startled butler, and end up hurrying him along, sans his usual coat and gloves.

"What is the hurry, my queen, and aren't you hours early?"

"I'm early to visit the court, yes, but I'm not here for that. I'm here to find someone in Tartarus and bring them to Mount Olympus."

"Never a dull moment," he says, chuckling as he inserts the skeleton key into the lock. The door within the gate opens and I slip out.

"I'll be back."

"Should I ready a hose and an outdoor shower?" Owen yells.

"Possibly," I holler, though I think I'm too far away for him to hear.

At the hut, the shades hold my robe open, and I slide my arms into the sleeves. I chafe at the delay as they take their time, gently shaking the front and back panels to achieve the perfect drape. Too bad their efforts will be wasted. They melt back into the stonework, and I grab the front halves of the robe, descending the stairs two at a time. Lights set into the walls barely have time to flicker on as I pass. At the bottom of the endless stairwell, I stop to catch my breath and make sure I haven't jostled my crown off-center.

I am ready.

Straightening my spine, I pull my authority to me and enter

the cavernous waiting room. Lost souls mill about, the random pattern they create interrupted by scribes traversing the space from one corridor to another. I make my way into the controlled chaos and bear to the right, to the arched opening that marks the threshold between this level of the Underworld, and Tartarus.

———————————————

Chapter 34

———————————————

THE STENCH OF UNWASHED BODIES, burnt metal, and nastier things assaults my nostrils. Shoving both hands into the robe's pockets, I find the small jar Joachim gifted me. I twist open the lid and dab menthol-scented salve under, and up into, both nostrils. It helps. A lot.

The long corridor angles downward. Wall sconces are few and far between. At least they're lit. I make a note to order more lights installed, and wonder if Tartarus has a cleaning crew or maintenance staff. Joachim would know.

I near the bottom. For the first time, I notice that the ceiling gets lower and lower the closer one gets to Tartarus, fostering a sense of impending claustrophobia. I still my rising panic by reminding myself I am queen here, and if I order lights, there will be lights. I'm not sure I can order the ceiling be raised.

Oh! What if I order potted ferns and sitting areas for visitors?

I smile at the idea. Stepping from the cave-like corridor into the misty gathering space, I startle as I encounter two guards, one standing on either side of the arch. They notice my arrival, and pound what appear to be ceremonial staffs once against the stone floor.

"Queen Persephone."

I don't recognize these individuals from the last time I was here when I first met Joachim. For one thing, their matching, deep maroon uniforms are fashioned from leather-like, high-end material, not pulled from an ancient storage closet. Their polished horns curl up from their hairline and back along their skull, indicating they're from the Reformed Realm. I'm relieved that my friend and their queen, Violetta, was able to send more of her guards on short notice. Both males have glossy wings drawn tight to their backs, designating their mated status, though they look too much alike to be paired with one another.

"Guards." I keep a neutral face, though I'm pleased at the speed with which they recognize me.

"How may we be of service today?"

"First, tell me your names."

"I am Kai Skarpsgärd, and this is my brother, Dag. We're two of the new hires. Queen Violetta herself chose us for this mission."

"Kai. Dag. I would like you to locate a prisoner and bring them to me. Her name is Arkė, and I believe she has been here from the time of the Titans."

"Let me check the database." Kai steps behind the column carved from the stone walls as Dag returns to scanning the long hallway behind me. Curious, I lean forward to see if Kai's consulting a book like the one in my library.

Shockingly, it's not a book, it's a tablet like those available in the aboveworld. "Do we get internet down here?" I ask, unable to keep the surprise from my voice.

"No, Queen Persephone. At least, not the internet the way you might be familiar with. This is a software program developed in our realm at the request of Captain Köhler. He tasked our queen's youngest son with creating a directory of Tartarus' inhabitants. Captain Köhler noted most prisoners seemed to prefer, or were confined to, one level or another. Also noted are their crimes and punishments; who was assigned to mete out the punishment; who was wronged in the first place, and if the topic of reparations has been broached."

"That is… extraordinary. I wonder why this hasn't been done before?"

Kai shrugs. "Sometimes it takes fresh eyes to spot a problem and design a solution." I watch as he scrolls, stops, and widens the entry he found. "And here we go. Arkė. Oh. Oh, wow."

"What do you mean, 'Oh, wow'?"

He steps aside and invites me to read the screen. "This Arkė was a goddess in her own right, born before the Olympians and sentenced by Zeus for crimes against his kin. One would think she would have been forgiven a long time ago, but according to the records, she's still here.

"At least, her body's still here," he adds, somewhat reluctantly.

"Her *body*? Does this mean she's *dead*?" If Arkė did not survive her captivity, I don't know what this means for what Hades and I want to accomplish, or for my hope to free Astrape.

"The most recent entries on her page state no one has seen any sign of movement from her in a very long time."

"Does this say where her body—" I pause to rephrase my question. I'm not ready to assume she is dead. "Does this indicate where she resides?"

Kai nods, then taps the screen. A face framed by horns appears. "Mimir. Queen Persephone is here, and she has asked me to locate a prisoner for her. Captain Köhler wants two of us at the gate at all times, and I need you to cover for me."

Mimir gives Kai a sharp nod and that portion of the screen goes black. I'm going to ask Joachim - Captain Köhler - if he thinks Queen Violetta's son could bring demon technology to House of Hades. Having better access to my friends during my lengthy stays in the Underworld would go a long way toward easing my loneliness and isolation.

I'm also going to let this guard know I'm not going to stand here and twiddle my thumbs while he retrieves Arkė. My curiosity is growing, and I'll be well-protected, making this the perfect opportunity for me to explore Tartarus further. "Kai, I'm coming with you."

"I don't think that's—"

Though he towers over me, I channel Demeter in body and voice. "Guard Skarpsgärd, I am Queen of the Underworld. Tartarus lies within my domain, and I wish to acquaint myself with every single one of its nooks and crannies, as well as its inhabitants. Please, lead the way."

"Are you sure?"

I lift my robes and show him my sneakered feet. "I'm sure."

FIVE MINUTES LATER, I'm less certain about this recent life choice. Maintaining a regal visage as rank air assaults my nose is a challenge. I apply more of the salve, remind myself to breathe through my mouth, and cover the lower half of my face with my sleeve.

That solution doesn't last. If I'm going to accompany Kai on this rescue mission, I need to see my subjects, and to be seen by them. Even if they don't recognize me as Persephone, they should recognize the symbolism of the robes I wear, and my crown, and—

"Ow!" Something soft and smelly splatters against the side of my head, drips onto my chest, and falls to the ground with a *plop*. Kai immediately pulls me behind him and snaps out his wings. I try unsuccessfully to peek around their taut, nearly translucent edges. "What was that?"

"I believe it was a piece of rotting fruit. Are you hurt?"

Being on the receiving end of this act of personal expression is a new experience for me. "Just a little bruise to my ego," I reassure my escort. "I'm fine."

Kai releases me and folds his wings against his back. "Are you sure you want to continue?"

"I take full responsibility for my presence here, Kai."

"While I appreciate the sentiment, Queen Persephone, while you are here, you are under the protection of your guards. Captain Köhler will be extremely displeased of anything happens to you, as will my commander, as will my queen."

"Nothing's going to happen to me." Touching my crown, I draw in some of the aquamarine's cool, calming energy for myself. "Let's find Arkė."

Chapter 35

"WHERE EXACTLY ARE WE GOING?" I should have asked this earlier. Some newly acquired character trait has me taking on challenges and situations I would have shied from in the past, and this qualifies as one of them.

"The catacombs."

I flash on images of holes dug into dank dirt walls and filled with human bones. Shuddering, I curl my fingers into fists to prevent myself from clinging to Kai's armor-covered arm. "We have *catacombs*?"

"Yes, ma'am.

Kai continues to guide me along the inside of the wide walkway, closer to the wall than the unprotected edge. He's taking us deeper into Tartarus, and I want to stop, take in our surroundings. I tap Kai's arm - I know better than to touch a demon's wings - as the gradual slope ends at a misty foyer of sorts, one whose floor is flat, and whose walls and ceilings I can't make out for the constantly swirling mist. The angled slope narrows as it starts up again, and the wide gap opening to our left is giving me vertigo. I add protective railings to my list of structural updates.

Kai shifts slightly. "We'll get to the catacombs once we've circled Tartarus three times."

"And is there anything below the catacombs?" I ask, pressing my hand to my stomach and forcing myself to swallow. I should have thought to bring bottled water.

"Fire?" he offers. I hope he's joking. "Are you all right to continue?"

At my nod, Kai moves forward. We pass alcoves carved into the walls to our right. Some have bars, some have solid doors. Others do not. Some are empty; others have one or more inhabitants in human form, and in other, more beastly forms. I'm deeply curious to investigate further - and I'm acutely aware of the time constraint set by Bronte.

We circle the pit a third time, and I notice the temperature is dropping. "This is it," Kai says. "I haven't been this far down before, which is an oversight in our orientation and training I think my captain will want to rectify." Kai extends his arm, blocking me from continuing. "If you don't mind, Queen Persephone, I would prefer to check each room before you enter or pass."

"I agree with your caution. Proceed."

Kai unhooks the big black flashlight attached to his weapons belt and clicks it on. The beam pierces the gloom and highlights the moody mist hovering above our heads. He swings the beam into the first opening and continues to the next. Some of these rooms are empty, some are furnished with narrows beds and piles of bones. Some are accompanied by plaques; some have been walled off. Kai expresses the opinion that each room should be catalogued as quickly and as thoroughly as possible, the information then cross-checked with the prison's records.

I agree. "Excellent idea. These plaques are so dirty, I can't read what they say. I'd like to know whose bones these are and give them a proper burial."

Two-thirds of the way around the catacombs' walkway, Kai stops. His body language tells me he's found Arkė, or her last recorded residence. He raises his hand to prevent me from moving closer, then presses a finger to his lips.

Nodding, my heart rate speeds up in anticipation. I have no idea what Arkė looked like when she was in her prime. How tall she was, the color of her hair or skin, whether her wings rose from her back, or from some other place on her body. I don't even know whether she resembles human, or bird, or beast. It's all I can do to keep from shoving Kai aside and seeing for myself.

"I believe she is alive. Her ribcage is expanding and contracting." He beckons me to his side, hands me the flashlight, and whispers, "You should be the one to speak to her first."

"You'll come inside with me?" I ask, cradling the hefty light, which is heavy enough to double as a weapon should I need it. Hopefully, I won't. Joachim will blame Kai, then himself, if anything happens to me while I'm down here.

"Yes." He draws on a pair of thick leather gloves.

"What are those for?"

Kai mimes sweeping the flashlight across the low ceiling and the walls. I follow his suggestion to see clusters of shallow scratch marks. Tiny, grimy feathers litter the floor. Swallowing hard, I approach Arkė. A chain runs upward from the base of her stone slab resting place and attaches to her ankle. She's curled in on herself, her back to the room's opening. Her skin is coated with oily, grimy dirt. What clothes she might have had rotted away eons ago.

"She's all bones and skin." I keep my voice low. I'm not sure what to do next. "And how are we going to get the chain off her?"

"I carry a set of master keys with me. If none of them open

the lock, I'll run back up to the guard post and find something to break the chain."

Break the chain. The light's beam falters. Kai has no idea his promise to free Arkė connects me back to that cathartic night on the Pelion peninsula, and while Arkė's situation differs from mine, she deserves a fresh start and whatever dignity we can provide.

I glance at Kai. His armor won't work for what I need. I unbutton the clasp at my throat, slip out of my robe, and spread it alongside Arkė's backside. "You work on her restraints. I'll stand here and catch her if she rolls over."

Waiting for Kai, scents rise from Arkė's body. Nothing herbal or flowery. Just dirt, old blood, and death. Resignation. Profound resignation. Metal clanks against stone and the demon rises slowly from where he crouched at Arkė's feet. Pointing to the robe, he mimes draping it over the goddess' side.

I follow his lead, bending my knees in anticipation of his next move. Kai grasps Arkė's ankles and turns her legs toward me, creating a spiraling motion up her body and turning her frontside toward the waiting robe. I catch her in its folds and draw her against my chest. Kai wraps the rest of the robe around her chilled, bony limbs.

Arkė has claws, obsidian black and chipped, not fingernails. Her hair - oh, Goddess, her hair, or what's left of it - is matted and so full of filth I think I'm going to have to ask Owen for help shaving it off.

"Give her to me," Kai says.

"She's light as a feather," I whisper, shaking my head. I feel instantly protective of the messenger goddess. "Let me carry her for now. I'll let you know if she gets heavy. Oh," I add, handing Kai the flashlight, "see if there's anything in here that might belong to her or that could tell us more about her circumstances."

He circles the slab, bending to pick up what looks like a rotting bag. He also removes the chain still binding Arkė's ankle to the stone. "Let's get her out of here."

Chapter 36

THE DEMON GUARD leads the way. A few curious inhabitants peer out of their rooms or pause on their way up and down the spiral walkway to see who we are and what is wrapped in my winter weight robe. We don't stop, not even when a half human/half reptilian-looking being sporting scales on their torso and a snake's tail in lieu of legs attempts a menacing look. I glare back, and they retreat.

I'm sweating with effort by the time we reach the guard station. Kai again offers to carry Arkė. This time, I accept his help, and pass my bundle to him. Next thing I know, the muscular demon drops to one knee and his eyes shutter closed. Shock moves across his features, followed closely by a peaceful smile. I have no idea why he's acting this way.

"Kai? Are you all right?"

"I am giving thanks, Queen Persephone, to the Spirits that guide our lives, is all."

Reaching for his armored shoulder, I sense there's more to his actions than a simple giving thanks. A lot more. There's no time to ask him to explain the thrum I feel through the segmented leather pauldrons. Once he rises, I lead the way out of the Underworld and up the seemingly endless stairs to my hut. Kai's breathing never strains, he never asks to rest. We pass through the hut, leaving a trio of curious shades in our wake, and follow the path through the fields of flowering asphodel. I ring the bell at the estate's main gate, intending to have Kai pass Arkè over to Owen's care.

I rethink that plan as my aged butler lumbers down the distant stairs.

"I can continue to carry her," the demon murmurs.

"Thank you, Kai. Normally I would ask Owen to take over from here. He's a dear man, but really, he's in no condition to carry much more than a basket of vegetables. Will you come inside and help me get Arkè into a bath?"

"Of course."

Owen quickens his pace when he catches sight of us. "What does my lady require?" he asks, swinging the gate open wide enough to accommodate the demon's wings and the bundle in his arms. I keep my instructions simple. I'm still considering the best course of action.

"You could lead the way to my guest suite."

My butler hurries alongside me and the guard, into the mansion and through the foyer, veering right toward my rooms. One of the cooks who chose to stay on, Torsten, I think, hurries from the kitchen hallway, and I ask for bone broth.

"For your supper, my queen?"

"No. For my guest," I tell him, not stopping. "She will need something warm and nutritious when she wakes."

"As you wish." Torsten spins on his heel. Owen barrels ahead to open doors and turn on lights. Inside the guest suite, I toe off my sneakers, peel down my socks while still in motion, and lead Kai into the bathroom.

"Any sign of life?" I ask, perching on the shelf encircling the extra-large tub. I plug the drain and get the water going. When the tub is half-full, I shoo Owen out and ask him to close the main door to my side of the mansion. "Kai, stay with me."

"If you could place a layer of towels on the floor, I will put her down and we'll remove your cloak."

The bathroom wasn't designed with demons' wings in mind, and Kai knocks a few items off the freestanding shelves. Nothing breaks, or startles Arkė out of her coma-like state. Carefully, gingerly, I unwrap her. Not only is she caked in grime but she's also smelly; her knobby limbs are bent at every joint and held tight to her torso like a featherless baby bird nestled in its shell. Kai draws my robe out from under the goddess, and together, we take hold of the corners of the top towel, lift, and lower Arkė into the waiting bathwater.

"Here."

The guard hands me the terrycloth covered bath pillow he knocked off the shelf. Supporting the side of Arkė's head, I slide it under her neck and press on the suction cups in back to keep it in place. I study her face for any sign she's waking. Her features are as still as in death.

"I need something to wash her with." And more padding underneath my knees. The fronts of my leggings are soaked, and the floor tiles are cold. Maybe I shouldn't have dismissed Owen as quickly as I did. A fire in the fireplace would go a long way toward making the bathroom more comfortable. Kai hands me washcloths and unwraps a bar of soap. I mention the idea of a fire, and he backs out of the bathroom. I note his reluctance to leave as another thing to ask him about later.

Arkė's body bobs slightly in the water. I lather up one cloth, intending to wash off the dirt. No matter where I begin, the water's going to get dirty fast. I start at her upper back, gently rubbing the cloth in circles down her bony spine to her sacrum. I prepare a second cloth and wash from one shoulder, down over her ribs to her waist. The water already needs changing and I've only removed the topmost layer of dirt.

"Kai? Can you position the rinse hose, so fresh water will fill the tub as the old water drains out?" He understands what I need him to do. He even asks Owen for duct tape. A few minutes later, we've rigged a new system. I turn on the faucets, adjust the outflow to the right temperature, and return to my task.

The second time I work the cloth down Arkė's back, I realize the bumps I felt earlier aren't clumps of dirt, they're scars, jagged lines on either side of her spine between her shoulder blades.

"I can't tell if Zeus ripped off her wings, or used a dull blade," Kai whispers, a mix of horror and compassion in his voice. Though my anger at Zeus is turning to rage, I need to remain calm, centered, and focused on Arkė.

I finish her back. The sight of the scars is so disturbing, I move to her feet and spend more time there than necessary until I collect myself. When it's time to turn her over and wash her arms and her other side, I must ask Kai for help. My arms are tiring, and this task is taking an unexpected toll on my emotions. I'm not sure Arkė will survive a trip on Galena's back, and I'm not about to deliver a catatonic goddess into the hands of someone I don't know, whose intentions haven't been shared.

"I think I can turn her if you hold her head." Kai straddles that end of the tub, gently holding the goddess' head above the slow flow of water. I stand, somewhat hunched over, and begin to rotate Arkė from her hips. Her limbs haven't unclenched, and this seems the safest way to move her.

Between one moment and the next, a breath judders through her body, her arms jerk upward, and the tips of her clawed fingers dig into my scalp. Her other hand grips the crown I forgot I'm still wearing. The magic that keeps it on my head resists her touch. The band tightens.

"Arkė." It takes everything I've got to keep my voice calm through the points of pain. "Arkė. You are safe."

She takes in another breath and tightens her grip. Blood slips along my scalp and down my cheekbones, dripping onto Arkė's sunken chest. I try again with the soft approach. "Arkė. It's Persephone. You are in my home, and I will keep you safe. You can let go."

She loosens her grip. I settle her back in the tub, on her other side, and let go of the breath I didn't realize I was holding. Arkė's clawed hands are still too close to my head for comfort. I wipe the blood from my face with the back of my wrist, then reach to the side and plug the drain. Maybe if there's more warm water around her, she'll relax. Kai puts a fresh washcloth in my hands. I soak it, squeeze, and gently stroke Arkė's shoulder, and this side of her back, revealing more of the horrific scars. Slowly, as though every movement hurts, the goddess brings her arms in toward her chest and closes her eyes.

I rock back on my heels. I need a break, a breath. Kai places a mug of tea in my hand, tells me to drink. I sip. Feel for my crown. Lifting it off my head, I hand it to the demon and ask him to give it to Owen for safekeeping.

So much for aquamarine's calming abilities.

I finish the tea and thank Kai for anticipating what I needed. "I needed a break too," he murmurs. "There is much here for me to absorb."

"Me too," I admit.

I finish washing Arkė's body, including her fingers and claws. Kai holds the showerhead over the goddess' hair as I work in shampoo, then rinse and repeat. Water runs dirtier than ever, and I keep stopping to clear the drain of debris. With patience, her hair might be salvageable, but cutting Arkė's hair is not my decision to make. I do the best I can, and when the rinse water runs clear, I declare Project Goddess Wash complete.

"Where would you like me to put her?" Kai asks, once we've wrapped her in a bath sheet. He offers to carry Arkė, and I let him.

"I think this bedroom will be fine. I'll have the staff clean the bathroom, plus, the kitchen's close by. I'll stay here with her."

I draw back the covers on the bed. Kai lowers Arkė onto the sheets. She's wrapped in the biggest towel I can find, with another wrapping her hair. Her knees are still drawn into her chest, and her arms still look like the armature of wings plucked clean of feathers, but she's clean, safe, and smelling much better.

"Thank you, Kai. I couldn't have done this without you."

"I am at your service."

"Does Queen Violetta mind you dividing yourself between her court and mine?" I ask.

"As long as she remains my Queen with a capital Q, I think she'll accept that a man - or a demon - can serve two rulers. Is there anything else I can do for you?" he adds. "For her?"

"I hope to get her to drink some water and broth."

"Perhaps bringing in a healer would be a good idea? We have excellent ones in the Reformed Realm."

"If Arkė requires more than our healers can provide, I promise I'll ask."

With my indirect dismissal, he gives a quick bow and leaves. When Owen re-enters the room, followed by the newly promoted chef wheeling in a tray, I'm still staring at Arkė. My belly gurgles in reaction to the smell of the hot broth, and I realize I'm starving. The two set out a bowl of soup for me at the small table by the fireplace and point out the container of broth for Arkė. I notice one of them kindly added a cup with a lid and straws.

"Owen, I need to get a message to Hades. He's on Mount Olympus, at his apartment." The butler has been briefed on how to make the journey if there's an emergency. To my knowledge, this will be his first time traveling there on his own.

"I am certain I can deliver your missive to the King. Would you like me to retrieve your official stationery, or is this to be delivered verbally?"

"Paper, please."

He and the chef depart, and I'm alone with my guest. I drag my comfortable chair closer to the side of the bed and eat my soup while watching Arkë's face and hands. Her skin's sallow, there's still some dirt embedded in her cuticles and along her hairline - and I'm flooded with guilt. This sentient being has been kept prisoner within a place I rule over. She's been chained, likely starved, and subjected to other horrors I don't want to imagine. And I had no idea she was there.

What does that say about me? And how many more like her does Tartarus hold?

Chapter 37

IMAGINING there are others like Arkė prevents me from
finishing my soup. I bring the bowl to the rolling cart and butter a
soft roll. Kai left the bag he found inside Arkė's cell on the floor
next to the bedside table. I finish the roll, pick the sack up by its
drawstring, and immediately drop it. I'm not sure if the slimy
sensation coating my fingers comes from the rotting leather
drawstring, or if the bag is spelled.

Owen knocks, then lets himself in. I ask him for a pair of
gloves, rubber or latex, whatever's easiest to retrieve, and explain
why they're needed. He dips into the bathroom and comes out
waving a pair of hot pink cleaning gloves.

"Allow me," he says, gingerly taking the bag.

"Do you feel any magic?" I ask.

"I think your aversion to touching the bag has more to do
with the state it's in." He spreads a towel across the end of the
bed, recognizing I want to watch, *and* I don't want to leave Arkė
alone. The bag is round and as the butler eases it open, I see
divisions like those you'd find in a pouch for storing jewelry.

Except they don't separate to reveal their contents, they remain stuck.

Owen asks me to hand him the unused knife from the tray and uses it to pry open one of the compartments, and another, until all gape wide for our perusal. He excuses himself, returning this time with a pair of tweezers and one of the lightweight wooden boxes he uses to keep spare buttons sorted. He hands me the tweezers and carefully, I pick each item up and transfer it to the clean box. "I don't think we should throw away her bag," I offer, "but maybe it can be washed?"

"I've seen leather in worse condition, my queen, but not by much. Leave it with me and I shall see what I can do."

"Thank you, Owen."

"She's a small thing, isn't she? Do you know her story?"

I share what I know, which reminds me I'm still on Bronte's clock and hours have flown by since Kai and I first discovered Arkė. "Let me write that note to Hades."

I'm stumped at what to say. Do I share my concern about the messenger goddess' condition? Tell him I'm second-guessing Bronte's intentions? I decide to write a simple plea for Hades to hurry and join me and lend his help to the search for the missing goddess.

He knows a good six hours or so have passed since we split up. I hope he can read between the lines, and I caution Owen to just hand the note to Hades, and to not elaborate.

"You have my permission to play dumb," I add.

With Owen off to Mount Olympus and no one I trust to relieve me, I'm stuck in this room. I could leave - but should I? What if Arkė wakes up, freaks out, and shreds the bedding or worse, injures herself with her claws? What if she escapes or disappears? She's suffered for her time in Tartarus, and I have no idea what kind of magic or power she can access even in her diminished state.

The aquamarine crown sits on the tray where Owen left it. I glance at the bed, and the open door. I'd rather the crown was back in its display case, so I hurry out the door, down the hall, and into the living room, and set it back on its shelf. I don't linger. Back in the guest room, Arkė's eyes are still closed, until suddenly, shockingly, they're not. From one step to the next, her eyelids fly open. Her gaze wobbles and her fingers contract. She can't seem to focus and her eyelids close.

"Arkė?" I move closer, my bare feet sinking into the carpet's soft pile. "Are you awake?"

"Water."

I bring her the cup with the lid and the bendable, paper straw. "Drink."

Her mouth opens, barely, and when I place the straw against her bottom lip, I'm not sure she knows what to do. I quickly remove the lid and straw, steady her jaw with my free hand, and tilt the cup until a bit of water wets her mouth. She swallows, and I give her more, and we continue like that until she's kept down most of it.

"Would you like soup?" I ask. "Broth?"

She nods, barely. I feed her the nourishing fluid until she's drunk most of the serving.

"Who are you?"

"I'm Persephone. You are in my home in the Underworld."

"Why?"

I blow out a breath. How much do I tell her? "I found you in Tartarus and brought you here."

"Why?"

"Because I was looking for you."

"Why?"

"Bronte and your sister, Iris, asked that I bring you to them. To Mount Olympus. But I—"

"No." Arkė grabs my arm. The tips of her claw cut through the fabric of my shirt. "I will not go."

"Arkė." I hold her wrist, not squeezing, and try to ease my thumb between my arm and her hand. I've had enough holes punched in me for one day. "I already decided I wasn't going to bring you there until you were awake, and I could ask you some questions."

"Do you have my bag?"

"I have your bag, but it's—"

"Bring it to me."

I slide two more fingers against her palm. This time, I squeeze her wrist and pull slightly. "You first have to let me go."

The claws withdraw slowly. I reach for the wooden case, which I'd placed on the bedside table, lift the lid, and show it to her. "The contents are in here, see?"

"My bag?"

"My servant is cleaning it."

She scans the box, her lips moving as though she's making an accounting of its contents. One claw taps the lid once she closes it. "It is not me Bronte and Iris want."

"What do they want?"

"Why should I tell you, the queen who neglects her subjects?"

I feel for the chair I dragged over earlier and sit, leaning forward, elbows on my knees. "I am sorry I neglected you and so many others. I am making changes to rectify my ignorance."

"Changes?"

I gaze at my clasped hands, at my smooth, uncalloused skin and perfect, polished nails. "I only became aware of issues within Tartarus a few days ago, and before I could do anything, my presence was required in the aboveworld."

"Because it is spring?"

"Yes, because it is spring."

"Do you know my story?" she asks, after a lengthy silence. I nod, and she continues, "I will not go to Mount Olympus and if I see Zeus again, I will rip out his heart and eat it."

"Zeus is taking his Godsrest."

"*Hmph.*" Arkė rolls to her other side, taking the covers with her. All I can see of her is the towel wrapped around her hair, and I barely hear her when she asks, "And do you know what happened to my wings?"

"I know that they were given to Peleus and Thetis as a wedding gift, then Thetis bestowed them on her son."

"Find my wings and return them to me. Only then will I consider meeting with my sister and her greedy lover. And it must be here, not there."

Arkė doesn't seem to have anything more to say to me. I'm torn whether to leave her alone or wait by the bed and keep close watch until Owen returns with Hades. I decide to take the contents of Arkė's bag with me to guarantee the goddess will stay. I lift the box from the bedside table, knocking my shin against the chair as I turn to go.

"Leave the box. I have nowhere to go. No one to see. I will not try to escape. You have my word."

I set the box down, and when I ask if she'd like more to eat, my question is answered with a soft snore.

I leave all the doors open behind me as I exit the bedroom, then the suite. To keep busy, I sort through my clothes to see if I have anything that would fit Arkė and come up with tops and bottoms I'd want to wear if I was in rough shape. All of it is soft, stretchy, and warm, in shades of blues and grays to match her eyes— and this is busy work, meant to keep me from looking more closely at Arkė's reference to Bronte as "greedy", and at my own feelings of protectiveness. For the first time in a very, *very* long time, I want Hades' opinion on what I should do.

That's almost worth going to the trouble to scry with Aušrinė for a sanity check.

I'm carrying an armload of folded clothes down the stairs when I hear a commotion coming from the hall leading to the foyer. I had left the main door to my side of the estate open, and Hades is the first one through, filled with purpose-driven intent as he removes his suit jacket mid-stride and hands it off to Owen.

"Your butler explained the situation, but I want to hear it directly from you. And I insist on speaking with Arkė." Hades swerves past the bottom of the staircase, only to complete a spin on his heel until he faces me again. "That was rude of me, though I do want to hear Arkė's story. Persephone, perhaps I should hear yours first?"

"She's sleeping right now, in one of the guest rooms. Let's talk in here." I gesture to my living room, relieved I don't have add an argument with Hades to my day. "Owen, will you please bring us tea and anything else the King would like to eat? Hades?"

"Uh—" Hades seems at a loss. "Anything, really, Owen, whatever's convenient."

Owen knows which teas I like, and he'll bend over backward to see I'm pleased. My hus— Hades continues to survey the room. He's perched on the edge of one of the velvet loveseats. I had both items upholstered in a delicious shade of rose gold. Velvet and shaggy sheepskin throw pillows in shades of pale lavender and pink sandwich him from either side. He's not even trying to cover his discomfort or his shock.

"Have you never been inside this side of the house?"

"No, I can't say I have. It's… nice." He leans into the cushion behind him and stretches his arm along the back of the couch. His arm jerks when his fingers encounter one of the many cashmere and mohair throws I keep handy, because I'm often cold.

I *almost* ask if he'd be more comfortable if we had this conversation in the Club Room. Quashing the momentary pleasure his discomfort brings, I drag the shawl out from under his arm to throw it around my shoulders before settling onto the opposite love seat.

"Arkė refuses to go to Mount Olympus," I say, starting my story. "She called Bronte 'greedy' and said it's not her they want, it's the stones in the pouch I found inside her cell. Arkė also said she won't cooperate until her wings have been returned."

I recount what I read about the messenger goddess in the book in our library, and what she confirmed. Hades' face grows stormy as I speak, and he jerks forward, planting his elbows on his knees and twisting the ring he wears on his forefinger. He takes the ring off and slides it back on as he thinks. "There's a very good chance Achilles still has those wings," he finally offers.

I was hoping he would admit that before I added a visit to Achilles and Patroclus' home. "Then we have to talk to Achilles. Today. Though I'm not sure if it would be wise to bring along Arkė."

Hades continues to spin his ring around the tip of his finger. "He and Patroclus owe me for making the arrangements for their surrogate. I did everything but donate the" —he blushes slightly and waves away the image I can't unsee— "I had planned to call in that debt when I needed a sizeable favor." He stops fidgeting and centers his gaze on me, like he's half-hoping I'll back down or confess Patroclus and Achilles are also in my debt.

Which they are not.

"This situation qualifies as sizeable, Hades. Wait until you see Arkė. She's all skin and bones and claws and bitterness. They had her in the *catacombs*."

He goes still. "There isn't exactly a— a prisoner evaluation program in place."

"Maybe there should be."

"Is that a responsibility you would like to take on?"

"Yes, I think I would. But that's a discussion for the future."

Clever man, thinking to distract me from the topic on the table. "Right now, it's more important you, or we, speak with Achilles."

Neither of us has touched the tray of food Owen left on the table between us. I pour a cup of tea, sweetening it with honey from a charming little porcelain jar topped with bright yellow bees, and add a bit of milk. Hades tucks his tie between two shirt buttons and snaps open a linen napkin. He lays it over one knee, helps himself to a sandwich, and eats half before I see any sign of tension leaving his body. Wiping his mouth, he nods at whatever thought he's having.

"What?" I ask, finishing the tea. I want to know what he's thinking, and I want to ask if he saw Astrape. Only, the stress and excitement of the day hit me like Hekate's hounds. Stifling a yawn, I go to set the teacup on the tray, miss the table completely, and watch the cup fall in slow motion. I fall too, sideways. My head bounces off the seat cushion, my forehead smacks the edge of the table, and I land on the floor with a *whump*.

Chapter 38

"PERSEPHONE?"

I retch onto the carpet. The acrid smell of my stomach's contents assaults my nose. My knees curl toward my chest reflexively.

"*Persephone!*"

Someone lifts me off the floor. Their arm squeezes my midsection and I retch again. Vomit splatters dark slacks and polished shoes. Hades will be angry I'm ruining his things.

"HYGEIA."

"What about Panacea?"

From the depths of my pain-filled state, I recognize the names of the two sisters, both healers. I don't know who I can trust, aside from the knowledgeable goddess I last saw on Bone Fire Croft.

"Airmid. Get Airmid."

Pain like knives in my belly, along with something more nebulous, insidious, pulls me away from that moment of clarity and hurtles me into a place without light, without sound, without up or down.

"I'M GIVING her activated charcoal through a nasogastric tube. This will bind any poison remaining in her digestive tract."

I am aware there is a tube in my nose and that opening my eyes or doing anything but focusing on taking shallow breaths will instigate another bout of stomach cramps.

"How did she—?"

"There was poison in her tea."

Owen would never poison me.

"I would never poison my queen." Owen's voice trembles with distress. I want to comfort him. "I— I just made her tea as I always do. Oh. Oh my." His voice tapers off and I sense him leave the room.

"Owen, where are you going?"

"I used the tea I found in the main kitchen, not the tea Gilda keeps for Persephone in *her* kitchen. I shall fetch the tin."

Chef Keldt. *That fucker.*

"Hold her shoulders." I'm lying on my side. Strong hands clutch my body. "Gently, Hades. *Gently.*"

The grip softens and the tube is carefully removed. I hope to never again need a tube shoved in or out of my nose or down my throat. I'm too weak to register that point out loud.

"Here it is, here is the tin."

"Hmm, there could be something in this. I will take it with me for testing." Airmid, at least I think it's Airmid I recognize in the quiet, commanding voice, sets down the tin. "I smell jessamine flowers. Does Persephone sweeten her tea?"

"She does, sometimes with sugar, sometimes with honey, and when I saw the pot of honey in the kitchen, I though the sight of the wee painted bees would bring my queen a bit of pleasure in an otherwise challenging day."

"Hand me the pot. And butler, stop your blubbering. This is not your fault." Sweet, flower-scented honey wafts toward me. My stomach muscles immediately spasm, pulling me back into a ball. Only there's someone sitting in front of me. My knees hit their hip and my face presses into the side of their thigh.

"Jessamine." Airmid speaks with such authority, I believe her. Though I don't know if Jessamine is a person or a plant. I do know I'm surprisingly grateful for Hades' minty cologne.

Mint. Good for nausea. The irony.

Now Hades is rubbing my back. This is more intimacy than we've shared in forever.

"Can you stay with your wife?" Airmid asks. "I want to have a look at the kitchen."

"For as long as needed," Hades responds, his voice heavy with responsibility and purpose. And maybe a little worry. "Chef Keldt keeps a garden off the back of the kitchen."

"Of course, he does. Owen? Please come with me."

My entire body is cold and tense. Hades continues to rub between my shoulder blades. His touch is gentle, hesitant, and he keeps his hand well away from my waist and hip. I finally relax my facial muscles enough to attempt to speak. My throat hurts as I whisper, "Thank you."

"Can I get you anything?"

I snuffle snort against his leg. "Normally when I'm feeling nauseous, Gilda brings me ginger tea with lots of honey."

"I don't think any of us will ever again serve you honey, not unless it's been tasted by someone beforehand."

"Are you offering to taste my food?"

"If that's what's needed. I'm going to have to speak with Keldt." Hades shifts slightly, teases sticky bits of my hair away from my cheeks. "Do you know where he is? I haven't seen him since we arrived."

"Didn't Owen tell you?" I ask.

"Tell me what?"

"I fired your chef and four of his assistants. Before I left for the aboveworld. I had Kronos over to dinner - Kronos and Dionysus - and Chef acted abominably toward me in front of my guests. It was the last straw, so I fired him." I turn my head enough I can see Hades' face. Shadows, and a clump of his hair, hide his eyes. "I suspect he's been trying for a long time to poison me."

"Why didn't you say anything to me?"

I just stare at him. I don't have the physical strength for this conversation, and I'm saved from trying to explain by Airmid and Owen's exuberant reappearance.

"Well! That demon has plants I've never seen outside growing the Eisochsen Realm and though I am loathe to tell a king what to do with one of his subjects, Hades, you would do well to place this *chef* of yours under lock and key."

"Consider it done. I appreciate your coming here more than words can express."

"Airmid?" I lift one arm and it flops back down. The healer moves closer to the bed. "While we have your expertise under our roof, would you be willing to examine another?"

"Do you think someone else has been poisoned?"

"No. I—" I struggle to get my elbow underneath me so I can sit upright. Neither my stomach nor my muscles cooperate. "I'm sorry, I think I've got to stay horizontal until I feel better. I have a guest. Her name is Arkė, and she was imprisoned in Tartarus for — for a very long time. I brought her here a few hours ago and one of the new guards and I managed to get her washed off. She drank a few ounces water, and about the same amount of bone broth, and when I left her, she was sleeping."

"Arkė? The messenger goddess and shadow sister to Iris?"

"Yes."

"Oh, my." Airmid sits heavily onto the chair beside the bed and rests the side of her head against her knuckles. "And here I was thinking the excitement induced by your presence on the croft had settled down enough I could get back to *my* work."

"I'm sorry."

"Don't be sorry. I would be honored to examine Arkė. And as for poisons, they're a fascinating area of research and the demonic realms contain plants grown for very specific purposes. Used here in the Underworld, or above, the symptoms they induce would be difficult for the average herbalist to detect. With your permission, I would like to bring my advanced students here for a session of show and tell."

"We would be happy to host as many students as you like for however long you wish," Hades interjects. "Now, would you be able to examine Arkė?"

"Yes."

Chapter 39

I TUG on the back of Hades' dress shirt. "Let Airmid go in by herself. Arké might react poorly to seeing you in the room without being warned. Or asked."

His spine stiffens. I let go of his shirt and pat his back, keeping my hand to the neutral place between his shoulder blades. "If you think that's best," he murmurs.

Airmid makes her way to the guest room, murmuring soft words the closer she gets to the door. I can feel her magic from here, a soothing wash of pale green and tiny, fresh leaves.

"What are we going to do?"

"*You* are going to get better. *I* am going to find Keldt and kill him myself."

"We have Bronte's deadline to worry about."

"We could stay married, Seph. I could— I will try harder, starting with the kitchen staff."

"Staff who neither like nor respect me is only a drop in the bucket of our problems, Hades. The only way out that I can see is a clean break. Once we've done that, once Bronte has put Zeus' seal to the papers, then we can negotiate."

"But what is there to negotiate?"

"Everything. And there will be more, now that I know Tartarus has such problems." I close my eyes and roll away from Hades' warmth. Someone must have washed my face after I vomited, which was kind, but I need a toothbrush, a hot bath, and clean clothes. "Can you help me upstairs to my bathroom?"

Before I can move, Hades has one arm under my knees and the other behind my back and he's lifting me up and holding me against his chest. "Tell me where to go," he says, using care to adjust his hold. "And let me know if I'm hurting you."

"Up the main stairs. My bedroom and en suite are down the hall to the left."

He carries me all the way into the bathroom, shoves the padded bench closer to the wall, and sets me down carefully. The tub is on the other side of the room, and Hades is at the faucets, drawing water and fussing with the temperature before I can protest.

"I like bubbles," I say, just to break the silence between us. "And after it's full, I add bath oil."

Hades pulls a stack of thick towels from the closet and sets them by the tub. He turns off the water and stands, facing away. "Do you need help getting in?"

I can't believe he's asking to do something that requires me to be naked in front of him. "No. I think I'll be fine."

"If I hear a crash or a splash, I'm coming in."

"If you hear anything like that, you'd better come in."

"I'll wait in the hall." He closes the door. I exhale. This day has gone from strange to weird and back again.

ARKĖ IS SUFFERING the effects of extreme dehydration, physical malnourishment, and social isolation. I'm concerned for her wellbeing, and if I had any say in this matter, she would be under a healer's care until she's better, or at least until she is physically able to care for herself and has some sort of community around her. The deeper effects of the mental, emotional, and psychic wounding will take far longer to heal, and she is going to need support."

"Were you able to get her to talk to you?" I ask.

"I was, and everything she said to me is confidential. I told her that she could trust you to see to her best interests." Airmid sets her portmanteau on top of the table in my foyer. The usual vase of flowers is missing, a reminder I'm supposed to be in the aboveworld. "As for your treatment, Persephone, bland foods for the next few days. I will leave a list with your butler. He's riddled with guilt, and you trusting him to make food and serve tea should ameliorate some of that.

"Non-stressful physical activity. This might be the ideal time to take up a soothing hobby, like decoupage or pressing flowers." She snaps the closures and slides the substantial bag's handles over her forearm. "Hades, my assistant will forward the bill. I know my way to Hekate's portal from here. I will show myself out through the kitchen as I would like another look at those plants before my next visit."

Airmid is halfway out the door when she stops. "Demeter will not hear of this incident from my lips."

"Thank you." I wait for the door to close behind the goddess before speaking. Hades beats me to it.

"'Flower-pressing'?" He's trying to not laugh, and he's failing. "I suppose you do leave petals wherever you go when you're the Goddess of Spring."

"Yes, I do, and if I had a team of minions following me around, I could command them to pick up my petals and save them for the royal crafting hour." A giggle starts to burble up out of my belly. "I could become a social media influencer. Get everyone into pressing their petals."

"Now *that* sounds kinky."

Hades and I do not banter. We do not tease each other, at least not lovingly. And we never, ever, talk about sexual intimacy, even peripherally. And here we are, doing all of that, and the happiness inside me is sending out these tendrils of affection, and my tendrils and Hades' appear to be meeting in the air between us.

"It does, doesn't it?" Yes, I'm smiling at the ogre I'm married to, the one I'm trying desperately to divorce. And the ogre, who I threw up on and who carried me up a flight of stairs and made a bubble bath to my specifications, is smiling too.

"Are you feeling up to having visitors?"

Aaand there's Mr. Serious. "Depends on who it is."

"Given what you just went through, I think it would be better to bring Achilles here. I won't bring him anywhere near Arkė. In fact, I can ask your butler to supervise whatever kitchen staff we have left to fix a light dinner and serve it in the Club Room. What do you think of that idea?"

"Is that your way of telling me you're worried about me?"

"Uh, yes, I suppose it is."

"It's okay to just say it, Hades."

"I'll— do better."

"Good. And yes, your idea makes sense. I'm not going anywhere without one of those fancy palanquins Zeus likes to travel in."

"Then I shall make arrangements with Owen on my way out and check in with you when I return."

"Should you send a messenger to Bronte with an update?"

"You want me to tell her we found Arkė?"

"Not exactly. Just let her know we're working on fulfilling her request. You know. Something vague and full of big words."

"Ahh, good thinking. Are you okay here?"

"I'm fine. You go, be persuasive."

I watch Hades dodge my stuff on his way to the door. Something's happening to the structure of my life, and I think I like it.

____

Chapter 40

____

OWEN BRINGS me a steaming pot of the curative herbal concoction prescribed by Airmid. Between sips, I spend a good ten minutes reassuring him he's not to blame for me getting sick and that his position in House of Hades is secure.

"In fact," I add, "what happened *confirmed* Keldt has been trying to poison me, which I've suspected for months. I was afraid to say anything because I didn't think Hades or anyone else would believe me. Really, Owen, we should be thanking you. Though I could have done without the vomiting and dizziness and all that."

"I shall endeavor to forgive myself, my queen."

"Good. I'm going to go and dress myself. Keep your ears open for any loud thumps in case I—" A horrified expression blossoms across my butler's face. "*Owen. I promise* I will not fall."

I offer him a hug, which he accepts, and once he's gone, I pull the bedcovers over my head and curl onto my side. Whatever was in the tea Airmid prepared soothes my belly and my nerves. I lift a bit of the blanket to bring in fresh air and start the inhale-

inhale-exhale practice I read about to support the whole Persephone De-Stressed theme.

It helps. And when my busy brain gets antsy and prods me into doing, I carefully unroll from my cocoon, sit up, and plant my feet on the floor. It's time to dress, and I think this evening's guest list, and purpose, calls for business casual. Because part of being a queen entails business-y things, like negotiations, and long-term plans, and keeping tabs on the employees. I add the demons of the Eisochsen Realm to topics I want to speak about with Hades and shuffle to my closet. I can almost, almost, stand fully upright. The muscles in my torso protest, and I massage my belly as I survey my fall/winter closet. Instinct says I should emphasize my current condition, rather than hide it from our guests, and use it as a bargaining ploy.

A stretchy, ankle length, long-sleeved black dress is perfect, especially when I add a black, watered-silk corset over the dress and pair the ensemble with low-heeled black boots. And though my beryl and druzy quartz crown would be an elegant addition, I open the deepest drawer of my jewelry chest in search of that crown's prototype.

The gold is pitted and dull, the red stones mismatched, and the quartz piece in the center is smaller, rougher. The bracelet I left at Habonde's would pair well with this crown. Still, there's something about it that calls to me. It's a work in progress, as am I.

I brush out my hair, twisting it into a messy chignon and securing it at my nape. When I put the crown on, its magic does more than hug the gold to my head. Molten warmth spreads down my neck and through my arms, swirling within my torso and pelvis and down each leg.

My mirror doesn't register much of a difference from one moment to the next, until the sensation reaches my toes. I go from looking like someone who was poisoned, to a slightly too-pale warrior woman ready to take on all challengers. All I need is a weapons belt and a sword.

Which makes me laugh. Physical prowess at any sort of sport has never been a talent I could claim. Maybe it's time to rethink my relationship with exercise.

Downstairs, I check on Arkė, who's still sleeping. I leave her door propped open and turn on the wall sconces lining the hallway, and a couple lamps in the living room. I don't want her to feel I've abandoned her. Before I leave, I pause at the table by the main door and swipe my hand over the mirror.

Aušrinė, I seek thee

Aušrinė, I reach thee

Aušrinė, I call thee to answer my—

"Persephone! Thank goddess, we've been so worried about you."

Aušrinė pauses to catch her breath. I know once she gets going again it'll be five minutes before she stops. I seize the moment.

"I'm fine." I don't add I'm fine *now*. Unless— "Listen, there have been some unexpected developments."

"Did you and Hades make it to Mount Olympus?" she asks.

"Yes, we did, and we spoke with Bronte."

"Was Astrape there? Did you get to talk to her?"

"She's there, and we barely spoke. Her sister has her locked down."

"What did Bronte say? Assuming she didn't immediately say yes and blow flowers up your butt."

I snort laugh. "Rini. From what little I know, she's definitely not the flower-blowing type."

"So, no rainbows and unicorns either?"

"Um, rainbows, yes. She was there with Iris."

"*Iris?*" I feel Rini's shiver from here. "Anyone who's all love and light and never shows their dark side can't be trusted."

"You might be right. I didn't get much of an impression of her, but here's what's interesting. Bronte agreed to put her proxy seal on the divorce papers *if* we find Iris' sister and bring her to Mount Olympus."

"Let me guess, you found Arkė, and she said no fucking way."

"Yes, and yes. And how did you know Iris had a sister named Arkė?"

"I'm a geek for Greek mythology? Ever since Zeus showed up to the croft at last summer's gathering and started waving his gold-plated dick around, I've been doing my research. Tartarus is filled with immortals he sentenced, and if you ask me, which you haven't but you know that if I have an opinion on something, I am going to share it, all those prisoners' sentences should be looked at with fresh eyes."

I clench the table's edge and lean in toward the mirror's surface. "We're on the same page. Which is why I'm calling."

Chapter 41

HAPPY THAT I connected with Aûsrinė, and knowing she'll share my update with Ciri and Bé, I head to the Club Room to wait for Hades to return. Light from the fire Owen lit brushes the surfaces of the leather chairs, adding a welcoming elegance to the space. I draw the doors closed slightly, to help the room retain its warmth. Circling through, I adjust every table lamp before stepping out to search for my butler and set him on another task.

"I know how Hades feels about flowers, which is that he sees no use for them. However, since he and I are entertaining together for the first time in forever, I would like to blend our aesthetics. Could you cut flowers and greens enough for three vases and bring them to the Flower Room? Keep the blossoms white if possible and see if you can find any of those bushes with the twisty branches."

"My queen, nothing would delight me more than to aid and abet your influence upon *that* side of the House."

Fire and flowers. What else is needed? Cashmere and mohair. Back in my living room, I gather up an armful of throws, check in on Arkė, and hurry back to the Club Room. I dump everything on the low table near the fireplace, refold the throws, and drape them over the backs of a select few chairs. Touches of pale green and ivory set off the polished oxblood leather.

Who wouldn't want to make themselves comfortable in here?

"Persephone, what have you—"

"Hades, you've brought guests. Achilles, Patroclus, welcome."

Achilles, visibly agitated, pauses between the doors. "I'm in shock, Persephone. This is all a lot to process."

I wrap my arms around the former warrior's midsection and give him a gentle hug. Leaning back slightly, I draw his gaze to mine. "You've just become a father, which is a beautiful thing, and I'm sure you can't wait to hold your child. Please, come in, sit down, and let me pour you a drink."

Achilles softens enough I'm able lead him to the quartet of chairs where Kronos and I recently convened. "What are you drinking? Should we open champagne? Or one of those bottles Hades hoards for 'special occasions'?"

Hades passes me. "I'll get the drinks, Persephone. Why don't you fill our friends in on— on everything."

"Everything, including our divorce?"

Patroclus drops into the chair next to the one I chose for Achilles. "Your *what*? You two can't divorce. Not after everything Achy and I went through to finally get married and have a child. Divorce? Gods, there's not enough alcohol in this house to temper *that* news."

Achilles leans forward, squeezes his husband's knee, and glares at me. "Pat. Darling. I'm sure they have their reasons."

"We do," I assure them, "and we need your help getting Zeus' official stamp on the papers."

Patroclus and Achilles shake their heads side to side like they're two puppets controlled by the same set of strings. "Not happening."

"Zeus is in his Godsrest," I continue, barreling through their resistance. "Before he went, he transferred his power to Bronte, and she has agreed to use Zeus' ring to—"

Patroclus rolls his eyes. "And which forty-seven hoops must you jump through before that cold-hearted tramp follows through on her promise?"

"There's only one. We bring Arkė to Mount Olympus."

"Good luck with that," Achilles mutters. Hades hands the immortals two glasses of wine and brings me another mug of the tea prescribed by Airmid. It reeks of green herbs and healing, and though I know it works, I would much rather be sipping the wine. "First you have to find her," the former warrior adds.

"I did find her. And she will meet with Bronte, but not on Mount Olympus and not until her wings have been returned."

"But those wings are *mine*." Achilles, looking more distressed by the minute, scrubs at his forehead. "They were my good luck charm through war after war. Through pestilence, through—"

"Until they weren't, my darling, and you got yourself killed." Patroclus sips at his wine. "Do you even know where you put the wings once they came off?"

Achilles lifts his nose in the air and waves away his husband's question. "I want them for our child. Those wings protected me, and they shall protect them. Those wings—"

One of the Club Room's heavy pocket doors bangs against its stopper.

"Zeus ripped those wings from my body. Do you have any idea what it's like to have a part of yourself, a... a hand or foot or limb removed without aid of a skilled knife? Without magic or herbs to dull the pain?"

The two in the matching club chairs go still as marble statues. Hades is at the bar, midway through opening a second bottle of wine. The squeak of the cork turning in the bottle's neck stops. I bring all my attention to Arkė, to where her clawed hand leaves pale scratches on the door's wood frame. She's dressed herself in the baggy cashmere lounge pants and hoodie I left piled on the end of her bed. Her feet are bare, and her damp, uncombed hair gives her the air of madness.

I make my way toward the goddess, grabbing one of the shawls and opening it as I move. I want to wrap Arkė up and guide her from the room. Tuck her in a place safe. She resists my efforts to comfort her, though she mutely accepts the added layer.

"Join us." I link my elbow through hers. "Everyone, this is Arkė, messenger goddess newly returned to us from her time in Tartarus. Arkė, meet Hades, Patroclus, and Achilles."

"Which one of you has my wings?"

Patroclus hands his glass to Achilles. "Your wings are close by." He speaks slowly, calmly as he points to one of the Club Room's tall windows. "In our house in Elysium. With your pardon, I shall retrieve them."

"Now?"

"Yes."

Achilles sputters. "But Patro—"

"Stop, my darling. Stop. Arkė's appearance so soon after the birth of our child is a sign, a… a closing of a circle. A time of reckoning. The manner in which those wings were gotten placed a curse upon every feather and I will not have them in our home or on my conscience a moment longer." Patroclus stands, smooths his slacks, and nods to Arkė as he leaves our company. "Save me a plate" trails him down the hallway. I'm not sure what to do next. Offer Arkė a drink? Escort her back to the guest room?

She decides for me with a decisive, "I would sit by the fire and wait."

"Would you like something to drink?" Hades asks. "Tea? Water?"

"Mulled wine." Arkė's gaze is fixed on the flames. I guide her to the same chair Kronos claimed when he was here, and the birdlike goddess slowly sinks into the cushiony leather and draws her knees into her chest.

"I'll see what spices I can find in the kitchen," Hades says, grabbing a bottle of wine by the neck and heading for the door.

"I'll help." Achilles jolts to his feet, nervously giving Arkė and her oversized chair a wide berth. I understand his discomfort.

"Oh, Hades, I think we can assume whatever ingredients you need should be safe from, you know——"

"Contamination?"

"Yes. That. Just avoid anything Keldt labeled 'Persephone' and while you're at it, make enough for all of us."

The two disappear into the hall. I can't quite wrap my head around the image of Hades making mulled wine, much less preparing anything at all, in the vast kitchen. With him and Achilles gone and Arkė dozing, I draw out my scrying necklace and bring it closer to my lips.

Aûsrinė, I seek thee

Aûsrinė, I reach thee

Aûsrinė, I call thee to answer my summons

Rini doesn't answer. I try the summons again, refusing to take her silence as a bad sign. If she's not responding, it's because she's out of the mirror's range, which means House of Hades is about to have more guests.

Chapter 42

"DID you know the king is in the kitchen? And that he is *cooking*?"

A stunned Owen appears in the doorway, bearing a tray laden with small bites. He shakes his head, walks across the room to set the tray on the bar, then busies himself straightening chairs and tables until everything is placed at precise angles.

"I do know that, and I am as surprised as you. And could you open up the seating arrangement? I'm expecting more guests."

The bell at the front door chimes, underlining my intuition, and the anticipation that's been building inside my chest plummets. Owen swerves toward the hall before I can volunteer to go myself.

Deep male voices boom, and when I step into the hallway, a trio of figures swerves right, into the corridor leading to the kitchen. I have no idea who's here, other than possibly friends of Hades. The mystery is solved before I can duck back into the Club Room.

Dionysus emerges, walking alongside Hades and fussing at him about the proper ratio of wine to brandy to spices. Achilles is close behind, followed by Kronos, who has his arm around Owen's stooped shoulders and the two look like they're plotting… something. Dread's hold on me lifts, and I lean against the door frame and watch the handsome quintet approach.

Kronos is the first to notice me. He slaps Owen's back and hurries forward, opening his arms for a hug. Either he's been to a professional barber and seen a tailor or someone waved their magic wand in his direction. He looks and smells like a wealthy, self-made man and I welcome his fatherly embrace.

"You're looking gaunt, my dear girl. Elegant," he adds, holding my upper arms and leaning back as he admires my choice of attire. Letting me go, he gently adjusts my crown, "but gaunt. Who do I need to rough up on your behalf?"

"Keldt, if you can find him."

"That bastard's back?"

"He left a surprise for me in the kitchen, and I was poisoned. But I'm fine, I'm fine," I add, seeing the alarm on Kronos' face. "They summoned Airmid, and she took care of it. What brings you and Dio here tonight?"

"We heard the good news about the baby, and on our way to congratulating the lucky fathers, we encountered Patroclus. He should be here any moment."

I tug on his sleeve, and place myself between the five impressive males, and the child-sized goddess asleep by the fire.

"I need all of you to tone it down," I begin. They bring their heads in closer so I can keep my voice low. "Arkė is here. One of the new guards helped me search Tartarus, and we found her in the catacombs. She's in rough shape, so please, be mindful and give her space."

"Message received." Dionysus straightens and takes the pot of mulled wine from Hades. "I'll serve this," he whispers. "It's only fitting, you know."

The door chime rings again. "And I'll get that," Hades says, turning in his heel.

"I'll go with you." Achilles' face is a mask, but behind that mask I sense he's grappling with something deeply personal. I hope he's not trying to figure out a way to keep the wings.

Inside the Club Room, Dionysus ladles wine into glass punch cups. He's monitoring Kronos, who's lowering himself into the chair angled beside Arkė's. Dio hands him a cup and sets another on the slate shelf surrounding the suspended fireplace. When Arkė opens her eyes, she'll see the wine first, Kronos second. I'm hoping there's no bad blood between them.

The next wave of visitors is moving closer. I take up position at the doorway again, thinking to remind them to stay quiet. Only it's not Patroclus who's returned, it's my girlfriends, and it's me who has to refrain from piercing the air with a squeal. I press a finger to my lips and hurry toward Rini, who's in the lead. She's always in the lead, and as I'm hugging her, I see Bé and Ciri.

And Astrape. Rini lets me go, whispering, "It worked! You were so smart, Sephie."

I quickly fill them in on who's in the Club Room. And when I face Astrape, whose hair has fallen loose from its golden bindings, that same heat I felt before suffuses my chest.

"Hi."

Persephone the Eloquent is in the house.

"Thank you for sending Galena. And Ciri. Your idea was brilliant, and it worked, and they got there just in time. The council is in chaos, Bronte's fighting for her political life, and Iris just… fled."

I manage one of those awkward sideways hugs with Astrape. Ciri holds up the bracelet Lidia had given me and waves it in the air. "The spell in here got us past the Sky Cloud Gate, and whatever magic they used on the golden girdle was just about drained of power. One more day, and Astrape would have been able to loosen the bindings herself."

"Do any of you need to freshen up?" They all shake their heads. Ciri returns the cuff and I slip it onto my wrist. "Then come in. Dionysus is at the bar. He'll serve whatever you'd like. That's Arkė over there," I say, pointing to the bundle in the chair. "Kronos is next to her, and Achilles is in the corner with Hades."

"How are things with Hades? Do we need to put him in his place? Turn him into a toad?"

"You can do that?" I ask Bé. I know that when she taps into the primal source of her power, she can manipulate rocks and soil and trees. I didn't know she could also transform animals. Or at least amphibians.

"It was a figure of speech, Seph. I just want to make sure you're okay."

"I'm good." Astrape's rubbing my back, right between my shoulders like Hades did, and I like how it feels to be this close to her. It feels… natural. Comfortable. I lean into her and rise on my toes, so my words reach her ears only. "I'm glad my plan worked too. I hated seeing you trapped like that."

"Whatever power Zeus allegedly transferred to Bronte wasn't even close to the power he normally wields," she says, bending closer. "Either he kept most of it for himself, or he was truly on the edge of losing it all."

"Let's not worry about Zeus right now." I slide out of our embrace and take her hand, drawing her into the room. "Get yourself something to eat and drink. I want to stay by Arkė."

I'm concerned about the messenger goddess waking to find all these unknown faces peering at her. I nudge aside the chair I'd been sitting in, and slide an ottoman closer. Keeping my back to the fire, I place my hand over hers. She's drawn the blanket around herself; her clawed fingers still clutch her knees.

Kronos sets his empty cup beside the half-full one Dionysus

poured out for the goddess and draws his chair closer. "Arkė?" Her eyelids flutter in response, then open slightly. "Arkė, it's me, Kronos." He clears his throat and I notice his eyes glisten. "I am here with you."

"Kronos?"

The Titan slides off the chair and onto his knees. "I thought I had lost you forever."

Arkė lifts her head slightly and tries to focus on Kronos' face.

"Kronos? What's going on?" I ask.

"I owe this beautiful creature my life. And somewhere, somehow, I forgot that. I forgot her. And you found her."

This was a story I was going to have to hear later. As Kronos and Arkė gaze at each other, the door chime goes off for the third time tonight. Or is it the fourth? "Let me get it," I say. "It's got to be Patroclus."

I haven't had any of the wine. I fortify myself with a sip, then head for the foyer. Whoever is here has gone from knocking to pounding on the door, sending spikes of worry needling under my skin. What if Patroclus couldn't find the wings? I press down on the lever handle. The door opens inward, and I quickly back up. Patroclus *is* here, and though he's carrying a box, it's too small to hold a set of wings. Behind him stands a worried-looking Kai.

"Queen Persephone, we have a situation. I'm sorry to show up like this, but we didn't know how to contact you directly."

"Come in, both of you. Patroclus, please wait for me. Kai, tell me what's going on."

Stress lines map the handsome demon's face. "Someone calling themselves Iris showed up in Tartarus and demanded to see Arkė. I assumed this Iris was the sister Arkė spoke of, and I remembered her saying that she didn't want to see her. I made an excuse, told the two other guards down there what I could of the situation, and figured out how to get to you." He took a deep breath.

"Arkė's awake. Come with us." I lock the front door and hurry ahead of the two. "Patroclus, I assume you have the wings?"

"I do."

"Then let's get them to Arkė and get her out of here."

Chapter 43

WALKING into the Club Room and seeing everyone sitting or standing, drinks and small plates in hand, one would think there was a family reunion happening, or that a Board meeting had just broken up. Achilles spots us as soon as we walk in and moves toward his husband.

"Thank you, my darling," he says. "I'll take it from here."

For a moment, they each cling to one end of the oblong box. Patroclus reaches for Achilles, strokes his wrist with a light touch. "Are you certain you don't want me to give them to her?"

Achilles closes his eyes and shakes his head. "The duty is mine." The former warrior seats himself on the ottoman beside Arkė's chair. Kronos, who'd been leaning in, retakes the club chair he first claimed and rests a hand on the arm of Arkė's.

"Goddess," Achilles begins. The others in the room quiet their conversations and gravitate toward the fireplace. "The return of your wings is long overdue." He sets the wooden box on his knees and undoes the delicate latch. The opening faces Arkė, and as Achilles lifts the lid, she cranes forward, eyes alight with hope and a longing so strong my chest muscles contract. She reaches forward, lifts one wing out, and the other, and cradles them to her heart. Her gaze never leaves Achilles' face even as she strokes the feathers.

The wings aren't any larger than raven wings. Any glossiness they might have had faded long ago, and feathers are missing from each.

"I am sorry they are not in better shape," Achilles says, his voice deep with apology. "If I had known this day was upon us, I would have had them repaired."

"Where on your body did you wear my wings?" Arkė asks.

"On my helm, most often, hence the missing feathers. Arrows, you know."

A secretive smile lifts the corners of the goddess' mouth. "Had you worn them on your back, as I did, you would have been better protected."

"And why is that?"

Arkė scans the room and settles on Kronos. "Did you never wonder where I got my speed?" she asks him. "How I was able to dodge any arrow?"

"I did," he responds. "And I chalked it up to luck."

"These wings allowed me to side-step through time and I would have remained free had not Iris spoken to Zeus of their gift." Arkė's face hardens. Her fingers tighten, highlighting the joints. "Zeus sought to make an example of me when he removed the wings from my body."

"Arkė?" I butt in. "I know this is all very sudden, but a decision must be made. My guard here, Kai, tells me Iris is in Tartarus and she is looking for you. Do you want to stay and see—"

She freezes, and her face pales to near white. "Get me out of here. Please."

"I can take her," Kai says, elbowing his way between Hades and Patroclus.

"Take her where?" *Quick, quick,* I'm rifling through sites I know and the immortals I'm connected with, searching for some place or someone who could effectively hide and protect the messenger goddess.

"To the Reformed Realm. We have healers who work literal miracles with our wings. They might be able to help Arkė, or at least—" Kai shrugs, never taking his eyes off the goddess. She studies him, her eyes bright, attentive, as though she sees something in the demon no one else can.

"I shall go with Kai."

And I'll owe Queen Violetta another favor. "But how are you going to get there?" I ask the winged guard. "Arkė's too weak to walk."

"The primary portal to my realm sits in the middle of Boston. I was there two nights ago, on my way here. Get us out of the Underworld, and I can take it from there."

A plan snaps into place. "Kai, you carry Arkė. Hades, do what you need to do to make this house safe. Astrape, come with me."

"We're coming, too," Bé chimes in. "We can help Kai and Arkė get to the croft. Astrape can escort them to Boston."

"Kai." Hades affects his King of the Underworld tone, and it works. He has the attention of everyone in the room. "No one can know you have Arkė. No one. Zeus has spies everywhere, including possibly the Reformed Realm."

"I know what to do," I interject. Arkė's not going to like my idea, but if it helps her escape undetected, it will be worth the potential discomfort. I lead the way to my side of the house. Arkė clutches the box with her wings; at her request, Kai locates the other wooden box containing the objects pulled from her ruined leather bag. I dart up the stairs, to my closet, followed closely by Rini, and pull out the largest rolling suitcase I can find.

"What's that for?" she asks. "Are you giving Arkė all your clothes?"

"We're putting Arkė in here. That way, Kai will appear to be just another demon on vacation. He can glamour his wings when they're among humans, and as soon as he gets to the portal in Boston, he can let Arkė out and lose the suitcase."

"That's a crazy idea."

"But you have to admit it's brilliant too."

"That it is." Rini drops to her knees beside me. "So, what else are we putting in here?"

"I keep brand new socks and underwear in that drawer. Grab some of each. I'd give her sneakers too, but her feet are so small, they'd drop off."

Within minutes, Rini and I accumulate a stack of basic clothing for Arkė. I add another small, soft blanket, one of those U-shaped travel pillows, and a sleep mask.

"What about toiletries?"

"Thank you for reminding me." In my bathroom are two drawers filled with those pretty zippered bags cosmetics companies hand out. They're filled with samples and necessities, and I find the roomiest one, dump everything out, and add what I think Arkė will need: toothbrush, toothpaste, nail trimmers and files, nail polishes in clear and red just because, a facial cleanser and moisturizer, a bottle of rosehip oil. A sturdy wooden comb.

"Shoot, I wish I'd brought the swag bags I made for us," Rini says.

"Oh, I have *oodles* of your stuff." I point to a different drawer. "In there. You've seen her skin. Choose what you think's best." I chuckle. "I can't believe that in the middle of trying to smuggle a goddess out of the Underworld, we're concerned with her skin care regimen."

Footsteps approach from my bedroom. "Persephone?"

It's Astrape. "In here."

She stops, framed in the doorway between my bedroom and bathroom, worry tugging at her gorgeously thick eyebrows. "We just got word that Iris is on her way. We've got to hurry."

"Shit, shit, shit. Okay, take that suitcase to Kai and help him get Arkė inside. We're coming right down, and we can pack clothes and stuff around her to keep her comfortable."

"You're putting a *goddess* in a *suitcase*?" Astrape's hesitation makes me question my decisions for the second time today. Nodding, I forge ahead.

"Yes. She's small and it'll work. Trust me."

She extends the suitcase's handle with a *snap*. "I trust you."

"Take the back stairs into the main kitchen and wait for us." I don't have time to explain why, I just point. Rini grabs the cosmetics bags and the underwear, and I lead the way. "Hustle, hustle."

The rear stairwell takes us to the ground floor hall with the two guest suites. We careen into the room I used for Arkė, unzip the suitcase and lay it flat, and line the bottom with the travel blanket. "Arkė, in here."

She doesn't hesitate. "Kai, lift me."

The demon carries her as though she's the most fragile, delicate package in all the realms. Rini and I drop to our knees and stuff clothing and the little bags around her. She holds the box containing her wings close to her chest. I try to tuck the edges of the blanket between the wooden corners and her body.

"What about my other box, the one with the objects from my bag?"

I hand Rini that box. She hesitates. "I'm not sure this will fit."

"Then take everything out."

Rini lifts the lid and pauses. "Arkė, may I ask what these are?"

"Coins for summoning, among other things."

"For summoning what?"

"That is a story for another day."

Rini nods, and without hesitation, distributes the coin-shaped objects among the three cosmetic bags, with Arkė watching intently. Once Rini sits back on her heels, Arkė looks to me, then to Kai.

"I am ready."

"Goddess speed," I say, once the demon zips the suitcase closed and gingerly rights it.

"Goddess speed," he echoes. "Now, how do we get out of here?"

———————

Chapter 44

———————

WE HUSTLE ASTRAPE, Kai, and the suitcase out the back door and onto the fieldstone patio. Sounds from a ruckus at the front of the estate filter through the night air. I grab Kai and Astrape by their wrists.

"You two are going to have to run. Head to the stone wall and follow it to the gate. Past the gate, it's a short walk through the meadow to the road to Elysium. The portal lies in the park, inside the gazebo. Patroclus confirmed tonight that it's still there."

Astrape just looks at me. I try to interpret what's going on in her nightdark eyes, up until the moment she shakes my hand loose, wraps an arm around my waist and cups the back of my head, and kisses me. On the mouth. In front of Kai and Rini. Her lush, warm lips taste faintly of mulled wine, and I decide this is the best way to drink. I'm too startled to do much more than wrap my arms around her neck and find a slightly better angle for our lips. Kai's quiet cough breaks the moment, and I tell Astrape I'll wait for her back at the croft. Grinning - that much I *can* see in the dark - the Goddess of Lightning sets me upright, then squats by the suitcase and locates the lower handle. She and Kai hoist Arkė between them, melting into the shadows without a word or a backward glance.

My heart is racing, and not just because Astrape kissed me. Again. "We did good," Rini says, keeping any comments about that very public kiss to herself. "What's next, boss?"

"We see who's at the door." Re-entering the kitchen side-by-side, I whisper, "I bet it's Iris."

Rini leans into my side. "And I bet she's got her sob story all worked out."

"We should hear what she has to say. The longer we can keep her here, talking, the more time that gives Kai and Astrape."

We detour to my side of House of Hades so I can close and lock the door to the room Arkė used. She was naked when we found her, so nothing of hers is in the house except the grimy leather sack that held her precious objects. I hope Owen had the good sense to leave it in the room he uses for repairs. I lock the door to the guest suites just in case we need another barrier.

I pause at my front door. "Do I look okay?"

"You're a queen, Persephone. It's your job to look more than 'okay'." Rini straightens my corset and adjusts my dress at the waist and shoulders. She finger-combs the hairs that escaped, and steps back. "Pull on your power and send it outward, let it coat your skin."

"Like one of those body shimmer lotions you make?" I tease.

"Exactly!" I close my eyes and breathe in, picturing the power of the Underworld rising from my core. Tingles stream along my arms and legs, my neck and face, even my ears. When I open my eyes, Rini nods her approval as she continues scanning me from crowned head to booted toe. "That's it. A moment ago, you *looked* like a queen. When you consciously draw on your power, you *radiate* queenliness and more than ever before in all the years I've known you, you're *acting* like a queen. Iris doesn't stand a chance."

Shoulders back and head high, I sweep open the main door to my side of the house. Rini follows, closing it behind her and stays two steps behind me through the wide, echoing hall to the mansion's grand foyer. Brilliant gold light leaks in through the glass panels to either side of the double front doors and the transom above. I reach for the handle, and Rini playfully smacks my hand away.

"Queens don't open their own doors. Rearrange that face of yours and look— I dunno, mean, or annoyed, or something."

I cover my mouth and nose to stifle my snort. Demeter does this thing where she lengthens the back of her neck as she's getting ready to deliver one of her speeches. I try the same action, sending my spine upward, rooting my feet downward, pulling on my connections to the Great Beneath and the Great Beyond. Hand on my belly, I connect with the Great Within, something the recent days have revealed I've been neglecting.

"I'm ready," I whisper. And I am.

"And… you're on." Rini turns the handle, sweeps the door open, and steps into the shadows. I like the look of the door opening all on its own. Adds a bit of drama. As do I, having repositioned myself at the center of the House crest embedded in the foyer's floor.

"Where is my sister?"

Iris has fashioned her own theatrical entrance. I resist the urge to blink, even as she ups the wattage of her dazzling light display.

"Welcome to House of Hades, Iris. Come in."

The Goddess of Rainbows huffs, and she puffs, and as she steps over the threshold and enters *my* house, her demeanor shifts from defiance to emotional exhaustion. I wonder who she's been studying with. Or maybe this is one hundred percent her. She throws herself at me, clutches my upper arms, starts sobbing. I can't hug her - I *won't* hug her her - though I can keep a bit of needed distance between us by placing my hands at her waist. These are dry sobs she's conjuring, emotionless, she's just producing sounds and pushing them out her throat. Nothing in her body suggests she's even remotely worried about her sister.

I disentangle myself from her cloying embrace. Her eyes remain dry, there's no snot running down her face, and her cheeks are fiery with something closer to rage than sorrow. All that gold light she produced outside is gone, except for a few shiny motes blinking out one by one.

"Would you like to freshen up?" Rini asks. She's added one of Owen's aprons to her ensemble and she almost looks like she works here. *Almost.* Iris tosses her a glance and decides my bestie's not worth sucking up to.

"Oh, it was awful, Persephone, you have no idea. Every Olympian on the Council is against Bronte, and it was all I could do to get out of there alive."

"I'm not sure why you came here. Hades and I have not been able to locate your sister."

She stiffens. "I know that now, thanks to the demon who escorted me through Tartarus. Did you know my sister was kept in the *catacombs*?"

Out the corner of my eye, Rini closes in like she's getting ready to herd us elsewhere. "Queen Persephone? May I remind you, your guests are waiting, and dinner is about to be served."

"Thank you." I nod in her direction, without taking my gaze off Iris. "I am sorry to hear your sister was housed in the catacombs. We will resume our search for her after we have eaten. In the meantime, I cannot offer you sanctuary, not in this time of discord. Word did reach us about what's happening on Mount Olympus, and it is incumbent upon me to remain neutral."

Wow, I'm surprised at how easy it is to lie.

"Then what am I to *do*?"

I tilt my head, pretending to seriously consider her question. "I suggest you return to your home, wherever that is. Those entering the Underworld without an invitation are allowed a one-hour grace period before they are turned over to our guards. Judging by the way your power faded when you entered my house, your hour is nearly up."

Iris gasps, and if a single look could diminish one's life force, I would be a withered hag. "I'm curious," I continue. "How did you enter the Underworld in the first place?"

"With this." Iris extends her arm and slowly opens her fingers. Nestled in her palm is a stone much like the ones in Arkė's rotted bag.

Chapter 45

MY FINGERS CURL into tight fists. I cannot react to what I'm seeing.

"A *rock* let you in?"

"This is no rock. This is a Coin of the Realm, granting the bearer access to any realm, at any time."

"And how many times can you use it?"

"As many times as I need."

"Then I suggest you use it now and leave the Underworld while you can."

Rini and I watch Iris depart down the gravel pathway. No golden glow accompanies her, until a single flash of light bursts as she nears the main gate.

"That was interesting."

"That was *very* interesting."

"What else do you think Arkè's coins can——"

"Persephone, is everything alright?" Hades appears behind us, then ducks into the closet and comes out with a trench coat.

"Iris has been handled, for the moment."

"Any problems? Do you think she'll be back?"

I pause to consider what to share with Hades. "Iris possesses a stone - she called it a 'Coin of the Realm' - that allows her to portal anywhere, including to other realms." Before Hades can ask why I didn't take the stone from Iris, I add, "Arkė is, and will be, very well protected. I felt that trying to keep Iris here and get the stone from her might signal I'd seen others like it."

"Good thinking. We will deal with Iris and Bronte later." He shoves his arms into his coat, shrugs his shoulders, tugs on the ends of the sleeves - all those little movements he always makes as he settles his clothing onto his frame.

"Are you going somewhere?"

His face pales slightly, a shade that almost matches the beige of his khaki overcoat. "Achilles and Patroclus have asked to see their child. I offered to escort them to the croft for a short visit, rather than bring the child here. I'm not sure how long an infant can be away from their mother."

I reinforce all the queenly energy I accessed when readying myself to face Iris. "If Minthe would prefer to accompany her child, please, let her return to the Underworld. I'm sure Achilles and Patroclus have a guest room." I'm willing to bend a little, not a lot. Allowing Minthe to come home is one thing; inviting her to stay under our roof would be something Persephone the Compliant might have felt pressured to offer in the past. Tonight, I am not that version of myself.

Hades swallows hard. "Are you sure?"

"Yes, I'm sure."

I close the massive door behind the king as soon as he leaves. It will take him at least thirty minutes to portal to and from Bone Fire Croft. Maybe more, if Minthe's packing for herself and the child. "I'm ravenous," I admit. Ravenous and gloriously untriggered by speaking with Hades about the nymph. I loop my arm through Rini's. "Wanna go eat?"

"Goddess and Spirit, I thought you'd never ask."

The closer we get to the Club Room, the more my mouth waters. Grilled meat. Yeasty bread. Roasted garlic. Strolling through the wide open doors - because running would be unqueenly - we're welcomed by a buffet table set with a repeat of the House's last dinner party, along with other mouthwatering dishes. Owen, consummate anticipator of others' needs, has deployed what's left of the kitchen crew and created a feast.

Vases of white flowers and elegant greenery grace one end of the bar and the two tables in front of the room's tall windows. Coals glow within the fireplace. Bé, Patroclus, and Dionysus discuss the challenges of gardening in the Underworld. Ciri explains to Achilles how she would go about crafting protective amulets for babies. And Kronos, Lord of the Table, sharpens a carving knife while devising future menus with Owen.

"This is nice," Rini whispers, nudging my side.

Nudging her back, I confess, "I'm not sure what's happening, but I think I like it."

"If what you said to Iris is true, the crew and I have way overstayed our welcome."

"I didn't exactly lie. There was a brief time when the Underworld was designated a vacation 'hot spot' and staying here was a rite of passage." I shake my head at the absurdity. "We had to institute drastic measures to keep out the overly curious. You, Bé, and Ciri are here at my invitation. Which means you can stay as long as I'm also in the Underworld. If I leave without you, you'll start to notice a sensation of coldness seeping into your chest. And what I said to Iris, about her edges disappearing, that was the truth."

"So why haven't you invited us here before?"

I'm stunned at her question, and it takes me a moment to find the answer. "I think I shut down whenever I make the transition from Goddess of Spring to Queen of the Underworld. But something is changing."

Rini barks out a laugh, causing a momentary cessation in the conversations. "That's the understatement of the week. Looks like all the food is on the table. Let's eat. You'll need more than just emotional fuel to deal with Minthe."

"*If* she decides to come back with Hades."

Rini throws her head back and laughs. "Oh, believe me, she'll come."

RINI'S PREDICTION IS CORRECT. Minthe arrives with Hades as Owen, Torsten, and Jutta are setting out dessert options, and the nymph is carrying a blanket-wrapped bundle in her arms. She walks into the Club Room, ignoring everyone she passes, and stops in front of me.

"Thank you, Persephone. You didn't have to do this, and I am grateful for your generosity."

Though I'm speechless - plus, there's a bite of custardy dessert melting in my mouth - I keep my mouth closed and nod at her, then glance toward the club chairs where the child's fathers wait. The two stand in unison. Dinner napkins slide to the floor. Patroclus beams and holds out both arms. Achilles bursts into tears.

The parents crowd together, cooing and crying. Kronos booms out his congratulations, and Hades jokes that the Titan is to maintain his distance from the baby. Kronos glares good-naturedly.

"I think my work here is done." I'm sitting with my best friends. My belly is full, my heart is full, and I'm deeply satisfied with the day's accomplishments. "Arkė's safe, at least for now, and the mystery of Hades' absences has been solved."

"What's next?"

I slip out of my boots, lean back into the comfortable couch, and tuck my feet under me. "Let's go back to the croft. Astrape said she'd meet us there, and I want to hear how it went with Arkė and Kai."

"And that's *all* you want to hear about?" Rini teases. "I witnessed that kiss she gave you. That was *way* more than a peck on the cheek, Sephie."

"Astrape and I have things to talk about," I agreed.

"You and *Demeter* have things to talk about."

"You're right." I look to my left, and to my right, and grab the nearest hands. "Any of you want to act as my proxy in the aboveworld for a bit?"

"Your *proxy*? Are you *quitting*?"

I gesture to the room. "I never, ever thought I would say this, but the Underworld is starting to feel like home."

"And Hades?"

I chuff out a breath. "And Hades is starting to feel like a friend."

Chapter 46

GETTING BACK to the croft takes some negotiating, mostly between the four of us, and Kronos and Dionysus. Seems my friends have impressed the gods and promises are made to gather soon for more conversations and culinary adventures.

Owen reassures me he will take care of cleaning and restoring Arkė's leather bag, and that he will keep it safe until we know the goddess' whereabouts. Hades takes me aside while Bé and Dionysus discuss grape-growing, hands over a folded paper, and pulls a hefty gold ring from his pocket.

"Is that what I think it is?" I ask, staring at his palm. I don't even bother trying to conjure a neutral face.

"Zeus' ring. Astrape slipped it to me when I answered the door. We can stamp the divorce paper ourselves, right here, right now, Persephone. If that's still what you want."

My hand shakes as I reach out take the ring, with its raised aegis, a radiant sun, the symbol of Zeus' place in the hierarchy of Olympians. "A divorce is what I want, Hades. A clean cut."

"And is there more you want?"

Nodding, I unfold the papers. The two lines at the bottom, with our names calligraphed beneath, await our signatures. I don't carry matches and sealing wax with me, so I invite him to my side of the estate and lead him into my office.

"Sit. Please." I indicate the chair across from my side of the desk. Opening the drawer with my stationery supplies, I remove a shallow brass dish, and the other items we'll need. I hand a fountain pen to Hades, along with a piece of scrap paper. "See if that works."

He uncaps the pen, taps the nib on the paper, leaving drops of ink, and practices his signature. The letters of his bright pink scrawl bleed slightly, and Hades chuckles. "Pink?" he asks, capping the pen.

"I think it's a very optimistic color," I tease. "Why, do you prefer black?" Waving away my question, I answer quickly, "Of course you do."

"No, for this occasion, I'm fine with pink. Are you ready?" At my nod, Hades places the paper between us and signs his name on his designated line. He turns the page one hundred and eighty degrees until it faces me, and hands over the pen. My hand is steady as I sign, *Persephone.*

In the space between our signatures, Hades drops molten wax until a sizeable circle lies ready. I wait for it to cool slightly, then press Zeus' ring into the wax. The aegis sits between Hades and Persephone, marking the moment I have wanted, and waited for.

"That was less painful than I thought it was going to be," Hades admits. "What's next?"

Shrugging, I tidy my desktop and refold the divorce decree. "I imagine this needs to get filed… somewhere?"

"I can do that."

"And we'll need to make an announcement."

"Shall we wait until you're ready to go public with your new role and your plans for Tartarus?"

Nodding, I see the wisdom in taking our time. "I should speak with my mother beforehand. She and I are about to experience a similar break up," I tell him, "and I'm under no illusion she's going to let me go easily."

"You're giving up your floral crown?"

"No, just renegotiating my position as Demeter's seasonal sidekick, for starters."

Hades leans back in the chair and props his chin on his fingers. He looks relaxed. At ease. "I look forward to hearing all about it, and to hearing your plans for the Underworld."

"And I look forward to sharing them." Standing, I lean across the desk and offer Hades my hand, along with the positively modern parting, "Let's stay in touch."

I SEND RINI, Bé, and Ciri to the croft ahead of me, explaining I still have to make my nightly visit to the Hall of Judgment. As Fates would have it, the Court is busier than usual and I'm there until after four. My trunks are still at Habonde's, and there is nothing I need to pack, so once the shades peel off my robe and disappear into the walls of my hut, I portal directly to Hekate's yew.

Stepping out from the tree's smooth-sided opening, I hear a soft whinny. Predawn light teases what little sky I can see between the branches, and I follow Galena's greeting to the other side of the tree.

Astrape sits propped against the trunk, a blanket spread out underneath her. Another wraps her shoulders. She lifts her chin and smiles up at me. "You made it."

Crouching, I settle my back against the yew. The lightning goddess fluffs out the big plaid blanket and invites me closer to her side. "It's big enough for two," she adds.

I lean into her warmth. Galena snuffles my neck, and I know

I disappoint her when I confess I brought no treats. "But I won't forget again," I assure her, turning to whisper to Astrape, "What does she like?"

"Apples, carrots, and peppermints." Astrape pats the ground to her other side, sets a rucksack between us, and removes a thermos. "Hot chocolate?"

"Please." The fragrant smell wafts upward, and my stomach gurgles in response. "Got any of Habonde's muffins in there?"

"Sure do."

Cradling tin mugs, with muffins on napkins in our laps, Astrape and I sip and eat and watch the sun finish its slow, glorious rise. Prussian blue paints the sky, along with lines of peach and pink, until clouds close in, and a soft rain begins to fall. I'm in no rush to move.

"What's next?" Astrape asks, pouring the last drops of chocolate into my cup and recapping the thermos.

"More dancing," I say, letting a smile play along my lips as I recall the hours we spent together in southern California.

"I can help with that. Anything else?"

Draining my cup, I shift slightly to face Astrape, and lick the corners of my mouth. "More kissing."

"I can help with that too."

She dips her finger into her cup and paints my bottom lip with melted chocolate. Tilting her head, she surveys her handiwork and grins. Persephone the Bold rises within my legs and arms and chest, and I straddle the object of my desire, take her jaw in my hands, and lower my lips to hers.

Astrape's throat vibrates - with pleasure, I hope - as I kiss her the way I've been wanting to. Flashes of golden light bathe her face, and I take the sun's reappearance as a sign my decision to pursue happiness has met with the Ancients' approval.

———

THE END
(for now)

Acknowledgments

Heartfelt thanks to editor Ali Williams (https://www.aliwilliams.org/) for her encouragement, inspiration, and sensitive reading of both *Persephone Lost & Found*, and *Demon Healer* (and for our Pink tent Zoom chats).

Gratitude to Alpha reader Kat Carruth, who always manages to find a 'yes' when I ask for her eyes on a story (I live for your sidebar comments).

Cheers to the Goddessverse Kickstarter backers who have waited so patiently for their copies of *Persephone Lost & Found*. Your support means everything!

Cover designer Elizabeth Mackey, it is always a pleasure to meld minds and work with you.

Beta reader Kim, I appreciate you more than you know.

Also by Coralie Moss

Join Coralie's mailing list

for news & ongoing short stories (www.coraliemoss.com).

Many of Coralie's stories are also available in "closed door" editions (meaning there is no adult content).

Visit her website for more information.

The latest books feature goddesses and other mythological figures navigating the modern world.

The Goddessverse Fantasy series includes:

The Goddess & the Woodsman - book 1

Persephone Lost & Found - book 2

Demon Healer - book 3

Pandora's (as yet untitled) story - coming late 2023

———

The Goddess by Proxy series includes:

• **Medusa's Proxy,** a paranormal romance novelette

———

The Shifters in the Underlands series:

• **Paper Dragon** (Jake Winslow Book 1)

- **Blood Dragon** (Jake Winslow Book 2)
- **Moon Dragon** (Jake Winslow Book 3)

———

The Sister Witches Urban Fantasy series:

- **Once Blessed, Thrice Cursed** is book #1 of the Sister Witches Urban Fantasy Series. Set in Northampton, Massachusetts, it introduces us to Clementine, Beryl, and Alderose Brodeur.
- **Demon Lines** (book 2) is the continuation of Clementine's story.
- **The Scarab Eater's Daughter** (book 3) gives us the sisters' continuing adventures from Alderose's point of view.
- **Beguiled, Bewitched, & Broken** (book 4) features the middle sister, Beryl.
- **The Sister Witches Urban Fantasy Series: Box Set 1** (includes book 1-4)
- **Witches Everbound** (book 5) completes the Sister Witches Urban Fantasy series.

———

The Calliope Jones series:

- **Magic Remembered** (book 1)
- **Magic Reclaimed** (book 2)
- **Magic Redeemed** (book 3)
- **Magic Restrained, a novelette** (book 3.5)
- **The Magic Series Box Set #1**

____

Join Coralie's mailing list for news & ongoing short stories (www.
coraliemoss.com).

About the Author

Author Coralie Moss likes to populate her fantasy stories with witches and other Magicals and plunk a surprise or five into their seemingly normal lives. She lives on an island in the Salish Sea - the site of much magical inspiration - with her husband and two rescue cats.

Join Coralie's mailing list for book news, giveaways, and the occasional homage to apples.